Also by Gennifer Albin

Crewel
Altered

UNRAVELED

CREWEL WORLD: BOOK THREE

UNRAVELED

GENNIFER ALBIN

Farrar Straus Giroux
New York

Farrar Straus Giroux Books for Young Readers
175 Fifth Avenue, New York 10010

Printed in the United States of America
First edition, 2014
10   9   8   7   6   5   4   3   2   1

macteenbooks.com

Library of Congress Cataloging-in-Publication Data
Albin, Gennifer.
    Unraveled / Gennifer Albin.
       pages cm — (Crewel world ; 3)
    Summary: Adelice returns to Arras, where the Guild's control is slipping
and Cormac Patton needs her help to reestablish order, but she soon discovers
that she is not alone and must choose between an unimaginable alliance and a
war that could destroy everyone she loves.
    ISBN 978-0-374-31643-3 (hardback)
    ISBN 978-0-374-31646-4 (e-book)
    [1. Science fiction.]   I. Title.

PZ7.A3224Unr 2014
[Fic]—dc23
                                                              2014008406

Farrar Straus Giroux Books for Young Readers may be purchased for business or
promotional use. For information on bulk purchases please contact Macmillan
Corporate and Premium Sales Department at (800) 221-7945 x5442 or by email at
specialmarkets@macmillan.com.

To James and Sydney,
who always want three stories

UNRAVELED

PROLOGUE

THE SEA IS DARK AND LOVELY AND it calls me to its arms. I can sleep there. But as I stop fighting, the water grows heavy on my chest, pushing me down, paralyzing my arms. My eyes fly open but there is no light. I am nothing. I am the ocean. I am everything.

There is no surface near enough to break through, so I have to learn to breathe underwater. I must be reborn. A dozen glass boxes dangle from my arms, binding me to my past. Inside some, my friends are trapped, crying out for help. In others, those I love reenact mistakes I cannot escape. Fragile reminders of gambles I have lost and games I am still playing hold my arms so I cannot swim.

I can change everything if I let go first. Release Jost and Erik. Trust who Amie has become. Abandon my hatred of Cormac. I must shed the past and emerge in a thick, new skin. To rise above, I strip off the weight that pushes against me and drags me down. I ascend through the water. I say goodbye to them and with each release of the past I float higher and higher, unburdened by the debts and stories that brought me to this point, because I am free.

Autonomous.

Independent.

Dangerous.

Nothing holds me back now. This is why the Guild should fear me. I've given everything away. I have nothing more to lose. I can save worlds, and I will.

The Guild may lie in wait for me, but I am ready for them.

ONE

I WAKE TO A DARKNESS THAT ENVELOPS me in comfortable oblivion. My convictions and memories jumble into a snarl of thoughts I can't quite untangle, so I call for the lights. The bed I'm in is strange and unfamiliar, and I can't quite sort out where my dreams end and my life begins. Then I remember I'm in Cormac's quarters on an aeroship bound for Arras.

My hands are in heavy gages, restrictive manacles that prevent me from using my skills. Without access to my hands, I struggle to rise like a bird with broken wings. Through a small round window I watch the crackle of light and energy bursting through the barrier as the aeroship glides smoothly along the Interface, the roughly woven boundary that separates Earth from Arras. Around me is possibility—the luminous pulse of the universe surging through the golden strands. Even though my hands are bound, I feel in control. Being separated from my arguably most powerful weapons reminds me that I have one defense left—one capable of inflicting much more damage: my mind.

Cormac and the Guild have underestimated me. Now as they take me back to the alteration labs and the Coventry looms, I know I have power. I must remember that, especially as I stand alone, torn from my friends, my family, and Erik.

Flexing my fingers against the steel gages that lock them into place, I study these glove-like shackles that are meant to cripple me. The gages look like a series of rings stacked on top of one another and then melded together. They appear simple in construction, but if I press too hard against them a shock of electricity jolts through my skin. On each gage's cuff a small blue light is illuminated. Taking a deep breath, I raise my hands to my mouth and try to bite down on the latch. The blue light flashes and a stronger bolt knocks the breath from my lungs.

I stop trying to take them off.

They've left me in Cormac's quarters, which are as slick and impersonal as Cormac himself. For a man who oversees a world as opulent as Arras, with its sculpted skyscrapers and cosmetically enhanced population, Cormac's taste is spartan. In the center of the room wait two ramrod-straight leather chairs with a steel table planted on the slate-tiled floor between them. The bed that I awoke in is perched on a low platform near the window. No artwork graces the walls. A small mirror shows me a girl with strawberry hair sharpening to fiery red, the remains of my cosmetic routine at the Coventry. For the moment, my face is clean, without a trace of cosmetics—pure and pale. But for how long? My eyes reflect the question back at me. They are still the same emerald green as my mother's.

The door to the corridor slides open and Cormac enters. He's changed out of the tactical gear he wore during our confrontation on Alcatraz and into his customary black tuxedo, though he's left his button-down open at the top, not even bothering with a tie. I assume this is what he calls casual wear.

While at first he looks exactly the same in his everyday attire, as he comes closer I notice faint blue circles under his eyes and more gray peppering the hair near his temples.

"I took the liberty of having something sent up for you to eat," he says.

I'm shocked to see he's holding the tray himself.

"You know how to lift things?" I ask.

"I do most of the heavy lifting," he says, setting my food on the gleaming table.

"Poor baby. Want a massage?" I offer.

"That would be lovely."

I lift my hands to remind him that his men have bound them. "Take these off first."

"Sure. I'll go ahead and give you the keys to the cockpit, too. Nice try, Adelice. Those gages are staying on until . . ." Cormac's eyes wander to the ceiling as he searches for an answer.

"Until?" I press.

"I'm trying to decide if I'll ever take them off."

I plop into one of the chairs near the table. It's as uncomfortable as it looks. With Cormac everything is about appearance.

I try to ignore the plate of food he's brought me, but my stomach rumbles angrily. Nearly a day has passed since I ate. The last meal brought to me at Kincaid's estate had been drugged and I had been warned not to touch it.

In a bid to discover why Kincaid was sedating me at night,

I'd discovered the truth. He was using the time to take my measurements, planning to alter me to suit his twisted plans for Earth and Arras. Caught in the rush to get away and find the man responsible for the Kairos Agenda, I'd forgotten to eat.

We'd had no food on our impromptu mission to Alcatraz. I had been too busy trying to rescue the scientist the Guild had imprisoned there, and other than a spot of tea brought to us by Dr. Albert Einstein, my stomach has been empty for hours.

Cormac's tray is loaded with roasted lamb shanks and buttery hot bread. I assume the cocktail is for him.

Then I realize I can't eat with these gages on. Cormac can't hold out forever. If he doesn't want me to have access to my hands again, there are worse things he could do to me. He needs my ability or he'd have cut them off instead of binding them. I don't feel any better though. If it's not gages to control me, it will be a prison cell, or alteration to make me docile, which leaves only one solution: I have to earn his trust back.

"Are you going to feed me, then?"

Cormac's mouth twists into a grimace at the request and his fingers squeeze the bridge of his nose. "You're already giving me headaches."

Apparently he's not into grand, romantic gestures like feeding the woman he imprisoned. I can see the conflict with each flick of his eyes between the plate and myself, but finally he cocks his head to the side to activate his complant. It's so like Cormac to call someone else in to do the dirty work.

"Hannox," Cormac calls, connecting his complant to his right-hand man. He's been ordering around the mysterious Hannox since the moment I met him. "Take Amie to a secure room and put two armed guards in front of the door. If anyone tries to get in, I want you to kill her."

There's a pause.

"Even me," he confirms. "Assume the possibility of Protocol One until we arrive in Arras."

"It seems like a bit much to kill someone for entering a room," I say as his head settles back into a more natural position.

"In your case there's no such thing as being overly cautious," Cormac says. "I should have learned that the night I met you. I've since learned who you really are."

I want to tell him that I knew exactly who he was the night he came to retrieve me from my home in Romen. He destroyed my family when my parents tried to run and save me from a life locked in a tower. Since then he'd only succeeded in showing me time and again how big a monster he truly was.

"Does that mean you're going to take these off?" I ask.

"I don't see why not." Cormac relaxes into his chair, smirking. "If you try anything, your sister is dead. You can't possibly save her."

Death threats always bring out the twinkle in his black eyes.

"Maybe I'll leave her behind," I hedge. "You've turned her into someone else. I don't know who she is anymore or what lies you've told her about me."

"She's the last member of your family, Adelice. I know exactly what you would do for her."

"She's not the last," I point out. Cormac knows that better than anyone. The Guild altered my mother, removed her soul, and sent her to Earth to hunt me. As a Remnant, she bears

9

only my mother's face. But she *is* still alive, no matter what she's done. I'd recently even met another family member, someone I didn't know existed: Dante, my biological father, who ran from the Guild so they couldn't force him to use his alteration skills. His brother, Benn, raised me as his own and died trying to protect me from the Guild. Cormac had taken a lot from me, but he hadn't wiped away my whole family. And there were other people I loved now, even if things were a bit complicated between us.

But despite my brave face, I try not to think of Amie. She's close to me at last. With my hands free I have all the weapons I need to reach her. It's possible I could enter her chambers through a window or an adjacent room. There might even be options for escape that don't involve walking past the armed guards. But rescuing Amie and returning to Earth won't get me anywhere. There will be no peace between the worlds—no peace for myself or those I love—until *I* create it.

"Amie may as well be the last member of your family."

I ignore Cormac's comment, focusing on gathering as much information as I can before he clams up again. "What is Protocol One exactly?"

"Don't tell me you spent all that time on Earth among Kincaid and his Tailors and you don't know," he says, licking his lips as though I've provided him with something delicious to savor.

"Humor me."

"It simply means that no one, myself included, can see Amie until we reach our destination and certain safety clearance has been granted."

"Why can't you see her?" I ask.

"What do Tailors do, Adelice?" He leans toward me, egging me on.

"They alter objects, and implant and erase memories," I say. "And?"

The answer is so obvious that it hits me like a well-thrown brick. "They change appearances."

"I don't know how far you've come with your alteration abilities. I know you can unwind," he says. Cormac witnessed me removing Kincaid's time strand on Alcatraz, revealing my newfound abilities to him. Now I wish I had let them fight their own battle instead of getting involved.

"I can't alter my appearance," I tell him, realizing that Cormac was warning Hannox that I might try to take his appearance and trick them into releasing Amie. "If I could, wouldn't I have done it before now? To avoid capture?"

"You had access to some of the most talented Tailors we've ever lost to the rebellion," Cormac says with a shrug. "I assumed you were too vain up until now."

"And now?"

"I think you were stupid. You could have taken anyone else's appearance."

What Cormac doesn't understand is that no good would have come from altering myself to become someone else. Arras's threat to Earth would still have existed, my sister would still be under Cormac's control, and I would still be hiding. Right now, being myself is my best asset, because Cormac seems eager to work with me.

"Do you have her bound as well?" I ask, bringing the subject back around to Amie. I picture her locked in a cell deep in the belly of the ship.

"I'm not scared of *Amie*," Cormac says. "She won't even know she's under safekeeping. I would guess she's reading the *Bulletin* or playing with her digifile. There are perks, you know, to being well behaved."

"I find being well behaved is overrated."

"Somehow that doesn't surprise me," he says. "In any case, she is secure. You can't reach her without risking her life. Is that clear?"

"Crystal," I mutter.

Cormac stretches toward me and swipes an access card across the blue light. It blinks red. Cormac removes the gages and tosses them next to my food tray. My dented flesh aches as I splay my fingers wide, cracking and popping the joints in my hands.

This is my chance.

I could run for it. This aeroship will be equipped with tethering gear and rappelling equipment. I could easily take out the guards, even Cormac, now that I have the use of my hands, and there's a good possibility I could even make it to the surface. I could make it back to Erik.

But returning to Earth only puts everyone I love in more danger. It's better to stay here and worm my way back into Cormac's good graces.

"How adorable." He traces a finger over my techprint. "The mark of Kairos. Souvenir?"

Despite Cormac's near-constant attention, it's the first time he's noticed the mark.

"I've had it for a long time," I say in a measured tone. I could brag more, talk about my rebel parents, but I know that could place Amie in more danger. Cormac is only trusting when he thinks he has total control. I can't risk that now.

"We'll have it removed, of course," he says.

I silently hope that he forgets about it. I don't want the small reminder of my past stripped from me. I pick up a fork and run it through a pile of mashed yams.

Cormac watches me over the rim of his highball. "This reminds me of our first meal together."

"Getting sentimental?" I ask, bringing a small bite to my lips and hating myself a little for feeling hungry, hating myself for accepting food from him. Even hunger feels like a weakness. I want him to fear me.

"You barely ate that day either," he says, swirling the amber liquid. "We had potential then, you and I. I'm afraid only one of us is living up to it."

I snort and allow myself to take a second, larger bite. My first meal with Cormac was at Nilus Station on the night of my retrieval, when the Guild came to take me away to become a Spinster. He had insisted that I eat that night, too. I hadn't been sure if Cormac would become a friend or not that night. One moment he seemed to want to earn my trust and the next he was threatening me. Now I knew the truth. Cormac Patton, now the prime minister of Arras, would work any angle he could to get me on his side. He made my own mother into a monster. He altered my friend to follow me. He even brainwashed my sister, Amie, into buying his idea of a perfect world. All while he stripped Earth of its fundamental elements in order to build Arras into an empire. I know he's going to destroy both worlds unless I can convince him to find a peaceful solution. Or I finally figure out how to destroy him.

Whichever comes first.

"I still have potential," I say finally. "And I'm ready to use it."

"A threat?" Cormac raises his eyebrows as he takes a draft of his bourbon.

"A *truce.*" It sounds strange coming from my lips, but I know this is exactly what he wants to hear. If I'm smart I can use Cormac like he's used me, but only if I play my cards right.

"You never stop surprising me, Adelice Lewys." Admiration colors his voice, and I feel dirty.

"I've had time to think," I say, pushing my true feelings aside. "I understand now that compromises must be made to help both worlds."

"I couldn't agree more."

I muster up a smile for him. This is how I'll get what I need. Earn his trust until he slips up or gives in. I can do this. I have to.

"There's one last order of business I need to discuss with you." Cormac reaches inside his tuxedo jacket and I stiffen.

"No need to be afraid," he says. "You're right that a truce is exactly what will bring these worlds together. And what better way of sealing our commitment to this compromise than by truly committing to each other?"

A small velvet box rests in his palm and my eyes fly to his, every bit of me willing him not to open it. But his thumb flips up the lid to reveal a ring.

"I told you before that I needed a wife," Cormac says, placing the box on the table.

"I heard you found one," I mumble. I abandon my fork and my meal to stare at the delicate curve of the golden band and the overlarge diamond cushioned in the center.

Cormac said we would work together, but I hadn't thought he meant this. Not after everything that's happened.

"She was deemed unsuitable in more ways than one." Cormac leans forward, steepling his fingers thoughtfully. His cold black eyes stay on me.

"Maela?" I assume. She was the person most likely to ascend to the position, and the person most likely to fly into a murderous fit of rage and lose her chance. I'd seen her instability more than once while she lorded over my training at the Coventry. I relied on it during my escape, when I couldn't reach Erik by myself. I let her push him into the tear I had created. All I had to do was mention kissing him.

"Never," he said with a groan. "She's too . . . eager."

"She's too cunning," I correct him.

"Either way, Maela would be a poor candidate for the position." Cormac laughs as though we're playing a new game.

I'd suspected from my interactions with her at the Coventry that something had gone wrong between Cormac and Maela. Now I'm certain I was right. I'd been on the bad end of Maela's temper while I was under her watch. She had often abused her position training the incoming Eligibles. I can't imagine the destruction she'd have caused as Cormac's wife.

But if it wasn't Maela, that left a frightening possibility.

"Not my . . . sister?" I ask, dreading his answer.

"Much too young," Cormac says. It should be reassuring that he sees her this way, but I also know this means Amie is still the same giddy girl who mooned over a bakery cake on my retrieval night. And Cormac has been molding her—altering her—for over a year to trust him and the Guild.

"I had an arrangement with Pryana," Cormac admits, drawing a long breath that says, *I'm guilty*. "My men—"

"Your Tailors."

"My Tailors," he says, barely missing a beat, "thought they could splice her with Loricel's genetic material. But she's never shown the natural talent Loricel—or you—had."

"Pity," I say carefully. I don't want him to see I'm upset over what he did to Loricel, the Creweler who guided me during my short time at the Coventry. Cormac collects information the way some men collect old *Bulletin*s. But with him it isn't a harmless habit. Cormac knows which stories—which inconsequential facts should be held on to—so he can use them against you later.

Cormac's mind stays on Pryana, though. "I've placed her back within the Western Coventry and canceled the wedding."

"I hope you hadn't sent the invitations," I say.

"Would it matter?" he asks with a snort.

Of course not. The Tailors under his command could remove the memory of the invitation, alter the information in the minds of the people fortunate—or rather, unfortunate—enough to have received one. Every action Cormac takes has a built-in fail-safe. He never has to worry about making a policy mistake or averting a disaster because he can wipe the memory of it away.

Tailors were the nightmares you couldn't remember the moment your eyes opened.

"Well, you are too old for me," I say, searching for something to talk about that doesn't revolve around that ring. In the end, I give up. "Why? Tell me why I should accept your . . . offer?"

"There's the little matter of your sister. Need I remind you she's currently in my custody?"

I shake my head. I'm well aware that he has Amie.

"Good. I knew she would come in handy, but there's more," he says. He straightens in his chair, ready to talk business. "The reason you should agree to it is fairly simple. There's trouble in Arras. If we're going to work together to ensure both worlds survive, we need to give the people something else to think about, obsess over—and what's better than a celebrity wedding?" He flashes me a blinding smile that's meant to be charming. Too bad it's never worked on me. But I know he's absolutely right. The wedding of Cormac would be the talk of every metro in Arras. It would occupy the *Bulletin*s and the Stream for months, even years, or however long it might take to divert people's attention from what's really going on.

"You want to distract them," I say.

"I need them in their places, Adelice. Our plans won't succeed if the citizens are scared."

"Exactly what is happening in Arras?" I ask.

"Nothing that can't be handled," he assures me, but he blinks as he says it.

Except he needs a wedding—*a huge distraction*—to handle it.

I push the plate away from me and rub my wrists. I don't know how much time I have until he puts the gages back on my hands, now that he's pitched his idea.

"You're finished with your meal," Cormac says. He looks at the gages, and I sigh, raising my hands to him. An aeroship

17

caught in the Interface between Earth and Arras is no place to try to escape. If only Cormac could see that.

"These protect me from you," he says, picking up the gages. "I saw what you did to Kincaid, which was admirable, but I'm not eager for a repeat performance. Not yet. There is another option, though."

He glances toward the box on the table. I still haven't touched it.

"If I say yes, no more gages?" I ask.

"When you put on that ring, Adelice, you'll be making a commitment. As will I," he reminds me. "To show you I am serious about our endeavor, as long as you wear that ring, there is no need for these." He waves the gages around and I look from them to the ring.

It isn't until I reach out for the blue velvet box that I notice my fingers are trembling. Are all girls this scared of a marriage proposal? It probably doesn't help that mine comes with a real till-death-do-us-part clause attached. I stare at the ring. It's flawless, but its loveliness is tainted by what it stands for: control.

Over me.

Over Arras.

"Allow me," he says, slipping it onto my finger. "I know you think of this as a means to an end, Adelice, but remember, there is no shame in compromise."

There is shame in lying, I think. But I swallow the words deep inside me with a frantic gulp.

"Perfect," he says. The ring fits precisely as though it were made for me. It probably was.

I fan my fingers in front of me, noticing the ring's weight

as the stone catches the light and blazes with fiery life, sending flickers like stars around the room.

"Do we have a deal?" Cormac asks.

"The proposal every girl dreams of," I mutter.

"I'm not getting down on one knee."

"Thank Arras."

I stare at him. Then I stare at the ring. Cormac needs a wedding to distract the citizens from trouble, whatever that means, but a wedding could buy me time as well. Time to figure out what Cormac is keeping from the people. Time to allow the Agenda on Earth to organize. Because time is a precious thing there, and I need to buy as much of it as I can for my friends.

"Yes," I say, pushing Erik's face from my mind and ignoring the twinge of fear I feel.

We regard each other for one wary moment and then I reach out and grip his hand in a firm shake.

"How businesslike," Cormac says, and he pulls my hand up to his mouth, but before his lips can touch it, the door zips open and Hannox enters. He freezes for a moment, no doubt stunned by Cormac's romantic gesture. Or maybe by the horror on my face.

"I'm sorry to interrupt, sir."

Cormac waves it off. "What's the trouble? Are those Agenda fools coming after us?"

I tug my hand from his at the mention of the Agenda, wondering if he's referring to Dante, Jost, and Erik.

"The problem isn't on Earth, sir," Hannox says, pausing to let this information sink in. "It's Arras. There's a blackout over the Eastern Sector."

TWO

I'VE ONLY EVER SEEN ONE BLACKOUT—when I was a child—but I've never forgotten it. The disappearance of the sky isn't something to be taken lightly, and past instances had been highlighted on the Stream as part of cautionary programming. The message in those programs was clear: stay calm. Blackouts lasted minutes at the most. At least, they were supposed to.

We had been warned about them during my training at the Coventry, the effect they had on citizens. Being responsible for a blackout was a sure way to lose your position at the loom. But a simple blackout didn't require the attention of the prime minister.

"Take her," Cormac commands Hannox, and he's out the door before I can ask him what I should do to help.

The gages are back over my fingers despite my protests and Hannox marches me out of Cormac's quarters.

"I don't need these," I say to Hannox.

"I'm in charge of your safety." His response is even, but he doesn't bother to look at me.

"And how do these keep me safe?" I ask him.

"Cormac placed you under my guard. I've been studying you for years, Adelice. I tracked you on the surface of Earth, and in that time I've come to one conclusion."

This should be good.

"The person who poses the most danger to you"—he pauses and meets my eyes—"is yourself."

I wish I could argue that point, but I can't.

Around us, officers in various styles of tactical gear rush in and out of corridors. Some carry weapons and others are in rappelling equipment. This is what a state of emergency looks like. Cormac can lie about the severity of the issues in Arras, but seeing this I know the situation is spinning out of his control. I wait for someone to give me directions but instead I'm led to the aeroship's observation deck, which is full of bustling crew who push past me and around me without a second glance.

"What am I supposed to do?" I ask Hannox as he turns to leave me.

Hannox isn't quite what I expected. I'd seen him before at the Guild mines on Earth, but now that he's up close to me, I don't know what to make of him. He's got a soft face with large brown eyes that crinkle in concentration. He's not smooth and polished and slick like Cormac. But Hannox is deadly, I remind myself. I can't trust his kind face. It's always Hannox that Cormac calls to handle his dirty work. He must be good at it.

"Sit tight and let us observe you," Hannox says to me.

"That's it? I can't . . . help?"

Hannox's eyes stay soft but his words are cold as he checks

the settings on the steel cuffs that bind my fingers. "I don't know what deal you've struck with Cormac, but when we need your help, we'll ask for it. We have a full-blown revolution happening in the Eastern Sector. I'm not about to parade the queen of the rebels in and trust her to help us out."

"What if I escape?" I ask him, a burning resentment bubbling through me. But I immediately regret my question. Hannox will certainly report it back to Cormac.

"I would love to see you try to escape with those on," Hannox says, gesturing to the gages, "but if by some miracle you do"—he turns my wrist and traces the control panel— "I'll blow your hands off. A Creweler isn't much use without her hands."

"No, she isn't," I say. I withdraw my hands and turn away from him so he can't see my face.

Hannox leans in to my ear. "And don't forget we have your sister."

I don't respond. I keep my focus on the activity around me, trying to discern what they plan to do once we get to Arras. We're moving across the Interface faster than I've ever seen before and in doing so we catch and rip at its strands, damaging many of them in the process. To my right a man is barking coordinates, his head tipped to the side, communicating via complant to someone far away. Men ascend the ship's overhead envelope, scaling its rungs with tethers and ropes hooked over their shoulders.

"Hold on tight!" The command comes from Cormac as he whistles past me. I follow him, desperate for more information about what's going on.

"Why?" I ask.

"Because we're about to brake," he calls over his shoulder.

"My hands are kinda engaged at the moment," I remind him. This stops him and he turns to stare at me, cursing under his breath. Before I can react, he flings his arm around my waist and pulls me to him as his left hand grabs a nearby railing.

"Your hands are engaged in more ways than one," he says as the aeroship brakes hard across the Interface, throwing me backward. But Cormac's grip stays tight around my waist, holding me to him. He presses me close to his chest. The ship makes a sharp scratching noise as we are forced to a stop, and all around us, several men lose their balance and crash into the deck of the ship. My eyes fly up to the men who were scaling the envelope a moment ago and I find them there, clinging to the steel ribs of the aeroship. As soon as the ship comes to a full stop, they spring into action, scrambling higher, until they can touch the Interface.

"What are they doing?" I ask, extricating myself from Cormac's too-eager embrace.

"No girls are working the looms in the Eastern Coventry, meaning we'll have to enter Arras in an undesignated space," Cormac explains.

"Why not have another Coventry do the work?" I ask.

Cormac rounds on me. "This event must be contained. The less people find out about it, the better."

"But how will we get into Arras through the Interface?"

"The men will create a passage," he says.

"A loophole?" I'd seen a loophole before, on an Agenda trip. The temporary tunnel allowed refugees from Arras to escape to Earth, but on that occasion the loophole had been created within Arras.

"Is that what your rebel friends call it?" he asks, beginning to walk the length of the deck. I follow as he checks the crew's progress. "*Loophole*—how poetic."

I clench my teeth to keep myself from saying something I'll regret. I won't get anywhere by reminding him of my ties to the Kairos Agenda, the growing rebellion intent on separating the worlds.

"How can they do it?" I ask him, not letting myself be baited. "I thought loopholes, er, *passages* had to be created within Arras. Doesn't the Interface prevent us from tunneling through it?"

Cormac doesn't answer me. Instead he paces the deck, waiting for the loophole process to complete.

"I can't create my own loophole," I remind him, certain he thinks I'll use the information to escape.

"I've seen you rip through a world to get away from me."

"That was different," I say. I know that the only reason my escape from the Western Coventry worked was because we were already close to the surface of Earth there.

"Perhaps you're right. You wouldn't survive throwing yourself through an average passage, and I've made certain there won't be a similar incident in the future," he says.

"We have a deal, Cormac," I remind him. "I'm not running off."

His eyes swivel to regard me for a moment before he relents. "They'll use a machine to create a temporary slub in the Interface between Arras and Earth and force a passage through. The Guild has the only technology to do so."

I know this can't be true, because the Agenda has access to

loophole technology. Cormac removes the gages from my hands, but I barely notice. Before I can decide whether or not to point this out to him, Cormac speaks again. "The Guild monitors all activity passing through the Interface."

If this is true, the Guild knows about every refugee who flees to Earth, something the Agenda is unaware of. But it does explain how easily Valery and Deniel had infiltrated Kincaid's estate while working as Cormac's spies. Kincaid might have been the most powerful man on Earth, controlling the vital solar trafficking trade, but he had a weakness for living toys. He collected refugees from Arras for his macabre theater productions. Both Valery and Deniel had sought asylum with Kincaid under false pretenses. Deniel had used his alteration abilities to find a place on the estate, but Valery, my former aesthetician, had become Kincaid's lover. Deniel had died before he could fulfill Cormac's orders, unwound by Kincaid's men, but Valery fooled us long enough to inflict serious damage. It was due to her that I was here now.

When the loophole is complete, we're separated into groups as an officer barks warnings. Given the circumstances, we have little time to get inside Arras before the loophole begins to collapse.

"Passage will be based on priority clearance," the officer shouts. "It is our mission to get these priority personnel safely to the surface. If someone tells you to run, *run*! Remember, the tunnel lacks a permanent rivet to ensure stability. That means you move fast and you move smart.

"A team has been sent in advance of group one to rivet the entrance into the Eastern Sector," the officer drones on as I half listen. "It's approximately one mile between the entrance and the exit. Move quickly, follow your leader, and get through."

I'm in the first group permitted passage into the loophole, along with Cormac. Since the advance team declared the passage safe, Cormac isn't wasting any time. I'm not sure if he's unwilling to risk being caught in a passage collapse by going later or if he's eager to get to the problems in the Eastern Sector.

I study the silvery web of protection patched over the Interface as we wait for clearance to enter the loophole. The mouth of the passage hovers next to the deck of the ship and a plank has been placed to allow us to enter the vortex. I only have to walk up the plank and into the tunnel, which sounds easy enough, though it looks terrifying. The officers leading us through carry a giant stack of metal hoops at least eight feet in diameter. When they reach the end of the plank, they pop the hoops apart and then back together. This time they aren't stacked, but fitted into an open sphere. A brass globe hangs in the center. It doesn't touch the rings. It merely floats as if suspended by air.

I've never traveled through a loophole before, and I have a million questions.

"What's that?" I ask Cormac, pointing to the strange contraption the officers are setting up.

"A bodkin."

I stare at him, waiting for a better answer.

"It's an armillary sphere. It maintains the loophole as we pass through," he says. "Stop asking questions."

A hundred butterflies take flight in my belly as we're led up to the mouth of the loophole.

We're released into it in our groups, one surging after the other, like great waves. The leader of our group guides the bodkin via remote control as we enter the loophole. Its hoops orbit in a whirring blaze of motion, cycling continuously to create a clean tunnel for us to pass through.

At first it's hard to keep my balance. A swirling kaleidoscope of colors spins, creating a sense of vertigo. Cormac curses as he stumbles, but I stay upright. When I stop looking at him and concentrate on the brilliant colors of the tunnel, walking becomes second nature. If I wanted I could touch the weave, change it. But that might cause the temporary passage to collapse. There's enough clearance for us to pass through without skimming the surface.

I wonder if I slipped off my boots whether my feet would feel the tingle of electricity present in the warped strands.

This is the universe in its full glory. As we make our way through, the coarse, colorful strands grow finer and begin to blur to pure light and I know the Arras rivet isn't far off. When I arrive at the rivet, it occurs to me what I'm about to do. I'm going back to Arras. I left devastation in my wake when I escaped this world. I'm not safe here. I hesitate in the mouth of the rivet, trying to absorb what lies on the other side.

A crippling darkness gathers and spreads along the sky, tainting the metro with gloom. It's unnatural, like everything in this world, but I know this isn't the work of a Spinster's hands on the loom.

It's the lack of them.

THREE

THE BLACKNESS YAWNS ACROSS THE SKY, extending like a floating abyss above us. I thought I knew darkness on Earth, but this is all-encompassing. Allia, the capital of the Eastern Sector, is rendered skeletal in the glow of emergency lights. It's a sketch of a metro that can't be real. If I reached out now to touch it, I'm sure my hands would meet with paper. Only the flicker of emergency lanterns gives the metro depth and dimension. I stop in the rivet, hesitant to enter this place, but Cormac grabs my arm and pulls me through.

"The power grids are offline, sir," an officer informs Cormac as he hands him a pair of goggles. "These are night optical devices that will allow you to see as we travel. They are equipped with infrared technology and will display heat signatures in orange."

"Heat signatures?" a young officer pipes up.

"Humans. Animals. Anything that's alive," his superior explains.

I take a deep breath, wondering what we'll find in the streets.

The officer passes out goggles to each of us. I'm fastening mine over my forehead when Hannox snatches them off me.

"Sir," he barks at Cormac. "I think Miss Lewys should stay behind with the guard."

"I should come along," I butt in, even though I'm not sure why I'm arguing. I'm not exactly eager to explore the dark corridors of the Eastern Sector. Maybe it's that I don't like being told what to do.

"That sounds like an excellent idea," Hannox mocks. He moves toward me and jabs a finger at my chest. "Let's take the *rebel* Creweler in to meet the *rebel* Spinsters."

"I didn't bring my *rebel* handbook to distribute, so I think it will be okay." I cross my arms over my chest, and we both turn to Cormac for his opinion on the matter.

"She won't be running around unsupervised," Cormac says, and I smirk at Hannox. He might have known Cormac for two hundred years, but I'm the one Cormac wants to keep happy.

"It's a precarious enough situation without dragging her into it," Hannox reminds him.

"Then veil her," Cormac orders. Hannox opens his mouth, but Cormac holds up his hand. "I'm not interested in debating this. The looms in the Eastern Sector have been disabled, but if you think her presence in the weave is a threat and you want to veil her, do it. Otherwise, get her in tactical gear."

"I'm not much of a shot," I tell him. In truth, I hate guns.

"I don't want you in tactical gear to use you as a sniper," Cormac says with a huff. "I only thought it would be nice if you survived until our wedding day."

Hannox mutters something under his breath.

Part of me wants to flash him my ring. The part of me that's feeling smug about winning out over the bossy Hannox. But since my engagement to Cormac is something I'm neither proud of nor looking forward to, I keep my fingers to myself.

"And her hands?" Hannox asks.

"Gages won't be necessary. Will they, Adelice?" Cormac says. "We've come to an arrangement."

The weight of the ring is heavy on my left hand as he says it. I've agreed to this, which means small mercies like unbound hands and trips into rioting sectors. I'm not sure if I'm coming out on the better end of this bargain.

"It's a bad idea," Hannox says one final time, but Cormac's angry look silences him.

When Cormac walks away, Hannox hands me tactical gear without offering to help me put it on. I struggle into the thick black vest and scratchy nylon pants, hooking and strapping while officers rush around me. The goggles pinch my nose, so I leave them perched on my forehead. It isn't long before the tactical teams in the sector meet us at the mouth of the rivet. Cormac speaks to them in a hushed voice, and I can't hear the explanation of what's going on within the sector.

When we finally set out to view the area, the streets are empty. Given the near panic of the ship's crew during our flight, I expected looting or mobs of angry people. But the capital is as still as death.

"I thought you said there was rioting," I say to Cormac as we ride through in a large motocade. I see no one, even though our van shines floodlights onto our path.

"There will be rioting soon," Cormac says.

"How do you know that?" I ask him.

"Experience." His mouth twists into a rueful smile.

"Oh." Had there been other riots? How had they started? What had he done in those metros? I want to ask him these questions, but I keep quiet, listening to the terse conversations between the officers in the truck and paying attention to Cormac's reaction to the empty streets.

A blackout happened once in Romen when I was a little girl. There was no warning. No way to anticipate what was about to happen. Amie was only a toddler, and we were both outside playing in the yard while our mother finished the dinner dishes. I picked blades of grass and held them to my lips, blowing a stream of air across them to create a high-pitched whistle. Amie laughed and clapped her hands while our mother watched us from the kitchen window. And then there was no sky.

It was as simple as that. In one moment I sat under the rose-tinged hues of sunset, entertaining my sister, and in the next, the world was black, blanketed in a sudden and absolute night. I remember the sounds of screaming, the wails of terror echoing through the darkness, but it wasn't until my mother lifted me onto her hip, Amie perched on the other side of her, that she shushed me with a gentle: "Quiet now. It will be okay, darlings."

I'd lost my screams in the dark, unaware that the sounds I heard came from my own throat. Dad met us at the stairs, and mercifully, there was still power in the house. But none of us could tear our eyes from the missing sky. It was the absence of it—how half of our reality had vanished—that made it hard to swallow. Dad ushered us into the basement and headed back upstairs as we huddled in our mother's arms against the wall.

I ran my fingers along the bricks behind her back. They were solid. They were real. They wouldn't disappear.

I had never touched the sky. It was too far from the ground, even on my tiptoes, even when the programmed clouds floated so close that they seemed within reach.

"Are the clouds real?" I asked my mother.

She blinked at the question. "Of course, Ad."

"But we can't touch them," I pointed out. I could touch this wall. I could touch her and Amie. I knew they were flesh and blood and stone, but I didn't know what a cloud was or why the sky was sometimes brilliant blue and other times dull gray.

Now I realize my mother could have explained more about the looms and why this was happening. Instead she simply said, "No, *we* cannot."

It wasn't an answer, even then. It was a clue. It was a different way to look at my world. *We* could not, according to my mother, but someone else could. It was the answer that stilled my breath as a girl. It stills my breath now.

Right now, in this metro, families wait behind drawn curtains or in cramped basements, and parents offer words of reassurance. But they repeat the practiced lies of generations: *This is normal. It will pass quickly. Don't be afraid.* And I know they say those things not merely to calm their children and stop the onslaught of innocent questions, but also to calm themselves. The population of the Eastern Sector has every right to believe this is a blip, a temporary issue that will resolve itself soon. But it's been hours since we received the news of the blackout and *soon* must feel like a lie even to those saying it now.

"Halt!" an officer yells, and the van squeals to a stop. In the middle of the road stands a man. He doesn't blink as our bright lights wash over him. It's as though he's daring us to drive forward and crush him.

A group of officers scramble out of the transport with their weapons drawn.

"PC!" an officer orders, but the man doesn't reach for anything.

"What's happening?" the man calls out instead.

"We need to see your privilege card," the officer says, ignoring the man's question.

The man steps forward, trying to see into the transport, but he's stopped with the butt of a rifle.

"My wife and children are scared. The sky has been dark for hours," he says.

"Return to your home," the officer says.

I catch my breath, silently willing the man to listen.

To stop asking questions.

"Your job is to protect us," the man says, shoving a finger in the officer's face. "I want answers."

"Sir, step back." His warning is ripe with violence.

"My daughter is four years old," the man says. "She wants to know where the sky has gone."

Nothing about the man seems dangerous. He's young but starting to bald and a sheen of nervous sweat glimmers on his skin. His questions come from a place of confusion, not rebellion. He's simply scared, and I can't blame him.

Cormac steps in front of the van, and I blink. He'd been beside me a moment ago.

"Tell her the sky will return soon," Cormac says. His back is to me, but I can imagine his practiced smile.

"Prime Minister," the man says, and I hear the shock in his voice.

"Go home," the officer next to the man orders again. The command is more insistent, almost nervous.

"No!" he refuses, and my pulse jumps up a notch. More rifles train on the man.

Go home, I beg him silently.

"I'm a citizen of Arras and I deserve to know what's going on," the man says.

A burst of laughter slices through the air, but it doesn't break the tense mood. Cormac is laughing. He finds this funny. A warning bell goes off in my mind.

"I'm not sure what's funny," the man says, but it's not confusion coloring his voice anymore. Now he's angry.

"I deserve to know what's going on," Cormac repeats mockingly. He strides up to the man and places his hands on his shoulders. "You really want to know?"

I don't hear the man say yes, but I dread where this is going. Before I realize it, I'm out of the van and moving toward them. An officer grabs me by the waist and my hands lash out toward his strands, but I pull them back before I hurt him.

"Your entire world is a lie," Cormac tells the man. "The Spinsters have abandoned you, and you're all going to die."

The man steps back and stares at him and so do I. Doesn't he know his men will talk about this?

Before I can process Cormac's reckless indifference, the man lunges toward Cormac, who sidesteps him. A split second later a shot shatters the air, hitting the man squarely in the chest.

"No!" I scream, pulling loose from the officer's arms and running toward the man.

He stumbles back, a fleeting look of surprise crossing his face. By the time I reach him, there's a pool of blood under his body. I press my hands to the wound and he covers them with his own.

"My daughter." His words are punctuated by gasps as airy as oxygen leaking from a balloon.

"I'll protect her," I promise him, but he doesn't hear me. He stares at me with unseeing eyes, glassy as the still ocean.

"Get rid of that," Cormac orders as he heads back toward the motocade. "I want us at the capitol building in five minutes."

He doesn't look at me when I follow him, but he waits for me to climb into the transport. Instead I stand in front of the van and plant my hands on my hips.

"That was unnecessary," I say. My voice is shaky, betraying my rage.

"You have blood on your hands," he says, gesturing for someone to bring me a rag.

"Someone should have blood on their hands tonight," I say in a low voice. "It should be you."

"That's what I do to traitors," Cormac says. "You'd do well to remember that."

"Then do it to me," I dare him, smacking my chest with my fist so he knows where to aim. "Because that man asked a question, and you killed him. *I ripped apart your world, Cormac.* It's only fair."

"Don't tempt me," he snarls. But it's an empty threat. Instead he pushes me aside and climbs into the transport. Cormac needs me to cooperate with his wedding plan to distract Arras and prevent future episodes like this in the other sectors.

Of course, he's after more than a bride. He's hoping for a powerful ally. But it will take more than threats to control me.

I don't follow him. Instead I watch as they drag the man's body to the side of the street. They don't bother to bag him like they did my father. In a few hours, his wife will come looking for him. She'll bring their daughter, because no mother would leave her young child alone in a blackout. Maybe she'll find him dead in the street, with no clue what happened to him. And then she'll turn to the Guild for security and hope. Never knowing it was they who betrayed her.

I've seen my father's blood pooling on the floor. I dream of it. The sticky blood, black like tar, that can't ever be erased. I'll live the rest of my life with that memory—burned into my mind at sixteen.

His daughter will live with death, too. She won't even have a childhood.

But as we move through the Eastern Sector another thought sends a chill down my spine.

The girl probably won't have to live with the memory for long.

FOUR

A TALL IRON FENCE WRAPS AROUND THE Eastern Ministry, the complex that contains the sector's offices. A guard steps out and clears us for entrance while two more men open the gate and then secure it behind us. Despite the lack of power for operating the gate, the capitol offices must have some type of generator because a few electric lights blink in the windows. To an ordinary citizen they probably look like beacons of hope. To me they're warning signals.

I have no idea what to expect once we're inside. Cormac was tight-lipped after our altercation in the street. The grounds of the Ministry are lush and wild in the dark. It's impossible to tell whether people and animals are moving through the gardens or whether it's the blackness playing tricks on my mind.

We pile out of the transport and Cormac taps my goggles. I pull them over my eyes and the world is red. Despite the total darkness, I can now see everything in front of me. Cormac glows like an ember.

"We'll check the perimeter," Hannox says.

"For what?" I ask.

"Bombs, armed rebels—"

"Cosmetic-less women!" I cry in mock horror.

"This isn't a joke." Hannox's eyes narrow. "If you can't get your priorities straight—"

"You have a blackout," I say, moving toward him. "The citizens are in their homes scared. You killed a man in the street. All because some women refused to do what you told them to? Get *your* priorities straight!"

"We have no idea what to expect in there. It's standard policy to check out a building and its surroundings before the prime minister enters it, even when there isn't an active rebellion in the immediate vicinity," Hannox explains through gritted teeth. I'm pretty sure he's visualizing strangling me.

"There's no rebellion here."

"What do you call this?" Hannox says, waving his hands at the blank sky.

"A few Spinsters taking a break?"

"Adelice." Cormac's invocation of my name is a warning, but I don't stop.

"Believe me, there's no armed revolution waiting for you in there," I say. It's as though they can't comprehend that someone chose not to obey, as though dissent could only be violent. I'm certain if a group had planned a full-blown revolution the streets would not be empty now.

"As if I would trust your insight," Hannox says. "May I please finish my job, sir?"

"It's a necessary evil," Cormac says to me, waving Hannox off to finish his work.

"Everything with you is a necessary evil," I say angrily.

"I'm not interested in continuing this petty fight."

I'm too furious to find the words to tell him that my being angry that he killed an innocent man is not a petty misunderstanding. Instead my hands ball into fists, but I force them to stay at my sides.

"That's better," Cormac says, grinning at my attempt to control myself. "I'm glad you've finally learned your place."

A wall of guards surrounds us, and Cormac paces the small space until the all-clear is given. Somehow I manage to bite back the told-you-so trying to escape my lips. A group of ministers wait as we enter. Circles ring their eyes and their suits are wrinkled. Cormac strides past most of them without even a glance. He only stops to shake hands with the man at the head of the line.

"Grady, what happened?" he says as the man falls into step beside him.

"The reconditioning program failed, Cormac," Grady responds in a what-can-you-do voice.

"But how did it come to this? My reports say there's been a full blackout for over five hours," Cormac says. The chumminess is gone from his voice.

Five hours. It's been less than an hour since we reached the loophole, but a considerable amount of time must have passed in Arras before the news reached us on Earth. Days go by in Arras before the people on Earth blink, thanks to the difference in the speed of time in each world. When the Guild created Arras, it forced time to pass twelve times faster there than on Earth in an effort to quickly establish supremacy over the world they had left behind. But the divergent timelines have prevented Cormac from receiving the initial reports in a

39

timely way. Three days have already passed. No wonder everyone is tense.

"It's complicated. I didn't expect you to come," Grady admits. He tugs at the tie around his neck. It probably feels like a noose.

"You hoped I wouldn't come," Cormac corrects him.

"No, but I don't think it's necessary for you to be here," Grady says.

"Because you have the situation under control?" Cormac asks. "You don't, Grady. Your city is shut down. Arras relies on your sector to provide seafood as well as paper supplies. Of course I had to come. When a sector minister loses control of his entire population, his boss has to step in."

"And he's your boss," I say in a mocking tone. If Cormac could have prevented this by stepping in, why hadn't he done it before?

"Stay out of this, Adelice," Cormac warns me.

"No," I say, wiggling between the men. "You don't get to come in here and act like this is all his fault. How long have I heard you whispering about problems in the Eastern Sector? If you want us to fix this, we need to address the real problem here."

Beside Cormac, Grady turns away but I spy a smile tugging at his lips.

"She thinks she's cute," Cormac tells him. "Adelice, do I need to give you another reminder of my attitude toward traitors?"

I shrink back a bit and glower at him, wondering who he views as a traitor in this scenario.

"The reconditioning didn't work, Grady?" Cormac asks, bringing the conversation back to its original topic.

"No, sir," Grady says, and the tension between them thickens. Cormac is asserting his authority over the man by reminding him how he failed.

Grady ushers us into his office and offers drinks, but even Cormac refuses as we take our seats. Cormac sits behind the desk, and Grady is forced to sit next to me. He doesn't relax into his seat, and from my vantage point I can see his feet are tapping nervously on the floor.

"How did this start?" Cormac asks.

"As you know, we've had some dissent among the working-age women in the Sector."

I'd heard Cormac speak of this before, on the night of the State of the Guild. It seems like a million years ago, and while I know that's not the case, I also know it's been an issue for at least two years.

"They were refusing to marry," I say out loud, recalling information Cormac had shared with me.

"They never stopped." Grady's voice sounds weary as though he's borne the weight of this for far too long. "We introduced new incentives—"

"You tried to bribe them," Cormac cuts in. "You gave them more pay, Grady. The only thing that taught them was that they could get what they wanted by being obstinate."

Grady's hands grip the arms of his chair and I wonder if he's trying to hold back from punching Cormac.

"I think that sounds like progress," I say.

"You would." Cormac dismisses my input. "How did it leak into the Coventry?"

Cormac can be dense sometimes. I think of my own mother, complaining about her boss and her poor wages.

"It became the vogue. It was impossible to determine if Eligibles had been contaminated."

Contaminated? Is he serious?

"And now we have a full-blown strike on our hands, Grady. If you had listened to me when I suggested—"

"Altering the entire population of the Eastern Coventry was not an option," Grady interrupts him. "This is a case of a few bad apples spoiling the bunch."

"A few?" Cormac roars. "Your looms are dark! Where are your good apples?"

"They can be reasoned with," Grady says. "We have some of the Spinsters responsible for initiating the blackout on the premises waiting for further questioning."

"I want to see them. What have they admitted to?" Cormac asks. He stands and heads for the door in quick, purposeful strides.

"Admitted? Nothing. They want to negotiate."

"Negotiate." Amusement mixes with arrogance as Cormac repeats the term.

"They're willing to go back to the looms, Minister," Grady says. "They simply want to discuss some possible changes within the structure of the Coventry."

"Do they?" Cormac asks. "Unlike you, I'm not in the business of listening to the complaints of a group of women."

"Really?" I say beside him.

"Do you have something to add?" Cormac asks me.

"Yeah, I do," I say. "What happened to working together and finding a solution?"

Cormac pushes me against the wall and lowers his mouth

to my ear. "Do not question me in front of my men. You do not understand the gravity of this situation."

"Because you won't tell me about it."

"Because you can't fix it," he seethes. "Now shut up and follow me, or I'll send you back to the transport with Hannox and believe me, you do not want that."

"Yes, *sir*." I emphasize the title. So much for working together.

"I want to see these women." Cormac releases me and tugs at the hem of his jacket.

"Minister, I think you'll find that they aren't asking for much—"

"I'm not interested in what they're asking for," Cormac stops him.

"But—"

"Nor am I interested in what you think, Grady. You've let this situation get out of control. I came to fix it."

I can't keep the question to myself. "Then why do you want to talk to them? If you aren't interested in listening to them?"

He stops and stares me down, his eyes as dark as the room surrounding us.

"To tell them what I'm going to do to them."

FIVE

THE STONES ARE DAMP AS I TRAIL my fingertips over the rough walls. I recognize the smell, how it prickles my nostrils. This cell is different from the one I found myself in when I was brought to the Coventry after my retrieval. It's large and set behind steel bars. I thought Grady wanted to *negotiate* with these women, but he must still see them as a threat. My goggles allow me to maneuver the dark corridors and as we round the corner, I make out several heat sources in front of us. The prisoners lie in puddles of umber, huddling together for warmth in the cold cells, but as we approach they move toward the bars.

"Ladies," Cormac greets them. He sounds charming and relaxed.

There is an acute inhalation in the room, like each person has sucked in a breath at the same time. I wonder how they're feeling now that Cormac Patton has come to see them. Do they think he's come as their savior or do they know him as well as I do? They must know. Even the Spinsters who pretended to be blind couldn't help but see.

One of the women finally dares to speak. "Minister Patton."

"Can we get some emergency lights on in here?" Cormac asks.

There's a buzz of orders throughout the room and a few minutes later a dim light flicks on overhead.

I wonder why they need to have a holding cell under the Ministry offices, anyway.

I don't have to think long about that question.

"Ladies." Cormac's politician smile is plastered on his face. "The whole of the Eastern Sector is in terror—"

"Sir," the woman dares to address him.

"What's your name?" he asks her.

"Hanna," she says. She's a few years older than me, with an upturned nose set over a wide mouth, and her brown eyes sparkle with rebellion.

"Hanna, don't speak until I tell you to." The smile slips from his face, showing them the Cormac I know and loathe. His fingers massage his temples. I guess I'm not the only one giving him a headache. "As I was saying, your actions—or rather inaction—have crippled this entire sector. I would love to hear your reason for abandoning your duties. You've left the entire sector in fear."

Hanna doesn't look abashed at Cormac's admonishment. She looks angry. She obviously hates him as much as I do. It occurs to me that in another scenario she and I might be friends. Except that I'm standing on the other side of the cell's bars, and I'm sure she hates me as much as him at the moment.

"We want basic rights," Hanna says. But the anger makes her voice tremble, weakening her strong words.

"*Basic rights,*" Cormac parrots. "You have clothing, food, shelter, safety. The last time I checked, those were basic rights."

"We want the rights you afford other citizens. We want to be able to marry and to have our own homes," Hanna says.

"Those are privileges," he corrects her.

"And we don't deserve privileges?" Hanna bursts out. She grabs the bars and presses her face into the space between them. "We work around the clock to ensure this world functions, and you lock us in a tower."

I knew I liked her.

"*And* you live in beautiful homes, wear designer clothing, eat delicacies," Cormac starts.

"Not all of us are eager to be paraded around like peacocks." She looks at me.

That's not fair. I'm dressed in tactical gear, for Arras's sake.

"And your plan to get these things that you deserve is to ignore your duties and terrify citizens?" Cormac asks.

"We want you to listen to us."

"I am listening, and I hear what you're saying," Cormac says. "What you need to realize is that *I don't care.* Your claims don't absolve you of your crime."

Cormac has already labeled them as criminals. This can't end well.

"I'm sure the Spinsters are eager to remedy the situation," Grady says, rubbing his hands together.

"It doesn't matter." Cormac turns away and speaks quietly to Hannox, who nods gravely at commands I can't hear.

While Cormac talks to him, I wander over to the bars.

Most of the girls look away from me, but Hanna faces me without blinking.

"Come to stare at us so that you can feel superior?" she asks.

I run my fingers over the cool steel between us. "I've spent time imprisoned by Cormac."

"And now you're by his side. Clearly, you're back in his good graces. Who did you betray for that privilege?" Hanna is clearly unimpressed with me.

"I understand being angry. I'm angry, too," I whisper to her.

"Oh, please," she says with an exaggerated roll of the eyes. "What could you possibly have endured?"

"Death, destruction, the loss of the people I love most," I say, and I refuse to blink. Hanna thinks she has me pegged, but she has no idea how I wound up here.

Or how far I'm willing to go.

"So you gave in to save a boy," she says in a mocking voice.

I don't tell her about my sister or the mother they've turned into a monster or the friend who escaped only by losing her own blood in a bathtub. Hanna needs to be angry. It fuels her so that she won't feel the fear in her belly. I know that fear. It never goes away. You can only ignore it or hide it under the fury.

But I have different reasons to play along right now. Ones she can't understand. Hanna only sees me on the other side of the bars and that makes me her enemy.

Still, a girl might go crazy locked away in a tower day after day. Hanna and her conspirators' perception of Arras has warped. It's easy to believe you understand the function of your world when it's at your fingertips every morning, afternoon, and evening. When the loom presents a piece of your world, it's easy to believe you see the whole picture. I held thunder in my palms and wove rivers into being. But I didn't understand what I was facing until I stood under the Interface and contemplated the reality of *both* worlds. Then I saw Arras for what it was: a parasite sucking away at the Earth.

"There's more at stake here than you or me," I say to her quietly. "It's the awful truth. You think you can run from it, but there's nowhere to go."

"I don't want to run from it," Hanna says, her eyes fierce. "I want to change it."

"You can't do that from a prison cell," I remind her.

"Adelice wised up," Cormac says, and I realize he's been privy to our entire conversation. "She and I are working to make life in Arras stable again."

"I can't wait to see how you're going to do that," Hanna says.

"It's too bad you won't be around to witness it," Cormac replies.

"What does that mean?" I demand, stepping in. I don't care what any of them think of me anymore. Not when things are spiraling out of control.

"You know how I treat traitors, Adelice. You've seen it yourself."

"But she hasn't experienced it herself," Hanna points out. "You've spared her. If we were all young and pretty, maybe you'd make an exception for us as well."

"You are young and pretty, Hanna, but I can't forgive everyone," he says. "Adelice will help me to heal the wounds your generation has inflicted on Arras by becoming my wife. That was the price she was willing to pay for peace."

"Better her than me," Hanna says, and then she unceremoniously spits at him. It lands at his feet.

Cormac takes a step back and regards the floor with disinterest. "If you want to know why I chose her despite her clear lack of respect for Guild authority, then I'll tell you. Adelice uses her intelligence to fight, which proves to me she is capable of reason. I'm less and less sure that's something most of you are capable of."

"When you say *most of us*, you mean women, right?" I say.

"Don't bother, hon," Hanna says. "You stopped being one of us when you partnered with him."

Her accusation doesn't sting like it once might have. Hanna has chosen her path and I've chosen mine. I have the benefit of experiences that she doesn't. Hanna is young and angry, but there's desperation in her actions and her words. It colors her ability to think rationally. The only way I can salvage this situation is to take the opposite approach. Reacting got me nowhere when it came to saving the man in the street. I can't focus on a strategy now. I have to anticipate Cormac's next move. It's clear Cormac plans to execute the Spinsters. But I'm not certain what that will do to the Eastern Sector. The blackout will continue. Food supplies will cease to arrive. How long before the people cross the borders? What will happen to them then? I have to convince Cormac to keep girls on the looms.

So even as Hanna tosses her accusations at me, they bounce off, unable to penetrate the thick skin I've constructed. I need to think so that I can plan. I need to bite my tongue. I need to play dumb until I know the correct words to change Cormac's mind.

Because I know they exist.

The other girls are watching our interaction with increasing dread. One has started to cry. Hanna is the ringleader. Several back away from her. I watch as they abandon Hanna, leaving her at the center of the rebellion.

"I will go back to the looms," the crying girl shouts.

Cormac smiles at her, but then he wags a finger. "It's too late for that. This whole sector has been tainted by disloyalty."

"B-b-but . . . but . . ." The girl stammers against the sobs heaving through her.

"Cormac," I say, taking his arm gently. "You've made your point."

"No, I haven't," he snaps at me, wrenching free.

I swallow hard and say the one thing that's always haunted me, that I've never brought up with him. "I know you are capable of mercy. You showed it to me once."

"I needed you, Adelice. I always knew you would be a Creweler," Cormac admits. "If you'd been any other Spinster, you would have shared their fate."

"What fate is that?" I ask, but he doesn't answer me. What will he do to them?

Instead he turns to the group of officers and officials surrounding him. "Protocol Two has been activated. Those with border privileges should evacuate now."

"You can't do that." Grady's face is ashen.

"I already did. The Guild can't continue to pretend this issue will be resolved. You've had two years to deal with this, Grady."

"There are innocent Spinsters here," Grady says. "Most remained in the towers. You can't punish them for the others' actions."

"I'm not," Cormac says. "I'm punishing them for their own inaction. Five girls didn't black out the sky. Five girls didn't cripple a sector. Inaction breeds rebellion. And the Guild has been inactive for too long regarding this matter. I take responsibility for that. It ends today."

"So that's it," Grady says, no longer trying to appeal to him. The fight has gone out of his eyes.

"Evacuate now, Grady, and try again if you can bear to show your face at the Ministry."

"How will you show yours?" he asks Cormac.

"Proudly. Because I've done something important here."

"Who has clearance to leave?" Grady asks.

"Those with border privileges. No one else."

"But my family!" Grady protests.

"You can have another."

"I don't want another."

"How sentimental of you." Cormac laughs at his colleague, dropping his voice to whisper, "Would you have said that about your last family or the one before?"

But judging from their confused faces, Hanna and the other girls hear the question, too. I shake my head at them, a message that this is not going to end in their favor. The Spinsters thought they were making a stand. They suffered under the delusion of their own power. It's a trap laid early in the Coventry. Make a girl feel pretty and important and she'll start to believe it. Distract her while you lead her into a tower and strip away her rights. And never show her what you've hidden.

The Guild miscalculated in thinking this would be enough

to keep the female population happy, though. They hadn't conceived of our evolution. But despite their mistakes, they'd kept their most important truths secret.

While I was on Earth I discovered how far they had gone to protect their power. I'm the only Spinster who knows the true depth of their power—and their history.

"You have no idea who you are dealing with," I say to Hanna sadly, "or what he's capable of."

Cormac flashes us a wicked smile. "They'll know soon enough."

SIX

SPECIAL TEAMS FLOOD THE CELLS. A GUARD jostles me out, pushing me against Cormac as a scream calls my attention back to the prisoners. Officers drag the Spinsters from their prison, herding them into a group. Hanna's eyes meet mine before security forces surround the girls. From the mass of black uniforms a collection of arms reach out, grasping toward freedom, but I'm pulled down the corridor of the tower and away from the swarm of girls.

Hanna's final accusatory look burns in my mind. She sees me as the problem—another girl not only controlled by the Guild but willing to do as they wish. I want to believe I'm dangerous—that my power should be feared—but who do I scare? The more I think about it, the clearer the answer becomes.

Myself.

Despite my best efforts, I'm no closer to solving this situation without violence, and as I watch the chaos, knowing that there's not much time left for the Spinsters here, my composed veneer cracks, fear and guilt seeping through it.

Cormac is only a few feet away. Whatever he is planning, I can still stop it. If I invoke our agreement, I can remind him that a compromise will be a better course of action. It's the best I can do, even as a tiny voice in the back of my mind reminds me this won't be enough.

"What are you doing?" I ask. He doesn't bother to look at me. He's too consumed with his business.

"We have no choice but to institute Protocol Two," he says. "Containment of the Spinsters is necessary, and this coventry and sector have been compromised."

"Can you transfer them out to other coventries? Separate the ones who didn't rebel?" It's less a question than a wish.

"I'm not interested in keeping a bunch of traitors." Cormac stops, but he searches the room around us. To him our conversation is merely another annoying side effect of the situation.

Grady stands to the side of the action. He doesn't try to stop the guards dragging the Spinsters away; he looks frozen.

"You have to stop this," I yell at him. "You know what he's going to do, don't you? Stop him!"

The troops march the girls past us and out the door of the Ministry. I have no idea where they are taking them, but it can't be good.

"Cormac." Grady finally speaks up. "Execute them if you must, but consider the people. They don't deserve to be punished for the actions of a few Spinsters. Without the Spinsters—"

Bile rises in my throat. He's willing to sacrifice those girls to save the population. Cormac rounds on him. His face is pale and there's a slight tremor when he raises his finger to point at Grady. "And let the taint in this sector spread through the rest of Arras? If we don't contain the rabid propaganda here and now, it will be Protocol Three next."

"It will never come to that," Grady says, but he slumps against a wall as if the weight of this possibility is too much to bear. "You've never been able to make hard decisions, Grady. I've made this one for you. You're absolved for now." Cormac waves a hand at him, shooing him in the direction of the exit. "Leave Allia before it's too late. I've ordered emergency rebounds into the adjoining three sectors and the termination of every Spinster in the sector."

Grady's face is slack, guilt hanging from it like oil pooling in a rag. Cormac may believe it's easy to walk away, but I feel the heaviness in the air. No one can justify what's happening here today. No one will be pardoned.

"What will happen to them if you order this? Who will work the looms? What will happen to all those innocent people if the Coventry sits empty?" I ask Cormac as Grady ambles out of the room. Grady made it sound as if everyone would be punished for the blackout.

"There's no *if.* It's done. You don't need to worry about it." He's too busy sending messages on his digifile to even look at me.

"Is that how this is going to work? I ask a question and you pat me on the head and send me back to the kitchen?" I plant my hands on my hips, hoping to appear defiant.

"I'll probably swat you on the ass, actually," Cormac says, grabbing my arm to pull me in closer, "especially if you take that tone with me in public."

"If you think I'm going to be an obedient little wife—"

"That's exactly what you're going to be," Cormac roars. His hand flies up in the air, but I don't shrink away from it. Our eyes meet and there's a fire burning behind his usually cold eyes. He doesn't strike me though, he merely waves toward a group of guards. They part to reveal Hannox, who pauses to nod at Cormac.

"You two should get married," I tell Cormac as Hannox heads in our direction. "You clearly have a very special relationship."

"You and I will after two hundred years, too."

"Oh, *promise*?" I ask, no longer trying to bite back the heedless spite that comes naturally to me. Even though I know it's reckless, I can't stop myself now. Cautious words and gentle reason have gotten me nowhere with Cormac. It's as though he can't even hear me.

"There's something you should understand now, Adelice," he whispers in my ear. The urgency of his words and the heat of his breath raise goose bumps down the back of my neck. "I am the one with power in Arras."

"I have talents of my own," I say.

"And they are mine now," he replies. Hannox appears beside us and Cormac points to me. "Get her to the transport. We're leaving for the Northern Ministry shortly."

"I'll have her transported back to the Western Coventry, and—" Hannox begins.

"No." Cormac stops him. "She stays with me."

Hannox lowers his voice. "Do you think that's a good idea?"

"Do not second-guess me, Hannox," Cormac snarls.

Hannox's jaw tightens and he glances briefly at me before snapping off a salute. "Yes, sir."

"Take her to the transport." Cormac shoves me toward Hannox and I stumble into his arms.

I've overheard enough exchanges between the two men to know things are tense between them because of me. The funny thing is that in some ways Hannox is a lot like me. We're both at the mercy of Cormac, a man who thinks a relationship consists of ordering the other person around. It's also clear that I'm not going to get any answers from Cormac about what's happening here.

As soon as Hannox leads me away, I ask him what's going on. Maybe Hannox can see that we aren't so different, too.

"If Cormac wouldn't tell you, why would I?" he asks.

"Cormac won't tell me because he thinks my ignorance gives him the upper hand."

"And you don't think it does?"

"I can't possibly stop him," I explain as he marches me out the exit of the Eastern Ministry.

"For the first time, I agree with you. Remember this: Cormac's fuse is considerably shorter these days," Hannox warns me. He gestures for me to lead the way, ending the discussion.

Outside the building, two shallow pools run the length of the path leading to the entrance. On each corner of the pools fantastical creatures with long hose-like extremities extending past marble spikes spray water. It ripples together, immediately becoming part of the pool. The fountains are like the coventries: both provide material directly to the source, parts flowing into one whole.

"Elephants," Hannox says beside me.

"I'm sorry?" I say.

"The animals are elephants," he tells me. "We brought some of every animal from Earth here initially. The elephants were my favorite."

"What happened to them?" I ask.

"Some animals died, others evolved with the changing conditions, and others were deemed unnecessary."

"And these?" I ask.

"No one saw a use for elephants. If an animal served no useful function, it was removed to allow Arras to prosper more efficiently."

"And elephants have no purpose?"

"I guess not." Sadness colors his words. Hannox doesn't speak again until he hands me off to the security guard waiting by the fleet of armored transports near the Ministry. Hannox didn't strike me as the friendly type when I first met him and I'm not sure why he would volunteer such a peculiar detail now. But sentimentality does strange things to people, I suppose.

As soon as Cormac joins us, we're evacuated out of the Ministry's emergency rebound chambers directly into the Northern Sector. But we don't go to the Ministry offices as Cormac insinuated earlier. He still hasn't given me any answers about what's going on. Instead we're whisked through the metro in a motocarriage.

I take a deep breath and push the words out of my mouth that I don't want to speak. "I think there is room for compromise regarding the Eastern Sector. You don't have to destroy it."

"There is no compromise," Cormac growls. "Our partnership doesn't extend to the governance of Arras."

"I thought you wanted someone to help you control the situation on Arras," I say.

"I do, but I'll tell you when and how you will be necessary for that purpose." He tugs at the vest strapped tightly around his neck.

"Then I'm not sure why you brought me here," I say. I don't shrink away from him even as he presses closer to me. There's a violent electricity in the air between us. One of us could snap at any moment, and I can't say how much longer I can play nice.

"Because you've never been able to see the big picture." His breath stings my nostrils as he gets in my face. "If this taint spreads through Arras, Earth will die along with it. I'll be forced to use more of its resources to rebuild our world."

"And the only way you can stop this threat is to destroy everything you built here?"

Cormac grabs my wrist so forcefully that it feels as though my bones will snap. "I have this under control."

"Are you sure?" My question is soft.

"Never presume that I'm not in control." His words are firm but his eyes tell a different story. He can't hide the fierce panic blazing in them.

"There are a lot of innocent people in this sector," I reason with him. "Are you going to desert them?"

His voice lowers to a whisper. This point is meant only for me. "Tell me, Adelice, how do you know when someone is innocent? Because two years ago I was called to a retrieval gone bad, and I walked in ready to face a traitor. And do you know what I found? A scrap of a girl who couldn't run fast enough to get away." Cormac trails a finger down my throat, and my hands curl into fists. "You looked innocent, and what a fool you made of all of us."

"You're wrong," I say in a quiet voice.

"You were innocent?" he asks.

"No, about me not seeing the big picture. It's not that I don't see it. It's that I see a different one than you." I pause, waiting for him to interrupt, but for once he's listening to me. "You're looking at the past, Cormac. Your world is falling apart while you squint and pretend the big picture isn't deteriorating rather than face the truth."

"And I suppose you're going to enlighten me?" he asks with a scoff.

"I can't do that, which is why you need me. You're holding on so tightly that you're strangling Arras. Call off the protocol and we'll figure something out together."

Cormac hesitates, his black eyes fixed on mine, flickering like he's trying to read a secret code. He won't find anything hidden there, because I believe every word I've said to him. "This sector isn't beyond saving," I continue. "Nothing in this world or the one below us is beyond saving. The fact that you brought me here proves you know that. You gave me another chance, Cormac. You can give those girls one as well."

Cormac's gaze falls to the floor and he straightens up, unable to meet my eyes. It's the first time he's backed down from me. It's the first time I've won.

I try to bite back the triumphant smile tugging at my lips as he cocks his head. "Hannox," he calls.

I think of Hanna's judgmental eyes. She scorned my methods, but I have gotten results through diplomacy. Cormac might be a twisted man, but he always does the best thing to advance his career. Abandoning the Eastern Sector wasn't going to earn him popularity points.

"Hold the protocol," he says. "Wait for my orders."

As soon as he ends his conversation, his eyes fall wearily over me.

My heart takes flight like a freed bird as we pass outside the central part of Cypress, past tall buildings and shops out to the cookie-cutter streets that comprise the neighborhoods. It's evening and the streets are empty, lights flicker in windows, but curfew is imminent. Posted signs warn us to turn back— that we're entering a restricted area. When we finally stop, Hannox helps me out of the back of the motocarriage. We're on a bluff much like the one Cormac brought me to during a good-will tour we took together. The men speak in furious whispers until Hannox climbs back inside the motocarriage, leaving Cormac and me alone.

"Are you here to tempt me?" I ask him as he appears by my side. He'd offered me Arras once as we looked over a cliff.

"No, we're here to witness."

"Witness what?" I ask, suspicion seeping into my voice.

He taps his wristwatch. "Soon. I thought it was time I showed you the big picture."

I stare out past the edge of the bluff. A metro stretches, sparkling, at the foot of it. The night is still, not a trace of wind in the air, but as my gaze moves upward there are no stars. No moon.

"Why are we here? I thought we were going to the Northern Ministry," I ask, not wanting to understand why he's brought me here, because I think I already know the answer.

"We are standing at the boundary between the Northern Sector and the Eastern Sector," Cormac explains.

This information sends a chill running through my veins, but I don't repeat my earlier question. The lights below are merely the candles and emergency flashes the population is using while the sector is in blackout. Instead I wait, dreading the answer that I know is coming.

I'm here to witness Protocol Two.

The black sky flashes rainbow. Colors streak across, lighting it in brilliant ruby and sapphire, each shade fading into another. Until it ceases to be. It's no longer empty air. It's more. It's become a gaping void. The space-time around us vibrates, filling the abyss overhead with the low hum of absence. Under it the metro tremors and fades, stripped before my eyes. My mind fills the silence with screams. But would they scream? Would the people of the Eastern Sector even know what was happening to them? Did they feel their removal from Arras?

Did they know they had been cast off from life? Through the lost cries echoing in my head only one thought is clear: Sebrina is in the Eastern Sector. I've failed Jost again.

I step closer to the edge, and when the air stings my tears, I realize I'm crying. "What have you done?"

"I've shown you who is in control here. Don't forget what you've seen."

I swallow my own scream as I stare across the expanse,

wishing I could explain to Jost what just happened. And hoping I never have to.

For a moment there is nothing, and I understand why Arras has strict boundary laws. Passage between sectors is controlled to ensure citizens stay where they are supposed to and don't see anything they shouldn't. But also because *this* might need to be done at a moment's notice. I feel certain it has been before.

"How many times have you done this?" I ask Cormac, forcing my hands to my sides even as they ache to reach out and rend him in half.

"Protocol Two?" he asks.

I nod, my eyes never leaving the empty space stretching before us. We stand on the precipice of this world. Past us lies nothing but a blank gap in reality.

"I'll never tell," he says.

I round on him, leaving no room between us. "You can't do this. There are innocent people there. There are children!"

My throat is thick with grief, and I choke on the final word, my heart splintering even further for Jost and Sebrina until I'm sure I will crack under the pressure of my guilt.

Cormac grabs my shoulders, squeezing them until my fingers start to tingle. "Do. Not. Question. Me."

Each word is a threat, spoken in a low tone that registers only in the shiver running up my spine. He drops his hold on me and steps away, opening and closing his fingers in rapid succession as he stares into the void.

There is more wrong here than an altered reality. No one is safe under the authority of Cormac Patton.

A placid gray washes across the vacant sky and the stars

reappear. As I watch, the world changes into a calm, still scene, erasing the violence that preceded this moment. Water ripples into place, flooding the space below the cliff. It is born of nothing, and it rushes in gentle waves until it reaches the edge of the precipice. Now I stand on a rocky beach instead of the end of the world, but the ocean is a lie. Now there are three sectors instead of four. Now I see Arras in a new and terrifying light.

We can destroy the world as quickly as we can build it.

SEVEN

BY THE END OF MY FIRST WEEK back at the Coventry I'm smiling, but only for the surveillance feeds that watch me. By the end of the second week, I begin placing orders from the catalogs left for my perusal. I learn patience as I try to forget what I've given up.

My freedom.

My destiny.

And Erik, who I force from my waking mind, but who haunts my dreams.

Days pass mechanically inside the walls of the Western Coventry, because I'm a prisoner here—despite Cormac's assurance that we are partners. It's not the same compound I remember coming to as an Eligible. The walls are still programmed with false windows that display relaxing settings, but the actual composition of the Coventry has changed. Now the threads that comprise the walls are knit tightly together and bound through with strange, artificial strands. Strands I can't penetrate. I wouldn't have tried if I hadn't been left to my own devices for so long that I'm sure I'm losing my mind.

My quarters are more lavish than when I first came here. Two of the walls in my bedroom are programmed to look like a window overlooking the Endless Sea. I'm not sure if it's meant to relax me or remind me I can't escape. There are five more rooms in my apartment on the top floor of the high tower, all decorated in shades of yellow. They're probably meant to boost my spirits, but the yellow is driving me crazy. There's a sunny bathroom, a buttery living room, a golden dining room, a lemony closet that could fit a small house inside it, and a second powder room, small, gray—the only contrasting color—for when Cormac comes to visit me.

I'm not allowed out among the other Spinsters, as though my rebellion is catching—a communicable disease without a cure. I suppose Cormac believes giving me a large cage to fly around in will convince me I'm free.

My staff is always changing and always silent, obviously instructed not to speak to me. Even the aestheticians who arrive each day to curl my hair and line my eyes won't chat with me. They go about their work without a word. Given what happened to my last aesthetician, my mentor, and my valet, I guess it's understandable that no one trusts me. I tried to talk with them at first, hoping they would have the information I need to break Cormac, but no one in the Coventry is interested in helping me. Cormac has made sure I have no allies or friends here. No one to help me find out the one piece of vital information I need: where Cormac stays when he comes here. Catching him asleep may be the only element of surprise I have in my favor.

I'm made up in case Cormac comes to call. It's the only information I've been given about my strange daily rituals. He's already preparing me to be the perfect wife: neat and fashionable and out of the way.

But I can tell when he's coming because my whole day shifts. Valets appear with decanters and freshly cut flowers. Maids scurry in and out, checking my supply of toilet paper and sweeping the pristine floor. New dresses arrive for my already stuffed closet. My only job is to pick one and stay out of the way of the gaggle of servants making way for the lord and master.

"Lord and master" is my new nickname for Cormac. I want to say it to his face with a sneer. I fantasize about it, but I'm starting to learn the value of some advice I once received from an old friend. I'll get more out of him if I play dumb.

By the time he finally arrives, I've had to reapply my own lipstick. Cormac bursts through the door to the apartment with the air of a man who owns the place.

He does, but it doesn't make it any less rude.

I watch as he loosens his bow tie, leaving it to hang askew against his unbuttoned collar. His fingers press into his temples as they often do these days. If I was meant to be a wife, I would be waiting with a cocktail poised in my hands, but I let the valet pour it. Cormac drinks longer draughts with each visit, a sign that his stress level is rising. We never talk about Arras or his job. I tried at first, but it became clear he no longer intends to utilize me or my skills. Now I'm left to play the role of the dutiful wife until I can gather the information I need to truly effect change in Arras, beginning with Cormac himself. The more secure he feels, the closer I can get to him.

We sit across from each other at a mahogany table too long for two people. The salad arrives and I spear the tender spinach leaves with unnecessary force. He doesn't notice.

"Headache?" I ask him. I focus on sounding concerned, even though the question unnerves me. I can almost see the edges of him fraying away and I'm not certain if it's actually happening or it's my imagination.

"I'm fine," he snaps, taking another swig from his drink and slamming the tumbler onto the table.

"Will you be staying long?" Despite my casual tone, my heart pounds like a drum as I ask.

"I'll leave in the morning." But to my disappointment he says no more about his plans.

"How was your week?" I ask, trying to channel my mother and how she spoke to my father at the dinner table.

His jaw tenses and he reaches for his glass again. It's empty and he's dismissed the valet, which means he'll be forced to speak to me. He twists his hands together, cracking his knuckles, each one popping ominously in the quiet room.

"I'd rather not discuss work."

"But I'm so *interested* in your job."

"You want to know, Adelice?" he asks, and I nod, stunned by his offer. This is the first time he's been willing to speak directly about the situation. "Containing the situation regarding the Eastern Sector is becoming impossible. Most of our seafood as well as paper goods traded through that sector. We'll have to expand another sector to fulfill those needs and that means opening up new mining sites on the surface and finding more girls to work in the coventries at a time when Eligibles have become scarce."

"It is a shame what happened in the Eastern Sector," I murmur.

"I don't deal with traitors." There's murder in his words.

"Which makes me feel fortunate," I reply in a gentle tone. I have to remind him that he can be merciful, because he seems to have forgotten.

He ignores the comment. Of late he's been less argumentative, less quick with his insults. If I didn't know it was impossible, I would say his job is killing him.

His head tilts to the side to take a complant call. This is the only way I have been able to learn things: that the rebellion on Earth is still strong, that Amie is being kept in the Northern Sector. The casual asides and conversations I overhear during our infrequent dinners paint a rough picture of what's happening within Arras and on Earth. He often listens for long periods on these calls, nodding solemnly, and that is how I know things are slipping from his control.

"Lobster is not my priority right now," he snaps, angry again. "I don't care what concerns it's raising. If it's that big an issue, do a full clean of the public. They can't miss something they don't know about."

Shellfish have never been so dangerous. Now everything feels like a risk. Each morsel on my tongue. Each casual joke. Perhaps it's only because I'm close to him that I see how the questions have become fissures in his foundation. How long will it be before they cause him to crack?

Cormac pushes his full plate away and calls for the next course. I manage a few more bites of salad before the plate is taken and a miniature tureen of soup is placed in front of me. As soon as I lift the lid, I can tell from the layer of gummy, melted cheese that it's French onion—Cormac's favorite. He knows I dislike it. I pick at it with my spoon.

"You aren't eating your soup," he says.

"I'm not fond of onion soup," I say as mildly as possible. Silently I add, *I hate it, and I hate you.*

"It's a delicacy. Onions are scarce."

"They are? I haven't noticed any shortage of onions."

"Because I ensure *you* don't go without," he says. Miraculously, he's eaten almost his entire bowl already. I shouldn't complain since it's one of the few things he consumes without alcohol content. "That is my job."

"Our job is to do what's right for Arras and Earth." It's a simple reminder, not a warning. Cormac brought me here to be his partner. I hold my gaze level with his even as he drops his spoon into the empty tureen. It clatters ominously against the porcelain.

"I wondered when you'd raise this issue again."

"Issue?" I repeat. "Cormac, people are dying. Your own people. We need to offer them a chance. I've seen the mines. You know this situation isn't sustainable—"

"You saw the mines when you were out playing rebel, so pardon me if I ignore your anecdotal evidence."

"Are you telling me there isn't a problem?"

"I'm telling you it isn't your place to fix it."

Blood roars in my ears. It's just like Cormac to bring up my place—it's my weakness. The one thing that I can't pretend to tolerate. "This wasn't our deal," I remind him. "I came to help you, not sit around."

"But you're so good at it," he says.

As if he knows what it's like to pretend, to play at life every second of the day.

Without thinking about it, I lift my full tureen and fling it across the room. The porcelain shatters against the wall, spraying stringy onion against the smooth, golden paint.

My hands splay against the wooden table and for a moment I consider using them. I could unwind him, wipe him from existence like he casually erases those who threaten him, but I won't make it out of here alive if I do. Cormac has collateral to ensure my good behavior, so I scratch my fingers across the wood's grain to stem the trembling in them.

Cormac presses the com near his end of the table, ignoring me. "Next course, and send a maid to the dining room."

"But then she'll know about our domestic problems," I say.

"I'll have her removed when she's finished cleaning up your mess," he says, and I fall back against my chair.

This is why I'm kept alone, because I'm always screwing things up for innocent people like Jost and Enora. The maid enters the room and gawks for a split second at the wall, but she replaces her surprise with practiced indifference and goes about cleaning up the soup.

"It slipped," I call to her. "I'm terribly clumsy." I keep my eyes on Cormac as I speak and he nods once like an approving master. I am but his humble servant once more, like everyone else in Arras.

Once the maid leaves I wait for him to make the call to have her altered or removed, but he doesn't place it. I've performed to his satisfaction.

The main course is a selection of vegetables—carrots,

potatoes, a squash of some sort—in a heavy tomato sauce. The first bite reveals complex tones of red wine and I savor it, before pointing out the obvious.

"There's no meat."

"I'm trying to eat less of it. Doctor's orders," he explains.

"You're immortal."

"I am not immortal."

"You've used other people's time threads to stay alive for hundreds of years," I argue.

"That's not immortality."

"What is it then?" I ask.

"That's privilege."

It must be nice to be a man.

"And privilege allows me to choose such spirited company," he continues.

I smile at him. "I can throw this plate against the wall if you like."

"There's been enough collateral damage for one evening, I think."

I shrug and pretend to pick up the plate but he doesn't crack a smile of his own. The Cormac who could appreciate my spirited company seems to be fading with each dramatic new development in Arras. At least the old Cormac was fun to fight with. Now his behavior is unpredictable.

"Despite your behavior this evening, I have a present for you."

"It's not my birthday," I tell him. Still no smile.

"You missed two while you were away," he reminds me. "I'm catching up." Now he is smiling, acting sweet, his attitude totally reversing in seconds. I can't wrap my head around it.

"Does that count?"

"I'm having it brought with the dessert course," he says.

"Is my present edible?" I ask. Chocolate might be worth getting excited over.

"Generally it's considered poor taste to eat one's presents."

"Unless it's chocolate."

"It's not chocolate."

"Damn."

When they arrive with the final course, my dessert is placed in front of me. I can't stop staring.

But my present won't meet my eyes.

"Amie will be residing at the Western Coventry for the foreseeable future," he says. I look to Amie for a sign that she's happy about this, but she's watching her plate.

"What do you think?" he asks.

"You said it wasn't chocolate. There is clearly chocolate on this plate," I say, smiling.

"The dessert is chocolate," he says.

"Amie loves chocolate." It's the only thing I can think to say in this moment. Her eyes flicker up to me and she gives me a tentative smile as though a real one would be too costly. She can't be here. Amie is a means of distraction.

"I see you have that in common," Cormac says. He gestures to the desserts in front of us—*torta di cioccolato*. The same as at my first meal at the Coventry. Now I'm eating it with my sister. The sister who was never supposed to wind up here.

"It's delicious," Amie says in a polite, if small, voice.

"There's more. Don't be shy about it," he says. "My girls are too skinny."

My stomach sinks at the way he casually throws out *my girls*. Neither of us belongs to him, yet we're both in his possession.

"What else do you like to eat?" I ask Amie, at a loss for what normal conversation would consist of between us. We can't talk about the last two years of her life, and I have no clue what lies Cormac has fed her about me. But I do know the surest way to lose my sister is to try to find out. The last time I saw her, she called me a freak. I'm not sure if time or alteration has softened her toward me, but I can't risk my second chance with her now.

"Curry," she says, her lips turning up at the edge again.

"Me too."

"And I like the onion soup."

Cormac smirks at this revelation. I don't tell her what I think of it. We manage a few more minutes of awkward conversation, but it only serves to remind me of the rift Cormac has created between us.

Once she had been my sister. Then she was Riya, a little girl rewoven into another family, and now she is here—Amie again. But not my Amie. She would never be my Amie after what they had done to her. She was too quiet, her bubbliness replaced by a timid subservience. If my parents hadn't trained me to resist the Guild, is this how I would have wound up: an obedient girl locked away in a tower?

When the plates are cleared, the two of them stand to leave my quarters and for a moment I want to ask Amie to stay. There's more than enough room and more can always be made. But I know Cormac will never allow it. He'll oversee our interactions, listen to our conversations, and chaperone our time together. He can't trust me not to undo all the work he's put into Amie.

"Will I get to see Pryana soon?" Amie asks Cormac.

"Of course. She was asking about you," he tells her. Amie bounces a little, clapping her hands, and I'm taken aback. Maybe the Amie I remembered wasn't gone. Behind her Cormac smiles at me, revealing rows of perfect teeth.

I can't bring myself to ask her about Pryana, the one person in the Coventry who has a real reason to hate me. I'd been responsible for her sister's death, at least in Pryana's mind. She couldn't see the lesson Maela wanted to teach us when she ripped most of an academy from Cypress: no one is safe from the Guild, and those at the loom least of all. Pryana had never forgiven me for my inaction. In truth, I've never forgiven myself, either.

Amie is led away from my apartment, to her own quarters, and I watch her go, wishing I could think of something better to ask her than what foods she likes now. But the questions I have for her can never be asked in front of Cormac.

Cormac pauses at my door, sliding his bow tie off his collar. For one horrible moment I think he's going to kiss me as he leans in, but instead he whispers, "Consider my present a reminder of what you have to lose."

I let him leave without bothering to point out that I've already lost her, but when the door closes behind him I rush to the bathroom. It's still the only place they don't watch me. I reach under the sink and feel around the pipes until my fingers close over the blade. I hid it in my sleeve at my first dinner when I returned to the Coventry, scared and uncertain of what to expect. But now I'm not thinking about defending myself, I'm considering how and when to strike.

I can't unwind Cormac, especially now that Amie is finally close. Attacking him like that would only undermine Arras's situation, and I don't have everything I need yet. I have to wait for the right opportunity—keep playing along until I can access the alteration information I need to fix my mother and recover the soul strand I hope is kept somewhere in the Coventry's repository. Once I do that, I'll need to incapacitate him to put my final plan into place. Arras needs a rebirth and it must begin with Cormac. He must change. If he refuses, I can change his mind for him. I settle onto the floor, the knife cradled carefully in my hand. It reflects the image of my engagement ring, and I choke back a scream.

With Amie here I'll have another source of information. She will hear things spill from his lips, and if I can earn her trust I will learn those secrets from her. But to do that I must trust her as well. Cormac may have twisted her to his purposes, but the old Amie is in there and I know how she works. I know her heart as well as my own. Cormac thinks he has the upper hand, but two can play this evil game.

Albert's words echo in my memory:

Destroy the looms. If you choose this path, others will follow you as Whorl. Embrace and trust them, but know their hearts. As you must know your own.

EIGHT

I'M UNCERTAIN WHEN I'LL HEAR FROM MY sister. I'm sure she's still scared of me after the night on Alcatraz when I unwound Kincaid, but the very next morning a note arrives. She's arranged for us to have a fitting for new gowns the next day, something I'm not looking forward to. But it's the first time I'll be alone with her since my retrieval, so I go with the flow and agree to host it in my overlarge quarters.

As soon as she arrives with Pryana at her side, I know this is a mistake. Pryana's eyes travel along the walls of my living room, taking in the upholstered sofas and carved tables, all the essence of elegance and wealth.

"Aren't *you* moving up in the world." Pryana isn't asking me a question. It's merely an observation—one that reeks of annoyance. This should have been her life.

"It's not really my taste," I say, leading them through the apartment to the bedroom. My closet is preconfigured for fittings, with mirror-lined platforms and ample space to work.

Amie dashes in and starts plucking gowns from the racks,

holding them up to her slender figure as she eyes herself in the full-length mirror.

"I don't think you're supposed to have taste as Cormac's wife." Pryana speaks in a quiet voice that only I can hear.

"I'm not terribly interested in mirroring my . . . fiancé's tastes," I say.

"How modern of you," Pryana says. She wanders through my closet, picking up heels from the shoe racks and examining them. "And stupid."

I snatch the shoes back from her. "I'm known for my abstinence."

Before the nastiness can escalate between us, Amie coughs politely. I don't want her caught in the middle of our feud, especially since I can't trust Pryana's motivations for getting close to her. But Amie might as well know how Pryana and I feel about each other.

The seamstresses arrive and maids take our dresses, hanging them to wait while we're measured and sized. Standing with my sister and my old enemy in nothing more than a wispy slip, I feel surprisingly vulnerable. I thought I would outgrow feeling awkward around Pryana, but she's still as poised as ever. One thing I'm definitely not.

"I love the lace on your hem," Amie says, darting over to study it. "I think it must be Chantilly."

It's such a silly thing to notice, and yet some of the tension in the room evaporates.

"Amie knows everything about textiles," Pryana explains to me after I give my sister a curious look.

"If I don't get chosen as a Spinster," Amie whispers to me, "I want to be assigned to make the dresses."

I smile at her. For a second, she's five years old and we're back in our living room in Romen, splayed out on the floor, watching Spinsters stroll the purple carpet at the State of the Guild address.

We were innocent then, seeing only the beautiful surface of Arras's elite class. Knowing Amie still studies dresses makes me feel as though a balloon filled with happiness is inflating inside my chest. Somehow, even with everything she's been through, this hasn't changed. It brings me hope.

"You would make beautiful dresses," I tell her. *And you'll be safe doing it,* I add silently. No one would spare a second thought for a seamstress.

"Perhaps she'd make a better Spinster," Pryana suggests.

"Oh, I still want to be a Spinster," Amie says, grabbing my hands. "Don't worry, Adelice. I'll make you proud."

Behind her Pryana raises an eyebrow.

That's about the last thing that would make me proud, but I don't say this in front of the group. To my surprise, the same concern seems to be reflected in Pryana's eyes.

They could only spare two seamstresses for our fitting and Amie insists on watching Pryana and me go first.

"This is my favorite part. I like to learn how they do it and it's hard while you're the one being fitted," she explains. Pryana and I glance at each other but we don't argue with her. I climb onto the platform and a girl begins measuring my arms. Pryana stands directly across from me and it's like looking in a warped mirror as the seamstresses stretch the tapes across our limbs. Over our busts. Around our waists. Pryana not only seems older to me now, if only slightly, but I realize, as we stand parallel to each other, that she looks older as well.

Pryana isn't the girl she was when I met her during orientation. Not anymore. That first day Pryana was wild, asking questions without pause and fluttering her eyelashes at the valets and officials. She was everything a Spinster *could* be. She believed in her role here, and her right to hold it. Now she's composed and polished. But underneath the veneer of self-assurance something is broken. I know how this happened, of course. I know she was set to be my replacement both as Creweler and as Cormac's wife. For a girl with as much ambition as Pryana once displayed, rejection must have destroyed something vital in her.

But she isn't trying to kill me. At least I don't think she is. It's a start.

"You've lost weight," the seamstress says to me, checking her chart. "It's been too long since your last fitting."

The measurements on file are not that old. I stood on a platform like this less than four months ago by my time, preparing to escort Cormac to the State of the Guild, but to the seamstress those measurements are two years old. A lot of time has passed in Arras since I escaped to Earth. But for me, I'd only been gone for a few months. I couldn't exactly explain that to the seamstress.

"She must not be eating enough," Pryana says, and for one second there is a flash of the old Pryana, the one who could be equal parts clever and cruel. A sudden thought sends a chill up my spine: Why hasn't Cormac altered her memory or wiped it completely?

The seamstress is encouraged by Pryana's participation and continues: "I can't understand why they would let you go this long between fittings, especially with the amount of traveling you'll be doing soon."

"Traveling?" I ask.

Amie looks up from the chart she's swiped from the seamstress and laughs. "Didn't Cormac tell you? This was his idea. He said you would need appropriate clothing for your trips."

They all wait for my reaction but I shrug. "He's not the most talkative."

"Not lately," the seamstress says, popping a pin from between her gritted teeth and fastening a swath of fabric around my waist.

"Maybe Adelice and Cormac are too busy to talk," Pryana suggests. Amie looks horrified but the seamstresses giggle.

"Don't," Amie warns. "You'll make me sick."

"You aren't excited about the wedding?" Pryana's seamstress asks Amie.

Amie looks torn between shaking her head and nodding. "I'm happy for them, but Ad is my sister and Cormac is like my father."

A wave of revulsion tumbles through my stomach. *Like my father.* Cormac is the reason she has no father. He took that away from her and now he dares to assume the role. I know better. Amie is a pawn—as expendable as anyone else in this twisted game. If he ceases to need her, she'll be tossed down to Earth or left to waste away in a coventry without a second thought. I can't imagine him expending enough energy to love a child.

"That does make things . . . complicated," the seamstress

says. I wonder if my relationship to Amie is common knowledge or not.

"But your bridesmaid's dress will be beautiful," Pryana says, directing Amie's attention away from the painful topic. "And I imagine you'll probably wear it on the purple carpet."

"Do you think so?" Amie practically squeals the question.

"I'm sure the wedding will be a gala event."

"What if I'm not invited?"

No part of me is looking forward to my nuptials with Cormac. But despite that, there is a little part of me that can see Amie fussing with my train and holding my bouquet.

"You're invited," I say. If I actually go through with the wedding, I dare Cormac to tell me my sister can't come.

"Oh, thank you, Adelice." Without thinking, Amie lunges forward and hugs me. It catches me off guard and before I can enjoy it, she pulls back, wincing. "Sewing pins!"

"You might want to save the hugging until I've finished," the seamstress says.

"Did I miss the hugging?" a voice calls in from the bedroom. I don't have to wait to see her to know that voice. I've heard it in a dark cell and in a quiet salon, whispered in my ear and shouted across a room.

She enters and I note she still has the violet eyes, but she's cultivated a striking streak of gray in her raven locks. Other than that, she doesn't look a day older than when I left. Apparently she's aging gracefully and *slowly*.

"What a surprise, Maela," I say.

Amie freezes for a moment and I can't figure out why. For a second I want to grab Maela and demand to know what she's done to my little sister. I've borne the brunt of Maela's anger before. I know the twisted feats she's capable of. But instead I press my scarred fingertips together and muster up a false smile.

"I heard I was missing a party, and you know how I love parties." Her voice is full of trills and bells, masking the darkness she hides. A darkness that sneaks up on you before you realize you're in danger.

"We should have invited you," Pryana says apologetically, but I don't believe for a moment that there's any love lost between them.

"I am your mentor," Maela reminds her.

That's new. Pryana had been assigned to someone else when I was here last.

"You *were* my mentor," Pryana corrects her in a gentle voice. The whole interaction is strange. Maela displaying her usual penchant for the dramatic interpretation of events while Pryana stays collected, even distant.

"She pretends to be Creweler for a few months and forgets the little people who helped her get there," Maela says to me.

I wonder what Maela thinks of me, if she's been allowed to remember our past. Regardless, she clearly still hates me.

The activity continues in the room, but the seamstresses have slowed their progress, obviously not wanting to miss anything that passes between the three of us. They listen, holding their breath like the pins clamped between their teeth.

"Are they designing your wedding dress?" Maela asks. Her voice is sugary like too-sweet tea, and equally hard to swallow.

I shake my head. "Not yet. We still have plenty of time for that."

"Oh," she says in a thoughtful voice. "I heard differently."

Trust Maela to come in and act like the most important

woman in the Coventry. She behaved the same way when she oversaw my brief training on the looms. I know better than to believe a word she says.

"There are plenty of rumors flying around the Coventry these days, Maela," Pryana says, almost as if she's coming to my defense. Apparently we both now view Maela with the apprehension she deserves, but that doesn't make us friends yet.

"I came to speak to Adelice," Maela says, not rising to Pryana's bait.

"You're in luck then," I say, tilting my head in invitation.

Maela's lips purse tightly as she glances at the other people in the room. "It hasn't been announced officially yet," she says with an emphasis bordering on warning, "but you'll be hosting a loom demonstration at the end of the week."

My heart slams against my chest and it takes every ounce of willpower not to smile, a reaction I don't quite understand. "For whom?" I manage to ask as my fingers begin to tingle.

Maela's lip curls up at my reaction. "For the Stream. Cormac wants to show you off."

The excitement leaches from me slowly, fading out until it reaches my twitching fingertips and is replaced by a chill that numbs my body. A distraction. He wants to use me as a distraction, and then I'll be locked away again.

"I'll be overseeing the filming," Maela continues.

But I already knew Cormac wouldn't be there. Something has his attention elsewhere—something terrible if he's using me as a decoy to distract Arras.

"Thank you for letting me know," I whisper.

Maela scans my face as though she senses the shift in my

reaction, but in the end she doesn't care. "I should be going. I have plenty of things to do."

As soon as Maela exits the room, Pryana lets out a low whistle. "I'm sure there are plenty of young Spinsters to terrify."

"I wondered when she was going to show her face. I was always a favorite of hers," I add. Pryana and I share a laugh.

Amie lets out a nervous giggle. She hasn't spoken since Maela's impromptu entrance, and I can't say I blame her.

"Maela can be very intimidating," I say to Amie, hoping to put her back at ease. "It's her most winning personality trait."

"I would hate to see her other characteristics, then." Amie twists a piece of lace around her fingers.

"Yes, you would," Pryana agrees.

"What other rumors are flying around the Coventry?" I ask. It's hard to find the courage to bring this up, because I don't trust Pryana. However, she's *out there*, and I know she hears all the gossip.

"Nothing new. Spinsters sneaking around with valets. Ministers engaging in dirty politics," she answers, without giving me any concrete examples.

"I want to know the rumors about Cormac." I'm taking a chance admitting this is what I want to know. Neither Amie nor Pryana has any loyalty to me. As it is, they might only be around to report back to Cormac. But my situation can't get any worse. I don't expect to get a straight answer from Pryana, but even if she is spying for him I have nothing to lose.

"They say he's going mad." Pryana's answer sucks the air from my lungs.

I'd thought the same thing. But how widespread were the rumors? There were always plenty of rumors at the Coventry. Usually they were tangled with a string of truth.

"He's losing his mind because the Whorl is coming," the seamstress says in a whisper. My eyes flash to Pryana's and she nods. I'm uncertain how to respond. How did a seamstress at the Coventry hear of the Whorl?

"Everyone is jealous," Amie says in a burst of annoyance.

"Jealous of what?" I ask.

"You," she says. There's a furious blush on her fair skin as she speaks. "They're jealous that he's marrying you and that's why everyone is spreading lies about him."

Cormac had thoroughly ingratiated himself with Amie in my absence. If anyone is going to tattle on me it'll be her, I realize sadly.

Still, Amie might as well know the truth. I have enough lies to keep straight. It isn't a secret that I don't want to marry Cormac. "They're welcome to him."

It was the wrong thing to say with Pryana in the room and I immediately wish I could take it back.

"He wants you to be happy, Ad," Amie says in a quiet voice. The room falls silent, and the fitting ends without any more words exchanged between us.

One of the seamstresses starts to hum an old melody my mother used to sing to me as a child. When I look at Amie, tears glisten in her eyes. She remembers it, I'm sure. But I'm not certain if she can place it; those little moments of our lives before may have been wiped from her mind. The damage Cormac did to her is severe and I'm not sure it can be undone. Valery overcame his tinkering, though perhaps only briefly.

For all I know she could have turned on Dante and the Agenda the moment I left with Cormac. I doubt it, though. Alteration can change many things about a person but still not affect her true essence. There's only one way to permanently alter someone's personality and I knew from my interactions with our mother that Cormac hadn't gone that far with my sister. Amie still has her soul.

There's an awkward pause we should fill with a hug, but neither of us is ready for that. Instead we say goodbye.

Pryana stops at the door, shooing Amie along, and I brace myself.

"I'm not going to hit you," she says.

"You've hit me before," I remind her, my fingers rubbing my jaw to relieve the echo of pain the memory recalls.

"Things have changed around here, Adelice." Each of Pryana's words is heavy, laced with a meaning I don't quite understand. "Keep your eyes open."

After they leave, I walk from room to room, surveying the emptiness that's more acute than ever.

And even more dangerous.

NINE

THE CREWS CLUSTER INTO THE STUDIO SPACE, setting up lighting equipment and cameras. The studio is bare and simple, but large enough to fit the dozen or so crew members who will film my profile for this evening's Stream broadcast. I tug at my short skirt, feeling too exposed already. I'm not eager to be filmed, but Cormac arranged this as a way to introduce me before we begin a publicity tour through Arras—a fact that makes me even less interested in performing for the cameras. I've been dressed in a pink wool suit with gold buttons on the lapels because Cormac says it's matronly.

Exactly how a sixteen-year-old wants to be described.

He wants me to look like a wife, not a teenage girl, but I'm not sure a wool suit will hide our massive age difference.

Maela is handling my preparation. As neither of us has killed the other yet, I'd say it's going well. But then she flies back into the studio, barking out orders and shoving past several cameramen.

"We're behind schedule already," she complains loudly. "Are none of you capable of working in a timely fashion?"

"We were waiting for you," I tell her. This isn't entirely true, but I can't imagine starting without her. She probably would have interrupted the broadcast to throw a hissy fit.

"The program is supposed to stream in five minutes," she says.

"Ma'am, we're ready to go live. If Miss Lewys is prepared to begin, we'll start right on time," a cameraman says. He glowers at her as he speaks, and Maela balks. I wonder if she's more upset that he dared to stand up to her or if she's angry that he called her ma'am.

"Adelice." She sweeps over to me and hovers. "You will simply be adjusting a rainstorm in the Southern Sector. As we discussed, another Spinster will oversee your work from the main studios."

Because I'm too dangerous to trust with a loom. I stare at the loom procured for my use. It feels like a million years since I've woven on one and its gears sing out to me, my fingers itching to touch it. I have held the naked matter of the universe, but it was never as peaceful as the act of spinning the refined weave of Arras. There is a harmony to the precise patterns used to construct this world and working with them is as second nature to me as breathing.

"Do you understand?" Maela asks in a harsh voice, and I look up to find her staring down at me.

"I'm sorry," I say. "I was thinking."

"Try not to *think* during the program," she says. "Cormac wants you to make an impression."

Of course Cormac does. He's betting on this charade to distract the citizens of Arras from the tension within the weave.

"You only want me to add some lightning?" I clarify. I long to touch the rain, but I've been told exactly what I'm expected to do.

"I want you to not screw this up," she hisses in a low voice meant only for me.

"It's a good thing I'm the one doing it, then," I say.

A commotion interrupts our exchange, and the Stream reporters part to reveal Cormac standing in the doorway. I shouldn't be surprised. He's obsessed with choreographing every aspect of my return to Arras—and of our sham engagement. The sheer fact that he would ask Maela to direct this shows how little he trusts me not to mess things up.

"Prime Minister." The respectful greeting is murmured by every man as Cormac passes through the room, heading straight to Maela and me. When he reaches us, he ignores Maela and leans down to plant a kiss on my forehead. He lingers long enough for the several cameramen who snap photos of the moment.

"I will answer questions at the beginning of the broadcast," he announces.

More than a few of the men grimace. Undoubtedly this will affect their Stream schedules and carefully planned programming. But no one challenges him. No one would dare deny the prime minister a chance to speak to his people. No one who wanted to keep his job, or for that matter, his life. I think of the man who dared to ask about my parents once at a rebound station, how he was carried away to an unknown fate.

Now I know he probably wound up on Earth, half the man he once was, forced to become a Remnant to fulfill the whims of the Guild.

"We go live in thirty seconds," a man announces from behind the camera.

Cormac looks to his side, spotting Maela still hovering in range of the camera lens. He groans and shoves her out of the way. It's inelegant and rude, and Maela's cheeks blaze with fury, but her gaze is leveled directly at me. I make a mental note to remind Cormac not to put me under her direction for future events and programs.

"And we're live," the man says, pointing a finger at the young reporter selected to interview Cormac and me.

"We're extraordinarily honored tonight to bring you an interview with Prime Minister Patton from the studios of the Western Coventry," he says, introducing the topic of the program.

"I'm pleased I could make it here to officially introduce my citizens to the young woman who has captured my heart," Cormac says. His stance is steady and everything from his gesticulations to his perfect smile prove how he weaseled his way to the top of the Guild.

"We've had the opportunity to meet Miss Lewys today," the reporter continues in a smooth voice, "and I think it's safe to assume she will capture the hearts of Arras, too."

Not a single one of these men has talked to me. Not even the one who adjusts the microphone system for the audio recording. I might become Cormac's wife, but that means nothing to them. I could be a prop for all they care.

"Prime Minister, I know everyone in Arras is dying to

know the same thing. How did Miss Lewys capture your attention?"

If one of them uses the word *capture* again, I'm going to scream.

I was the one who was *captured*, and it definitely wasn't romantic. But like everything in politics, a shiny veneer applied to the surface of the story is meant to divert the listeners with its sparkle so they can't see the ugliness beneath.

"Miss Lewys came into service with the Western Coventry in a truly remarkable way."

That's an understatement.

"Her talent caught my eye almost immediately. She's an exceptional Spinster, but I soon discovered she had other talents and characteristics as well."

Imagine a woman having other talents.

"Can you elaborate?" the reporter asked.

I keep a smile on my face, even as I choke back the mirthless laugh bubbling to my lips. I'd love to hear what traits caught Cormac's attention. Was it my penchant for talking back or my obvious distaste for the Guild and everything it stood for, including him?

"Well, she is quite beautiful," Cormac says, exchanging a nod with the reporter.

Yes, that is definitely my most winning characteristic—to Cormac. I'm pretty sure he hates everything else about me. At least our marriage will be based on a foundation of mutual disgust.

"She is beautiful," the reporter confirms out loud as though they are discussing a statue behind them.

"And she has a rare treat for you tonight," Cormac says.

"We usually don't show real-time weaving on Stream programming, but this evening Adelice will be weaving a rainstorm throughout the Southern Sector. If you're in the area, you've probably been anticipating these showers all day. If not, you haven't checked your weather programming."

Cormac gives a stern look to the cameras and then relaxes into a grin. "I'm only kidding, of course."

I know better than this. Cormac is incapable of jokes. Everything is a thinly veiled threat with him and this one is very clear. He wants to make sure the citizens of Arras have their priorities straight. He needs everyone to have their eyes on me.

"Adelice." Cormac's arm opens wide as though he's presenting me. Somehow I feel more like a sacrifice than entertainment.

I smile widely and murmur a soft hello. I've been warned not to speak. This program isn't about hearing me speak. It's about giving Arras a face, one they've seen before if they've been allowed to remember it, while further glamorizing Spinsters. Now young girls can dream of beautiful clothing, luxurious lifestyles, *and* the possibility that they, too, could marry the most powerful man in the world one day.

On cue, the loom whirs to life and the Southern Sector's weave glides silkily onto it. Most of Arras won't be able to see the strands of life on the loom, but I'm told the producers of the program have illustrations that will be overlaid to show what I'm doing. But none of that matters now that there is a woven piece on my loom. The storm is set to occur over the entire sector. Most likely as a demonstration of how much power the Spinsters can exert over an entire population at one time. My zoom function isn't enabled since my work is merely cosmetic. I can add some lightning and not much else. But when I touch the weave with my bare fingertips the rain shivers into them, cool and wet. I let my fingers linger in the lush tapestry, savoring the smooth, damp texture of the strands.

Reaching down to the tray at the edge of the loom, I pluck a single strand of lightning from the few dozen threads I've been given for this program. It tingles through my hands, sparking with electricity as I delicately wiggle it into a cloud hovering somewhere near the center of the sector. I imagine a bolt of light splintering the sky, followed by a *crack* booming over the homes of those watching the Stream from their living rooms. Before I can think, I add another, farther away, my fingers moving deftly.

I don't want to leave the loom. I want to go down to the studios and weave food rations. I want to lose myself in the precisely timed rain showers and snowstorms. I want to escape to a life of anonymity.

I could fold into this reality and forget everything. That's how addicting, how singular this experience feels. It consumes me. It motivates. For a moment I would do anything to knit my fingers into the slate-gray rain strands every day.

And as that desire pours through my blood, spreading like poison, my fingers ache for something new: destruction. My hands twitch toward the strands on the loom. Cormac wants a demonstration of my abilities, but shouldn't Arras see what I can also do? What all the girls trapped here can do? I suck in a breath and force myself to see the delicate weave in front of me. It teems with life, sparkling as it intersects with every piece around it.

I am not death. I am life.

"What an amazing demonstration," the reporter says, intruding on the euphoria of my work. The loom clicks off and the piece of tapestry fades away.

I miss it immediately. My center aches, hollow but for the longing to become part of something greater.

This is why the Spinsters do their work. This is why they don't abandon their duties. Because in the glorious moment when you can touch the fabric of the universe, you are one with it. You become it as you create it.

And this is why what the girls in the Eastern Sector did is spectacular to me. They walked away. And even now, with what I know, part of me wants to beg Cormac to bring the loom back for a few more moments.

I turn on my stool, crossing my legs in a prim posture for the camera, and smile again. But I wonder if the women watching at home spy the ghost of emptiness in my eyes.

"As you can see, Miss Lewys is a great asset to our looms and our world, and her role will continue to grow after she becomes my wife," Cormac says.

"Will she be working outside the looms?" the reporter asks. There's some hesitation to the question, but I'm not sure if it's because he doesn't want to ask or if it's because Cormac's insinuation is stunning, even to me.

"Not only will she be working outside the looms, she'll be working outside the home. It is our dream to move this world forward to more power and prestige. Each year Arras has advanced technologically, but it's time our greatest powers joined together in a new path. As you know, Spinsters are not allowed to marry. In many ways, Miss Lewys and I are embarking on a new world together, not merely a new marriage."

"And what is your hope for this new . . . world?" The reporter stumbles over the question.

I don't listen to Cormac's answer because I know it's lies. He's feeding the progressive dissenters what they want to hear: *Look, I'll give a woman some power on the Stream. We're moving forward, so stop worrying your pretty heads about the fate of the future generations.*

But anyone with half a brain would notice I'm not allowed to speak. They would see my pristine costume, specifically chosen to look demure and womanly on the camera, and know I have no more power than they do. Cormac's plan is to show them that even a woman of great power is willing to lay it aside and become a wife. But I can hardly expect them to know that when even Cormac doesn't take my power seriously.

And yet, he placed me on this loom tonight. If I were a true rebel, I would never have done what he asked. I would have wreaked havoc over the entire Southern Sector, throwing it into an uprising. But even as I think this I spot the techprint on my wrist.

That's not who I am. Unlike Cormac, I have no desire to abuse my skills to hurt the innocent. He knew that when he placed me here tonight. He's calling my bluff, but he doesn't know the cards I've hidden up my sleeve, especially not the access card I swiped from one of the guards. Cormac knows I'm a Tailor, though I don't think he's considered exactly how I could use that to my advantage.

But I have.

TEN

THE DREAM IS THE SAME. I am in a white room. When I look closely I see them. Frozen. Trapped. The faces of those I have loved and lost. My father. Enora. Loricel. They stare at me with dead eyes from translucent faces. Their mouths are twisted open, but struck dumb.

And still I go to each of them and ask them how to help. Nothing changes, so I return to the loom. On it are strands, but they are bloody. A bow is tied across the polished top of the loom, a single card dangling from it, reading: *Choose*.

The threads are dying, oozing away on the cold steel, but when I reach out to fix them the bands of the loom slice open my hands and fingers.

To save them I must bleed.

I reach forward and catch the sticky strands between my thumb and index finger and I see them.

Jost and Amie and Dante. They're dying.

Erik. His beautiful face contorts into a mask of anguish, and I begin to work without hesitation. Spurred by the ache in my chest that pulses with each cut of my fingers as I try to help him.

I twist and I tangle and I try to stop the blood ebbing from the strands, but as I do, I bleed more and more and more. A puddle forms at my feet and I know there's no way to save them all.

I begin to shake but then I hear a voice. "Adelice, wake up!"

The world blurs into focus and I open my eyes to find my sister standing over me with a frown on her face. I must have fallen asleep in a chair.

"You were dreaming," she says. "It sounded like a nightmare."

It was, but I don't tell her that. Instead I reach out and hug her close to me. For a second it's awkward, but she settles into my embrace. Her soft blond hair tickles my skin. We are right again.

"Are you okay?" She pulls away and looks at me with concern.

"I'm fine. I don't even remember the dream," I lie.

"I came to tell you that you were amazing on the Stream. I wish I could've been there, but Cormac forbade me."

I frown at this. Since when does Cormac care what Amie does? He's given her the run of the place since she arrived.

"I can leave if you're tired," she says, misinterpreting my frown. I shake my head. The dream sticks to me like the blood on the loom. I want Amie to stay because I need her. She strokes my hand, reminding me of our mother.

"What's this?" Amie reaches out and runs a soft finger over my techprint.

"Credentials," I say without thinking. I immediately wish I could take it back.

"From when you were with the revolutionaries?"

"Yes," I say hesitantly. Amie wasn't there to see Benn—the man we both knew as our father—print me on the night of my retrieval. She doesn't remember that our parents were the ones who pushed us into those tunnels.

"Adelice, you're lying to me," she says in a low voice. "I know it. You keep lying to me. It's like you forget that I'm your sister sometimes. I know you well enough to know when you're telling me the truth."

I sigh. This Amie isn't the one I whispered to at night or opened Winter Solstice presents with. She's different now. Hesitant where she was once vivacious. She doesn't run to me like she did when we were girls at academy. We don't share the same memories or experiences. Even though I want to trust her, I can't keep the Guild from using her against me.

"Amie, they monitor everything we say to each other," I tell her, choosing a logical reason to keep things from her.

"They're listening to us?" she asks. She's still very girlish sometimes in her trust of the Guild, so she doesn't see the twisted mechanisms at work here.

"Yes. And I don't think Cormac wants me to talk about my time on Earth," I say, knowing I don't want to tell her, either. "It's not safe for you to know, and I don't want to relive it."

"Was it terrible?" she asks.

It's a testament to how dependent she is that she doesn't see I'm unhappy here.

"No it wasn't, but it's in the past."

"And that's it? I was out of your life for years, and you won't share what happened to you? Or why you don't look any older than you did the night they came for you?" Her lower lip trembles like when she was a girl and our mom told her no.

"I can't," I say. Her face sinks and she stands to leave. "I can't tell you about *all* of it."

Amie sits back down and waits with an eager expression.

"This isn't a secret," I say. "At least, not one that Cormac cares about."

"Is it good?" She used to ask me that question at night when we swapped stories as girls.

"There's a boy," I say.

"Not Cormac?"

"No." I laugh at her question, but she leans forward and grabs my hands.

"Tell me!" she demands.

"His name is Erik."

Amie releases my hand and bites her lip in excitement. "I like that name."

It's exactly how I imagined it would be once I started courtship appointments. If I hadn't come to the Coventry, Amie and I would have giggled over boys late into the night. Now this is as close as I'll ever get.

"He has long blond hair. It's a little bit wavy. And bright blue eyes the color of the Endless Sea."

"He sounds cute," she says, squeezing my hand.

"He is," I say. "You saw him on the island."

The words escape my mouth before I think them through. I shouldn't bring up that night. Not now while our relationship is as fragile as glass.

"I don't remember much about that night." She's lying and

I know it, because despite all that's changed about Amie, I recognize how she tugs at the one strand perpetually loose from her pinned-up hair. The same strand that wiggled free of her pigtails and ponytails and braids in our childhood. She would curl it around her delicate fingers, twisting at it, when she got nervous.

"Do you love him?" she asks me.

"I do." The words sit like a lump in my throat. "It doesn't matter, though."

The excitement fades from Amie's face. "What about Cormac? Do you love him?"

There are things I'm willing to lie to Amie about, but this isn't one of them. "I don't. But my arrangement with Cormac was never about love, Ames. It's about what's best for Arras."

"Even if you aren't happy?" Her eyes are wide and earnest as she asks.

I wish it were that simple. I wish I could tell Amie that love and happiness win in the end, but that would only be another lie. "Arras is more important."

"And that scar on your wrist? What does it mean?" she asks one more time.

I recall the words my father said to me the night I was taken: *Remember who you are.* I try to remember who I am, but I've discovered too many things about myself since that night. I'm not even sure I'm the same person anymore. I've evolved in many ways from who I was in that cellar.

"Decide who you are," I say to her. "That's what it means now."

"Who are you?" she asks in a soft voice.

"I'm still deciding," I admit. My eyes search my sister's face and I'm amazed—despite the lost time, all I see is young Amie, as though she's always been this age to me. "Who are you?"

"I want to be a Spinster," she admits. Her eyes flash briefly at me but then she looks away.

Her confession is bitter as I swallow it, but I'll never win her back by belittling her dreams. "And why can't you be?"

"Cormac has let me try to use the looms already," Amie admits, making my chest constrict. She shouldn't be on the looms yet. She isn't even sixteen years old.

"And?" I ask.

"I keep trying to see it," she says in a sad voice, "but I can't. And he's so disappointed. He's had me examined by doctors and everything."

I know Cormac has had Amie's memory altered, but this sends a chill shivering down my neck. I wouldn't put it past him to try to alter her to have my skills. It's a terrifying possibility given how much control he already exerts over her. Perhaps this is why he hasn't pushed for me to be altered yet. He already has a test subject.

"I've been going down to a private studio," she continues. "Cormac gave me permission, but I had to promise I would inform him if I saw anything."

"Let me help you," I suggest. "Cormac can't see the weave himself, so he isn't a good person to advise you." I hate using her like this, but I need to get on a loom. I'm curious about what Cormac has shown her of the looms.

"Would you?" For a moment, Amie is the adoring sister looking up to me for wisdom, and I almost break.

Instead I push back against my guilt and tack a smile onto my lips. "Of course."

ELEVEN

"HERE IT IS." AMIE RUNS HER HAND over one of the new security panels and the door creaks open. She pushes her way into the stone room as the lights automatically turn on, flooding the small studio. There's an empty loom directly in front of us, but I force myself not to run toward it. Amie enters her access code and the loom whirs to life. I could see so much with the loom, not to mention change those things, but I have to tread carefully with my sister.

I look at Amie, whose eyes bore into the empty work space on the loom.

"There's nothing on it," I tell her in a soft voice.

"Oh!" She's embarrassed but she manages a giggle.

I reach over and set the loom to pull up her most recent coordinates. Unfortunately, the last place she looked was an ordinary metro in the Western Sector. I can make out the entire metro—neighborhoods, the metro center, parks, academies. Try as I might I can't get it to pull anything else up, except for security warnings. I shouldn't be surprised that the looms are so carefully controlled and monitored now. I'd hoped to find a hole in Cormac's tight-knit security system, thinking he might have a blind spot when it comes to Amie. I revert to the original coordinates and sit back so Amie can look at the loom.

"Do you see anything?" I ask her.

She shakes her head. I zoom in to take a closer look at the outlying neighborhoods and ask again.

This time her lip trembles as she says no.

"It's okay if you can't do this," I say, putting a hand over hers. *It's more than okay,* I add silently.

"It is not! What use will I be to anyone?" she says.

"I thought you wanted to design dresses."

"I do! But Cormac will be disappointed in me. He has faith in me and I'm going to prove him wrong." Amie wipes at the tears dribbling down her cheek and turns wide, tearstained eyes on me, looking for comfort.

"I will take care of Cormac," I say. "Let's try one more time."

I zoom in as close as I can to the weave, allowing the machine to default to a surveillance feed. We are looking at someone's living room. Amie sucks in a breath and I'm certain she can see this, but when I turn there are tears glistening in her eyes.

"Nothing," she whispers.

I drop my arm over her shoulder and hug her close to me, shushing her as she sobs against my shoulder. How can I ever tell her this is something she doesn't want? Especially when it's the last bit of the old Amie left after Cormac's alterations?

So I let her cry and no part of me rejoices that she can't see the weave or work the looms. I always thought it would be a relief to know my sister couldn't be a Spinster, but my fears have only been replaced by her pain.

"I have an idea," I say. "Let's sneak into the kitchen and find some chocolate."

Her eyes meet mine and a smile creeps over my sister's face as she nods. I pull her gently to her feet and we walk arm in arm down the hall. As we pass the studios, I notice what I missed before: heavy bolts and security panels—even on the rationing and weather studios.

I'm not the only one under tight control.

No wonder they're whispering that Cormac's mad, that the Whorl is coming. A month of this would make anyone dream of change. No one stops us as we duck into the kitchen. A few maids bustle past and a young girl stops to point us in the direction of the sweets.

"Mom would never let us have chocolate this late at night," I whisper to Amie conspiratorially. She giggles and I join her, choosing to ignore the dull ache in my chest at the thought of our mother.

I open the cupboard to discover a stack of chocolate bars, bonbons, and truffles. More chocolate than the entire sugar ration allotted in our childhood. I whip around to show off my discovery but Amie's back is turned.

"Ta-da!" I call out. But she doesn't turn toward me. Taking a step closer to her, I place a hand on her shoulder, urging her to look at me. Instead she steps to the side, revealing a large white cake with lacy lines of frosting that dip and weave delicately across its surface.

I can almost feel the too-sweet sting of the icing in the back of my throat.

"Why does this cake make my heart feel like it's going to explode?" Amie asks in a small voice.

I can barely tear my eyes from it to look at her, but when I do the pain is written across her face. They've taken the memory but not the pain.

"There was a cake the night I was retrieved," I remind her.

"I can't remember," she says. "Why can't I remember?"

"What?"

"Mom. Dad. They're here." She taps her forehead. "But they're not."

I have a choice. I can tell her the truth about Cormac and alteration. I can tell her he has stripped her of most of her childhood and adjusted her life to leave out the horrific events of that night. Or I can continue to lie to her.

"Because you miss them," I tell her, and in a way it's the truth.

"What happened to them?" This time her question is demanding. I know Cormac fed her a story about them. Given that she's been altered on more than one occasion, he's probably told her several stories about her life. But I don't know what she remembers or how she remembers it. I can't anticipate how she'll react to the information she desperately wants.

Telling Amie the truth serves no purpose. It might turn her against Cormac, but in the end, if I can't find a way to save Mom, then she'll also have to live with the knowledge of what's been done to our mother. Amie's innocence has already been twisted enough by Cormac. I must carry the burden alone. "They're dead. They died when I tried to escape from the retrieval squad."

Amie takes a step back as though I've hit her. "They died because you ran?"

In many ways this is what happened, but the guilt pressing on my chest tells me that even I can't blame myself entirely. Amie remembers little about our parents, even less than I knew that night. But I can't bring myself to tell her they had connections to the Agenda any more than I can tell her about Dante or that our mother is still alive. There's so much more to the story that it wouldn't help if she could remember it. It doesn't matter, though, because Amie believes the little I've told her. And she hates me for it. I can see it in her green eyes, the cool, hard emerald—she looks exactly like our mother when she's angry.

"How could you?" she asks.

"I didn't want this life." Even though I'm willing to protect her from the story of what happened to our parents, I'm not willing to pretend a Spinster is more than a false ideal. She needs to know there is a world so much larger than this.

"What's wrong with this life?" a soft voice asks behind us. Startled, Amie and I turn to find Pryana watching us.

"It's a lie," I tell her.

Pryana already knows this. She's smart enough to have always known.

Before Pryana can speak again, Amie chokes back a sob and rushes toward the door. I begin to stop her, but the weight of the truth holds me back. It's better this way.

"Every life is a lie we tell ourselves to help us sleep," Pryana says with a mirthless laugh.

"I never chose this lie."

Pryana takes a step closer to me and I can smell coconut on her skin. "I have news for you, Adelice. Every life is a choice. We don't get to pretend like we're forced into this world, this job, anymore. You chose to come back. I chose to play along."

"You're right," I say, meeting her steady gaze. "We have choices—you and I and Cormac. But there's a good part of the population who are powerless to stand up to the Guild, and they don't have a choice. You know that."

"Of course I do. I think of nothing else," Pryana says.

My breath catches in my throat not because she's agreeing with me, but because of the implication of her words.

"I see you've been sneaking cake," Pryana says, changing the subject.

"I was trying to cheer Amie up."

"Why was she upset?" Pryana's voice pitches up an octave.

"She can't see the weave on the loom. I thought I'd help her, but I couldn't."

"It's tricky," Pryana says, her eyes glued on mine. "Alteration does funny things to abilities. But I don't understand why you didn't tell her the truth about your retrieval."

"Why *would* I tell her the truth?" I reply as I pace the small space in front of the icebox.

"Because you hate Cormac," Pryana says. "He's the only one who gains anything by your keeping it from her."

So Pryana does know what Cormac did to my sister. "Amie gains something."

"And what's that?" Pryana asks.

"Innocence."

"Her innocence was robbed from her long ago," Pryana

says, and her tone reminds me that Cormac and the Guild have robbed it from us all.

"She doesn't know that, though," I say in a quiet voice. "I can't quite explain it. If I tell her why she can't remember and about what happened to our parents, she has to live with that."

"We all have to live with that," Pryana reminds me.

"Yeah, we do, but she's my kid sister. Someday she'll know. I won't be able to keep it from her forever. But right now she feels safe. She doesn't have nightmares. She doesn't blame herself."

"And you would rather she blame you?"

I take a deep breath, willing myself to broach a sensitive subject. "Wouldn't you do that for your sister?"

"I don't know," Pryana admits. Her voice shakes. "The Guild took her from me before I had the chance."

"You could have told Amie the truth. Why didn't you?"

Pryana hesitates as she twists her fingers together. "I'm not sure. It's not my place."

"Why are you being kind to Amie?"

"I don't have a sister to be nice to anymore," she says, opening the old wound we share. I'd lost my innocence about the nature of our world long before the day Maela ripped Pryana's sister and her classmates from their Cypress academy.

"Blame Maela," I say.

"I do blame Maela," she says, practically spitting the words at me. "Did it seem like we were best friends back there?"

I give her a grudging no. It sounds like whatever passed between them in my absence was as bad as what I'd endured under Maela. It also feels like Pryana still resents me.

"It's Cormac," Pryana says at last. "Maela hates anyone who catches Cormac's attention."

"And you were engaged to him," I say.

"Briefly." She shrugs. "I'm not exactly sorry to be rid of him. It was only a way out of here."

"You didn't want to be Creweler?" I ask, not hiding my surprise.

"I thought I did, but . . ." Pryana trails off. Her dark eyes meet mine. She doesn't need to finish the thought. We both know the burdens of being Creweler.

"All of this over a scumbag like Cormac Patton," I say.

"I was surprised you didn't know."

"I hadn't seen Maela for a long time. I thought she was mad about Erik."

"Don't get me wrong. She still hates you more than me, and Erik has a lot to do with that," Pryana says.

"How would she know about what happened between Erik and me?"

"She saw you kissing him in the garden," Pryana reminds me.

"I didn't mean that. Lots has happened since that night . . ." My thoughts trail away to memories of dancing in a moonlit courtyard and stolen kisses on the rocky shores of Alcatraz. I'm lost thinking of him, and I don't realize I've said too much.

Pryana takes a step back and studies me, then laughs. "You're in love with him."

"I . . ." But I don't know what to say, because if I lie, she'll know. I try to fight off the blush stealing over my face.

"The rumor was that you ran away for Jost." Pryana looks impressed.

"It's complicated."

"It usually is when you're in illicit relationships," Pryana says, but she's smiling all the way up to her eyes. "You do have good taste. His hair—he hasn't cut it?"

I allow myself a small grin and shake my head. Even though the thought of them both, Erik and Jost, of not knowing what's happening to them, whether they're safe—it's almost too much to bear.

"I'm not being nice to Amie for revenge," Pryana says, circling back to the question that sparked the conversation. "I like Amie. She reminds me of my sister."

"Pryana." I pause, unsure how to say this now. It's much too late for an apology. "I've made a lot of excuses for what happened that day, but I'm genuinely sorry about your sister."

"Me too, and . . . it's not your fault."

This morning I would never have thought she'd admit this to me.

"There are things that no one in Arras knows about," I say, feeling compelled to share something with her now. "Horrible things. If Amie knew—"

"Knew what?" Pryana presses me.

"Our mother isn't dead," I tell her. It's a relief to confess this to someone. No one on Earth really understood how difficult it was to find out what my mother had become. Even Dante forced himself to believe my mother was worth saving when he let her go, believing that a part of her was still in there. I wasn't so sure. "She's a—"

"Remnant?" Pryana guesses, and my mouth falls open. "I told you things have changed around here."

"You've always had the good gossip, but how in Arras do you know about Remnants?"

Pryana raises an eyebrow and then gestures that we should leave. As she turns to go, she flips her silky curls over her left shoulder to reveal the nape of her neck and the faint hourglass mark printed there. "Does this answer your question?"

I lunge for her, grabbing hold of her arm and whispering furiously, "You're Agenda?"

Pryana's pace remains steady and controlled, not wavering in the slightest at my accusation. "Shhh! *Things have changed.*"

We continue toward the tower and as the shock wears off, a smile sweeps over my face. "I have questions for you," I tell her. "There's a lot I need to know."

"Not right now," she says, parting ways with me at the elevator.

"When?" I clutch her arm, but the elevator doors begin to slide shut and I jump away as she mouths one word.

Soon.

TWELVE

WHEN PRYANA APPEARS IN MY DOORWAY THE following day, I remember what Albert told me—that people would follow me as the Whorl. This is my chance to see if that's true.

Pryana slides a thin bracelet over my wrist and yanks me into the hallway. "It's a mask," she explains. "It disrupts surveillance. Temporarily."

"For how long?" I ask.

"Thirty minutes. Where do you want to go?"

"The clinics," I say without hesitation. "And Cormac's suite."

"I can't guarantee we'll have time for both."

"The clinics then." I hate having to choose, but getting information on previous alterations, especially on what's been done with my mother's soul, has to come first. If things go wrong with Cormac, I might not get another chance to find it.

We move through the main tower and into the rest of the compound, passing the locked studios I saw last night. No one walks the halls. The Spinsters are on the looms. "They've fitted these walls with an artificial program."

"I know," I say. "There are no windows here at all."

"Not just that," Pryana says a trifle wistfully. "It's one big camera now. Rule number one about life at the Coventry: watch your step. Because they certainly are."

My eyes flick to the walls, half expecting to see eyes peeking through the plaster at me.

"But they can't see us because of this?" I ask her, holding up my bracelet.

"Nope. Present from the Agenda," she says, flashing me a grin.

"How did you get them?" I try to keep suspicion from seeping into my tone.

"Rule number two: the Agenda is everywhere."

How? It didn't make sense. No one else had rebelled when I escaped. Then I think of the hidden information on Enora's digifile. Erik helped her with it.

The seeds of rebellion were planted when we escaped, and they grew while we were gone. I realize that for the first time the accelerated timeline of Arras is working in the Agenda's favor.

"What are we looking for?" Pryana asks me as we wait quietly by the doors that lead into the medical wing of the compound. Before I can answer she raises a finger to her lips. Two nurses exit, chatting, and Pryana catches the door with the toe of her shoe, swinging it back open for me.

"I want to know what they've done to Amie," I lie, not ready to share all my plans with her. My alliance with Pryana is still too fragile for that.

"You already know that," Pryana says, glancing over at me. "They altered her memory, wiped it out of her."

"But I want to know exactly what they did . . . in case there are side effects," I say, hoping to sound more convincing.

"And that's all?" Pryana prompts. She's not buying it.

"I want to try to reverse what they've done to her."

Pryana's eyes widen. "And how will you do that?"

"I know some talented Tailors." I don't mention my own ability. The less Pryana knows about my plans, the safer we'll be if she's caught.

"We should look at the files first," Pryana says. "I know where they are."

As soon as we enter I remember everything, right down to the antiseptic scent that burns my nostrils. We pass the cold steel examination table, but when I look above it, I can't see the helmet of gears and tubes that mapped my brain for the Guild. How necessary are measurements and maps to alter someone?

Pryana has already hacked the main companel by the time I peel my attention from the ghostly room.

"Amie Lewys." Pryana moves over so that I can look through the files.

I skim the reports, looking for anything that will indicate how much damage they've done to Amie, until my gaze catches on the words *experiment terminated*. A long sigh escapes my mouth. I hadn't even realized I was holding my breath.

"They're not trying to alter Amie anymore." I motion to the companel screen.

Pryana reads it over my shoulder, but instead of looking relieved, her eyebrows knit together.

"What is it?" I ask, even though I dread the answer.

"You're right about Amie, but what does this mean?" Her index finger trails along the screen and I lean in to see:

It is recommended the Cypress Project experiments be expanded to candidates regardless of age or gender.

Our eyes meet and I know we're both thinking the same thing. Whatever this means, it's nothing good.

"Do you know what the Cypress Project is?" I ask her.

"No, but I don't like the sound of it."

Smart girl, I think, considering whether I should tell her and whether the Guild might have a violent response to a Spinster knowing about the Cypress Project. If the Agenda starts sharing info about it, Cormac will know it started with me. "Spinsters aren't natural. The Guild created us through genetic experiments."

"But if they did that . . ." Her voice fades away as she bites her lip. "Why girls?"

"Control," I say in a flat voice. "Any of the boys who showed the ability were erased from existence."

"Tailors?" Pryana guesses.

I nod, impressed with how much she's learned from the Agenda in Arras. Then again, even my parents had known this. They had merely chosen not to share the information with me. I ignore the tremble that races up my back at the thought of my parents and the secrets they kept from me. It hardly even bothers me anymore.

"But I don't know what they mean by expanding the experiments," I say as I push away from the desk and stare at the clinic's white walls. They glare back at me like a blank canvas waiting for me to make my move. The longer I look at them, the more questions tumble through my brain until one latches on and then breaks past my lips. "Do you think it's strange that they keep this information here?"

Pryana shrugs as she scrolls through the files on the companel. "They've probably done some of the experiments here."

I recall the metal helmet and the blinding light, followed by a series of questions meant to map how my mind worked. I'd been brought here for that. If I hadn't escaped when I did, I would have wound up on one of those slabs while Tailors altered my memory to make me more docile. This is where they would have taken Loricel on the night of my escape.

"Have you been back here?" I ask her.

"Yes." She turns away from the companel and stares me down. "The night you escaped. When they tried to alter me. Cormac wanted to splice me with Loricel's genetics so I could take over as Creweler. Any more tests for me?"

I don't even blink. Pryana must know how suspicious her change of heart seems. "One."

"What's stopping you? I'm dying to know how I can prove myself to you." There's hurt in her words.

"Why didn't he wipe you? You knew too much to be trusted. Why didn't Cormac alter your memories?"

Pryana snorts, shaking her head. "He did. At least he thinks he did. There's one thing you should know about the Coventry, Adelice. This place is teeming with Agenda."

"And the Agenda saved you?"

"A Tailor did," she says. "You have no reason to believe me, but who else can you trust?"

Albert's words echo in my mind. *Know their hearts.* I'm not sure I could ever know Pryana's heart.

But Amie does. "If Amie trusts you, then I do, too."

Pryana doesn't seem terribly moved by my admission.

Instead she focuses on the companel. "We don't have much time. You need to tell me what you're actually looking for."

"I told you—"

"Don't try to sell me that line about finding out what happened to Amie. We both know what happened to her. You need something else from here, and I'm dying to find out what it is." Her dark eyes sparkle as her mouth curves into an arrogant grin.

The problem with Pryana is that we're alike in too many ways. It's hard to fool someone who thinks the same way you do. That doesn't mean I want her to know I'm here to find information about putting the pieces of my mother back together. She would say it's endangering the Agenda.

"A girl's gotta have her secrets," I say with a shrug.

"She also has to have her allies."

Her choice of words stops me. Enora told me the same thing, and so did Albert—two people much wiser than myself.

"My mother's soul strand is here somewhere," I confess. "If I can find it."

A shadow crosses over her eyes. "I know where the strands are. When I found out about Remnants, I went looking for information on Ursula."

She's never spoken this name to me before, but I instantly know who she is from the twist of pain in her voice.

"Your sister," I say. "Did you find anything?"

"There was nothing left to find. Maela shredded her academy. Nothing was salvageable."

I consider wrapping my arm around her, but guilt weighs me down, preventing me from lifting a finger.

Pryana draws a long, steadying breath. "Finding your

mother's soul strand is a noble goal. I can help with that. But what's in Cormac's suite?"

"That's more complicated. Let me show you." I slide my fingers over the companel's screen, but before I can pull up any files on altering someone's appearance, the light overhead pulses red and a calm female voice calls, "Unauthorized access" repeatedly.

"How long was that mask supposed to work?" I ask Pryana as we scramble to our feet.

"Thirty minutes," she says before tacking on, "theoretically."

"You might have mentioned the 'theoretically' before."

The screech of boots echoes on the linoleum in the hall-way. Our only chance is that they don't know which room has been breached. Hopefully the mask can at least get this detail right.

"This way!" Pryana calls, shoving me into the small observation room attached to the office. My foot catches on the metal examination table and I plunge forward, knocking over a nearby cart. Pryana catches me and forces me back on my feet, dragging me along behind her before I can even recover from my stumble. At the door we pause, peeking out to check the hallway, which is, miraculously, empty. I hesitate for a moment, but Pryana rushes toward the door that leads back into the main area of the compound and I'm left with no choice but to join her.

As we clear each set of swinging doors, the muffled shouts following us grow closer until Pryana grabs my arms and pulls me through the doors to the dining room. "In here."

As soon as we enter she pushes me toward an empty seat and takes the one next to me. The dining hall has changed.

The large mahogany table that occupied the space when I first came to the Coventry is no longer there. Instead there are rows of individual tables. At each one a Spinster eats alone. As in the lower studios, every girl is confined to her own space, which keeps them from speaking to one another.

A few heads turn toward us and I smile brightly. The other girls turn back to their meals without returning the gesture. Plain chicken and a chunk of bread are placed before me. In the past extravagant feasts were presented at mealtime: curries and pastries and soups. This is utilitarian, nourishment and nothing more.

Pryana catches my eye and motions to the food. Picking up my fork, I try to eat even as my pulse races. As I chew on the dry meat, I study the other Spinsters. Their dresses are as plain as the food. A few have pinned up their hair, but hardly any wear cosmetics. Pryana and I look like peacocks in comparison, which only unnerves me more.

It's obvious we don't belong here right now.

Turning my attention to my plate, I force myself to eat. To blend in.

The door opens behind us and a group enters noisily, causing every girl in the room to sit up and look around. I catch my breath and force myself to do the same.

A handful of guards linger in the doorway and my stomach drops as Maela pushes past them. She scans the room, her eyes landing on me.

"Ladies," she calls out. "There has been a security breach. Please line up against the wall."

No one breathes a word. There's not even a sideways glance as each girl does exactly as she's told, myself included. Pryana squeezes in next to me, but I don't dare look at her as Maela paces down the line, studying us. She doesn't stop in front of me, even though she must know who breached security. Maela is playing with us.

"One of you entered a secure area without permission," she says. "Who was it?"

I want to step forward, but I hold myself back. Cormac isn't here to save me from Maela's wrath.

Maela wags a finger at the group. "Come now. If you don't confess, I'll be forced to deem everyone here guilty. I'd hate to send all of you to the clinics."

Enough people have been wiped thanks to me. I shift my feet but Pryana holds me back.

"It was me."

I lurch forward in surprise to look at the girl who spoke. There's not a spot of color on her dark skin and her full cheeks make her look even younger than Amie. A few girls around her cast confused looks, but no one says anything.

"Gillian?" Maela raises an eyebrow as she plants her hands on her hips. "You broke into the clinics?"

Gillian nods, her gaze fixed on Maela. "I thought I could escape."

I take a small step forward, knowing I can't let this girl lie to save me. I don't know why she's doing it. But I do know the punishment for girls who try to escape. But as I move out of the line, Pryana's nails dig into my arm and drag me back.

"Very well." Maela nods to the guards. They don't shackle the girl. Instead she falls into step behind them, as though she knows exactly what's expected of her. A shiver races down my neck.

Maela waves off the rest of the group. "You may finish your meals."

As she turns to leave, her eyes meet mine. The tilt of her head would be imperceptible to anyone else. No one here knows Maela like I do. The message is clear: it's my move.

When the dinner shift ends, Pryana and I race back to my quarters and we're barely through the door before I drag her into the bathroom.

"Nice trick," she says as I turn on the faucets to drown out our conversation.

"I learned how to survive around here. It seems you have, too."

She shrugs. "We do what we have to do."

"Including letting an innocent girl confess to treason?" I fight to keep my voice lower than the running water, even as blood pounds in my ears.

"I didn't see you step forward."

"I tried to! I want answers!" I demand, losing control over the volume of my voice.

Pryana's jaw clenches and her coffee-colored eyes flash to mine. She looks away and shakes her head. "Gillian sacrificed herself for the cause."

"What cause?" I manage. "What cause does the Agenda have that requires suicide?"

Pryana's eyes roll back. "Don't play dumb, Adelice. You know what we're fighting for. Gillian did what she had to do to protect the Whorl."

"Get out," I say in a low voice. "Get out and tell whoever else is playing rebel here this: I don't need protecting."

Pryana's eyes narrow, although she doesn't challenge me.

When she leaves, I move to the sink. Placing my hands under the running water, I splash it on my face and watch it stream across my skin. I rinse my face and my neck and my hands until I'm as clear skinned and pure as the girl who stepped forward for me today. But no matter how hard I scrub, I'll never wash her blood from my hands.

THIRTEEN

A KNOCK SOUNDS AT THE DOOR. No one except Pryana and Amie knocks when they come to visit, and I'm fairly certain they're both upset with me. People only come to deliver food or clean or check my companel and they never wait for me to let them in. But when I open the door, I know the person is here to see me.

"May I come in?" Maela asks.

I step aside and allow her into my living room. She flits into the space, picking up a vase from the mantel over the fireplace. I half expect her to try to shove it into her pocket. It's written on her face: these should have been hers. Her quarters. Her job.

Her Cormac.

But that doesn't explain why she's here now.

"Can I get you something?" I ask her. "A drink? A map back to your room?"

"It's lovely to see you, too," she says. Maela doesn't take the hint. Instead she drops into a recliner, crossing her legs like she's getting comfortable.

I give up hope and sit down across from her. "I thought you might visit sooner."

"Cormac has you under lock and key. I wasn't allowed," she explains.

"You've never let that stand in the way before."

Maela sees rules as optional. She showed her flexibility with them more than once during my training—ripping an entire academy, torturing me with razor-sharp thread. It's not like her to do as she's told.

"But when I saw you in the dining room earlier, I assumed it was permissible for me to call on you."

"An interesting meal." I meet her eyes directly. "I don't recall interrogation being part of the courses before."

"Times are different at the Coventry, Adelice."

"They're different in all of Arras," I correct her.

"You've proven to be quite the catalyst." She peers at me, waiting for my reaction. I keep my face blank, despite her accusation. She's not the first to mistakenly blame me for the unrest in Arras.

"I think there's a lot more going on here than anything I've caused," I say.

"And yet, here you are. In the penthouse of the high tower. Ring on your finger," she says.

I twist my engagement ring around, hiding the diamond in my clenched fist. Most days I forget I'm wearing it. Since Cormac comes only once a week, I rarely have to face my impending marriage.

"Why are you here?" I ask. "Or do you just miss torturing me?"

"I have missed your flair for the dramatic."

"My flair? That's sort of the pot calling the kettle black," I say.

"Don't worry, I'm not looking to be friends with you, Adelice," Maela says.

"That's a relief. I'm not taking applications."

"And yet you let someone like Pryana into your quarters without a second thought."

"Pryana is a friend." It's not exactly the truth, but it's close.

"You should reconsider who you trust," Maela warns me.

"That means a lot coming from someone I don't trust."

"I have nothing to gain by lying to you." Maela leans forward as though she's sharing an intimate bit of knowledge. "Cormac does. Pryana does. Even Erik does."

"Erik isn't here to lie to me," I say, managing to get the words past the lump in my throat.

"Your trust has trapped you," she says.

"What trapped you, Maela? What made you into such a frightened little bird?" I ask. Doesn't she know she's in a cage, not in control? Can't she see the bars and locks and secrets that keep her here?

Maela flashes me a pert smile, something wild peeking from behind her eyes. But before she can answer me, a tutting noise distracts us both from the fight. Cormac stands in the doorway. I'm not happy he's caught Maela torturing me. When Cormac has gotten involved in the past, it only led to more trouble from Maela. Now I know why, of course. But knowledge is far from power.

Maela avoided my question before, but the answer is written all over her face when she looks at Cormac. If I thought her capable of it, I might almost believe it was love smoldering in her eyes. Now I know why she never rose further. She built her own prison.

"I'm sorry to interrupt your visit," he says. "I was told Adelice was alone."

"Believe me, you aren't interrupting anything," I say. "Maela was leaving."

Maela gives a hollow laugh as she stands. But when she brushes past Cormac, her fingers slide across his shoulder and she whispers something I can't quite hear.

When she's gone, I raise an eyebrow.

"You don't want to know. Maela and I . . ." He doesn't finish the thought, but I don't need him to.

"I don't care about either of your sordid pasts," I assure him.

"You should. You are marrying me, after all."

"To what do I owe this very unexpected pleasure?" I ask, changing the subject from his past conquests. "I haven't ordered dinner yet, but I certainly could."

"No, don't bother. I'm here on official business. I won't bother you for long." But even as he says it, he shrugs off his jacket and throws it over a chair. Next he'll pour a drink. Then he'll avoid my questions. Our interactions here have become like clockwork.

"You aren't bothering me," I lie in a practiced tone that reeks of obedience and inferiority and all the things he craves from me.

Cormac reaches for his jacket and retrieves a thin box. "A gift for our upcoming engagement gala."

"You shouldn't have," I say as I lift the lid to find a pair of shimmering black satin gloves.

"I'm told gloves are coming back into fashion, and my future wife should be the height of style." He pulls at his bow tie, loosening it a little without taking it off.

"Thank you. They're lovely." I lay the box aside, knowing this isn't why he came. He could have sent the gloves with my aesthetician. "Why are you here?"

"There are concerns for your safety within the Ministry," Cormac says.

"You have me in total lockdown in a building reinforced by Arras-knows-what technology," I remind him, pausing to allow him to contradict me. But when he doesn't, I add, "I could go on."

"That's quite enough," he says. "In order to keep public focus on the wedding, I will need you to travel. Therefore I'm bringing in someone to keep an eye on you . . . to protect you."

"To watch me," I correct him.

"Damn it, Adelice. Do you want to get killed?" He's yelling at me, his fingers balling into fists, but all I can do is stare at him. Calmness sweeps over his face, and he continues in a slow voice. "Believe it or not, I don't want you killed by some revolutionary."

"You think the Agenda will kill me?" I ask, shaking my head at the ridiculous idea.

"The Agenda is unpredictable. I think they might try to take you away. Not only would that void our agreement, but it would also undo everything we've worked for."

"You're being overprotective," I say, grinning at his choice of words. Even in private moments, Cormac is such a politician. But then he grabs my arm and shakes me so hard that my vision goes blurry.

"Don't laugh at me," he warns, cold fury creeping into his words.

I wrench myself away and stare at him, trying to focus. What was that about?

"I wasn't laughing at you," I say.

His eyes remain furious but after a few minutes he calms down and showers me with a litany of apologies.

"So I'll have my own guard?" I ask.

"Yes."

"Good. I've always wanted a guy in a suit to follow me."

"Alixandra is hardly a guy," he scoffs.

"Alixandra?" I repeat, narrowing my eyes.

"Did you think I'd leave you alone with a boy after what happened before?" he asks me.

He has a point. Not that I'm looking for romance at the moment. "I'm surprised you trust a woman with something as important as this."

"Alixandra knows her place," Cormac says. "Maybe you can learn a thing or two from her."

"When do I meet her?" I ask.

"She'll arrive tomorrow and then escort you to the gala at the end of the week. She will remain with you at all times."

"Like when I go to the bathroom?" I ask.

"Of course."

"Will she watch me sleep?"

"And floss your teeth, if I ask her to," Cormac says, cutting off my questions. "You aren't being cute, darling."

"I'm not aiming for cute."

"I won't allow anyone to hurt you—not even yourself."

"Then what about our deal?" I plead.

Cormac brushes off my objections and picks up his jacket. Before he leaves he says something I already know.

"Deals change."

FOURTEEN

THE ENGAGEMENT GALA IS A TYPICAL GUILD affair right down to the flashing cameras and my choreographed entrance into the Northern Ministry on the purple carpet. Pressed linen tablecloths and structured flower arrangements are displayed carefully around a slate-gray dance floor. Even my gown had to be approved by Cormac in advance—a gray silk dress that skims my negligible curves and swishes in soft waves to my feet. It's beaded with silver crystals in triangular patterns that accentuate my waist and catch the dim light in the hall. Martinis are passed on trays. I grab one immediately but put it down after I taste it.

"Don't be wasteful," Cormac says, motioning to the abandoned drink. He presses his hand against the small of my back.

"Cormac!" A tall woman in a wine-colored gown dashes over and throws her arms around him, startling us both.

"Dawna, how nice to see you," he greets her smoothly as he pries himself out of her embrace. His eyes scan her vibrant dress, and then narrow. She must have broken his carefully articulated dress code.

"Your bride has such lovely taste," she says as she motions to the ballroom filled with Cormac-style objects, and I realize she must not know him very well. Anyone who did would see this is all Cormac's doing.

"She does indeed," he responds. He looks past Dawna, scoping out the crowd for someone more important to speak with.

"Actually," I say, plastering a smile on my face, "Cormac planned the entire event."

"But Cormac, you have to let the bride plan these things. It is her wedding after all." Dawna tut-tuts at the end for emphasis.

Me plan the big day? Not if either of us has anything to say about it.

"Would you like that, Adelice?" Cormac says, and he shoots me a look that says, *Two can play this game.* He can fake the doting fiancé bit, too.

"I wouldn't dare dream of questioning your wishes." I push the words out of gritted teeth, never once letting my smile slip from my face.

"I see how she landed you," Dawna says, smacking me a bit too hard on the shoulder. "Such a lucky girl."

"Aren't I, though?" I murmur, smoothing a wrinkle from my long satin glove.

"These are darling." Dawna brushes her hand over my wrist. "Are gloves coming back in fashion?"

My eyes flicker to Cormac, but he's busy searching the crowd. "So I'm told."

"Then I must get myself a pair," she says.

"Pardon us, I see Minister—" Cormac doesn't even bother to finish his excuse before he pulls us from her clutches. As soon as we're a safe distance away, he twists my wrist. "Stop telling everyone you don't want to marry me."

I pull against his grip but fail to extricate myself. "I didn't say that to anyone, and we've only spoken to one person so far. Stop being dramatic, darling."

"We need the four sectors focused on the wedding—"

"Three," I remind him softly. "There are three sectors now."

"Of course," he snaps. He tugs at his bow tie, but I bat his hand away.

"Don't undo that. Everyone will assume you're drunk already and then they'll think *you* don't want to marry *me*."

"It's tricky, isn't it?" Cormac asks.

"What?"

"Pretending you want to marry someone. Stressful even."

Before we can break up at our engagement gala, a group of men approach.

"Shut up and smile," he orders.

Thanks for the reminder. This is already turning out worse than I feared.

I lose track of who is who and who runs what, and eventually give up on keeping each new person straight. Enora quizzed me on this once, I realize with a pang, but so much has happened since then. And she's not around to help me now. I turn my attention to the crowd instead. In the two years that I've been away from Arras, it looks like Cormac's been cleaning house. I spot Alixandra watching me out of the corner of my eye. I couldn't get away from Cormac now if I tried.

I consider going over to her. She's the only person I recognize here. Although, after nearly a week under her protection, I've discovered that Alixandra is not a talker. She dresses like a Spinster when we're together and the official story is she's my personal assistant. But everyone knows she's my security detail. She broods even in a ball gown—though I'm still not buying the story that Cormac is worried about my safety. She's not my bodyguard.

She's my chaperone.

Alixandra is petite with long blond hair and a button nose. It's not going to be hard for her to stay undercover, but I still can't imagine she'd actually be able to fight if it came to it. But looks can be deceiving. If Cormac trusts her, she has to be deadly. I know little else about her.

The afternoon we met her eyes swept over me, sizing me up with a cool disinterest. I had the distinct impression I'd failed whatever test she'd administered.

"I'm Adelice," I finally said, as she continued to watch me. I stuck my hand out, feeling it was proper.

Alixandra didn't shake my hand. She circled around me.

"So you escaped the Guild," she said in a cold voice.

"I'm not interested in discussing my history with you." If she wanted to dredge up the past, I didn't have to participate, but even so, my fingers traced my techprint for comfort.

"I'm not interested in your smart mouth," she said, her voice never rising above the same steady tone. "You ran off with two boys."

"Two brothers as a matter of fact," I said. I had no idea why she was insisting on talking about that.

"Yes, I know." Alixandra stopped in front of me. We were

134

about the same height, but something fierce in her eyes made me shrink back. "I'm surprised Cormac is marrying you."

"Join the club," I said, biting my lip. Most people were nice to my face. But I knew most of Arras must disapprove of Cormac marrying someone as young as me. Alixandra was the first person to show it.

"I mean, he can't believe that you kept purity standards while you ran around down there, can he?"

"He can," I retort, tilting my chin up defiantly, "because I did."

"Is that true?" she asked.

"It is."

"I've seen those boys. I'm surprised." Nothing about the conversation was friendly. I wasn't sure if she believed me about the purity standards, and I definitely wasn't sure why she would even care.

"It's important that you realize I'm not your friend, Adelice," Alixandra told me. "My job is to keep you secure and to keep you out of trouble."

"I'm not planning to get into any trouble," I said. I meant it. Making things difficult at the Coventry or in Arras didn't fit into my plans. I hadn't come back to make trouble. I knew if I wanted to keep the people I loved safe, I needed to play along.

"I'm glad to hear that, but all the same, remember I'll have my eyes on you," she said.

Alixandra didn't like me. That much was clear.

"So you'll be with me at all times?"

"Yes, per Cormac's instructions," Alixandra said.

"And after we're married?"

"I'll do what he asks me to do. I wouldn't count on him relaxing the security surrounding you, though, especially once children come along."

I gagged a little, but managed to cover it with my hand. Children hadn't been part of our discussions.

"You don't look excited about having children," Alixandra noted.

I wasn't. "Things are happening very quickly. It's a lot to take in."

"Cormac will want an heir, of course, and then . . ." She let her words trail away and didn't finish her thought.

I wanted her to continue, but I couldn't stomach any more talk of my future with Cormac. I avoided conversation after that.

"Adelice!" Cormac's voice calls me back to the present, and I blink at him. "Minister Swander asked you to dance with him."

"Of course," I murmur, trying to remember who Minister Swander is. The name sounds familiar, but to my surprise the man who steps forward is young and handsome. I recall the last gala I attended at the Coventry—when Erik reminded me that every official was married. Swander's wife must be nearby. I take his hand, ready to get it over with.

Minister Swander leads me onto the dance floor, keeping a proper amount of space between us and dancing formally, which is to say, stiffly. For a moment I wish I was dancing with Erik, but I immediately put the thought out of my head. Then I notice that with each careful step, he is leading me farther across the dance floor, farther from Cormac.

"Cormac has finally landed himself a new Creweler," he says in a light tone.

I study him closely. He's exactly how I imagine Cormac would have looked at the same age. Too slick, too quick with a smile.

"I suppose he has," I respond. "Pardon my saying so, but you seem a little young to be a minister."

"You seem a little young to be a Creweler."

"Touché."

"I was born into Ministry service," he explains to me. "My father was an official."

"Was?" I ask.

A confused look passes over the minister's face. "He died."

"I'm sorry."

"Don't be." He waves off my regrets with the ease of someone who never mourned the loss.

"You weren't close?" I guess.

"No, we were," the minister assures me, "but that's life."

But it's not life, I think. Not for the Guild. Officials don't just die and ministers don't forget what happened.

"How did your father die?" I press.

"Old age, of course."

I can see I'm not going to get far with him, so I change the subject.

"Is your wife here?" I ask.

"I'm not married," he says.

I can't help myself. "That's unusual."

"I suppose I was married, but my wife is gone." He stumbles over the confession, blinking as if to clear his head.

Suddenly I know where I've heard his name. The old memory resurfaces and my stomach rolls over.

She had an accident.

Amie's words. Before I can compose myself, he stops and drops his hands from me.

"The song has ended. I suppose I must return you to your fiancé." He offers me his arm. His gaze stays unfocused, as though he's searching for something in the distance as he leads me back to Cormac and thanks him for the dance.

"Of course," Cormac says. "It looked like you were having a nice chat." I can tell Cormac wants to know what the minister said to me. Of course he does.

"He was telling me how his father died," I admit.

"He was?" Cormac asks. I can't gauge his reaction.

"Actually, he was *about* to tell me," I say, turning to Minister Swander expectantly.

"Excuse me, I see Brient," he says, avoiding the question once more. "Thank you for the lovely dance."

He hurries away, and I can't help but notice that he dashes straight for the washroom.

"How did his father die?" I ask Cormac. "I thought the Guild had gotten around that inconvenience."

"We can still die, Adelice," Cormac mutters.

"You could have fooled me."

"Death is a tricky thing. He wears many faces."

I wonder what face death will wear when he visits Cormac. I wonder if death will look like me.

"And his wife?"

Cormac shrugs.

"There was an accident," I say. "You made an example of her."

I recall the reverent account Amie gave about her teacher, at our dining table. I remember the hushed fear in my parents' voices. I remember everything about that night.

"You do love your stories," Cormac says, taking my elbow and steering me out of earshot.

"The truth is much more interesting," I say in a low voice.

"Truth takes time," he warns me. "Someday, when you've lived a lifetime, you'll understand that."

"And how long will it take you to believe it?"

He flashes me a murderous look, and I duck back toward the crowd, my heart beating fast as my past and present collide.

The dinner is served in courses. The first is the onion soup I despise. I slurp it loudly, pretending to relish every drop. Cormac ignores me, chatting with the other guests at the table. I pick at my roasted pheasant and finally abandon it.

"When is the wedding?" the wife of one of the ministers asks me from across the table.

I blink at the question. We haven't set a date, which is fine by me. It gives Cormac more time to milk this distraction and me more time to figure out what he's hiding from me.

"I'm not sure," I say in a syrupy voice. "Cormac is preoccupied with other issues at the moment. I wouldn't dream of distracting him with my silly wedding plans."

Cormac's hand lands on my leg and squeezes it tightly. I'm being warned.

"But you must be excited." The woman folds her hands under her chin, a dreamy look coming over her face.

"I am," I lie. "I hope it's soon."

Cormac leans in toward me. "I wouldn't dream of making you wait much longer."

I force a smile onto my face, hoping it looks right. I don't find his words reassuring.

He stands and raises his champagne flute, waiting for the other tables to quiet. A few people tap their own glasses with forks and soon all eyes are on him. The conversation in the room dies down, but I spot a few people whispering and even a handful of eye rolls.

"Friends," he addresses them. "I'm honored that you chose to spend the evening with us."

I'm guessing there wasn't much of a choice when they got the invitation.

"My beautiful future bride and I are eager to start a new chapter in Arras. Joining the Guild and the Coventry in marriage is rather, shall we say, unprecedented."

He waits for the few chuckles this elicits before he continues. "Our great nation is changing and even an old bachelor like me can see this. I've been married to my work for a long time. Adelice has shown me that our values and priorities must be realigned. The value of the family cannot be understated, and I look forward to finally contributing"—he winks—"to emphasizing the place of the family in Arras. With the help of my lovely future wife, of course."

I try to cover my face with my napkin. Perhaps it looks like I'm crying, because the woman sitting next to me pats my shoulder.

"So please join me in raising your glass to the beautiful and talented Adelice. The woman who captured my heart so fully I couldn't let her escape."

Truer words were never spoken. I lift my glass, but never get a chance to take a sip. A blast rips through the room, knocking me against the table. The crowd erupts in panic and I look to where Cormac stood seconds ago.

He's gone.

FIFTEEN

SMOKE UNFURLS ACROSS THE BALLROOM AS PEOPLE cough and scramble toward the exits. A woman is knocked down but no one helps her up, each person too concerned with his or her own mortality to notice. I push through the mass, trying to reach her, but the crowd jostles me farther away. I'm pulled out by Alixandra.

"What's happening?" I ask. I choke on the smoke burning my nostrils and my throat. It leaves the taste of ash on my tongue and my mouth is too dry to swallow against it.

Alixandra shushes me, peeking out the door and into the chaos.

"I can't see Cormac." From her it's a cold, hard fact: no emotion invested, no anger or concern. It's all a business transaction. She has secured one precious commodity and now must secure the next.

"We should look for him." I move to step out the door.

"No, my responsibility is to protect you."

"Fine," I say, leaning back against the wall, "but at least tell me what I need protecting from."

"Revolutionaries, obviously. We haven't had any issues since Cormac dealt with the Eastern Sector, but this is an organized attack."

"Is it the Agenda?" I try to keep the hope out of my voice. Not only because I don't want Alixandra to hear it, but because I don't want to feel it myself.

"Up here? No way."

"Then there's a different revolution in Arras?" I say, playing dumb.

"I was told you were present at the severance of the Eastern Sector." Alixandra eyes me like I'm a small bug she doesn't know whether to ignore or squash.

"And I was told that was an isolated incident and that the quarantine would prevent it from spreading into the surviving sectors."

Alixandra snorts. "Don't believe everything they tell you."

"So there's revolution everywhere then?"

"Ask Cormac how many sectors there were when they created Arras."

"Wait! What?"

But Alixandra goes back to ignoring me. She hikes up her skirt to reveal a holster tightened around her thigh and withdraws a compact gun. Tilting her head, she calls for transport.

"But we don't have Cormac," I remind her. I'm not exactly concerned about his safety, but a small part of me worries about the chaos that would follow if he's assassinated.

"My priority is you. Cormac has his own security team. In fact, he probably already left," she says.

"But—"

Alixandra raises a finger and takes another com. "Priority one. Access Alpha Two."

As she rattles off the security clearance, she turns away from the door and I see my chance. Before she can stop me, I duck back into the smoky room. A few people have collapsed on the floor, but other than that the room is deserted. The lingering haze stings my eyes, but I move forward, looking for Cormac, unsure whether I want to find him among those on the floor.

The cock of a gun stops me in my tracks. I raise my hands dramatically. "You found me," I say to Alixandra.

"Turn around," a male voice commands, and icy fear races through me. The man is wearing a gas mask and I can't see his face. I can see the gun extended to my forehead, though.

As soon as I face him, his hold on the gun slips. Before he can say anything, Alixandra cracks him on the head with her weapon.

"C'mon." She grabs me by the arm. "Are you trying to get killed?"

"He was lowering his gun," I tell her, trying to work through the confusion I feel.

"It's good to know that a group of armed mercenaries won't shoot an innocent girl," she says, dragging me out a back exit.

"No, it was more than that. It was like he wanted something from me."

"He probably did, and it probably wasn't anything pleasant," Alixandra says. Outside, our transport screeches up and two officers in tactical vests rush out to help us into the back of the van. Alixandra shoves me inside before I can protest.

"Our orders are to escort Miss Lewys directly to Minister Patton's private residence," one of the guards tells us.

"Look at that, Adelice," Alixandra mutters with a grim smile, "you're going home."

Cormac's house sits on a hill overlooking the Cypress metro. It's a concoction of glass and steel beams that jut out in strange ways. As we pull closer, I can see him through the window, pacing. The interior is bare. The *click* of our footsteps on the slate-tiled floors echoes in the large empty foyer, and the scent of bleach clings to the air, no doubt a side effect of keeping the home's surfaces so gleaming, pristine. There are no pictures or artwork. No sign that the man who lives here has led an extraordinary life. Perhaps Cormac knows the meaningless-ness of objects in a world where anything can be conjured. Or maybe he simply has nothing to cling to—even after two hundred years.

The officers march me past three different security doors. As soon as they deliver Alixandra and me, they leave.

"I'm fine," I tell Cormac when he asks if I'm okay. "Don't worry about me."

"I knew Alixandra would get you out of there," he says, almost apologizing.

"I went back, looking for you," I accuse.

"Well, that was very stupid."

"Don't worry. I learned my lesson," I say. "It won't happen again."

"And what were you doing letting her out of your sight?" He turns on Alixandra.

"She's quick and she doesn't listen," she says.

I like to think this is the understatement of the year.

"What do you know about this attack?" he asks her.

"Security is sweeping the scene," Alixandra informs him. "If revolutionaries managed to get in, I'd guess they have someone on the inside."

"I'll have to deactivate the personnel we used this evening."

"Sir?" Alixandra visibly pales at his threat.

"Not you," he roars. "I want you to check the reinforcements we installed there and double-check the Coventry—"

"I can assure you that the Coventry can't be breached from the inside or the outside," Alixandra interrupts him.

"Check again." His tone is impatient.

Cormac gestures for me to take a seat and Alixandra leaves the room to make her calls. He hasn't stopped pacing since I spotted him through the window. His bow tie hangs loose and he's lost his jacket. It's the most disheveled I've ever seen him. I have to admit he's been through a lot this evening.

"We need to assume that was an assassination attempt," Cormac tells me.

Yeah, I figured.

"But we don't know their target," he continues.

I stare at him. "I have a pretty good idea."

"I'm not interested in jokes right now. This is serious," he says.

"Pardon my delivery, then, but I *am* dead serious. You can't possibly think they were after anyone but you."

"They could have been after *you*," Cormac says. "You're a

146

high-profile target now and your death would cause major upset among the population."

I think back to the man in the gas mask. He was definitely lowering his gun. "They weren't after me."

"It doesn't matter."

"If I were you I'd stay focused on how they got into the ballroom." There was security everywhere. Cormac can no longer trust his own men.

"Alixandra and I will deal with those issues," Cormac says. "It's time to take decisive action."

"The last time you took decisive action it cost Arras an entire sector," I seethe.

"This time my action will be about unity," he says, "not destruction."

I don't like the sound of that.

"I'm moving our wedding up," Cormac says.

"Okay. Why?" I ask. It's honestly the last thing I expected to hear, and the last thing I think we should be worried about.

"To send a clear message to Arras that these are joyful times."

"Oh, definitely," I say in a flat voice. "Why not just alter everyone?"

"It's not merely a message to our citizens."

"It's a warning to the terrorists, too?" I guess.

"Exactly. I want them to know they can't scare me."

And yet these are clearly the actions of a desperate man. Surely the revolutionaries will see that.

"So when?" I ask.

"I was thinking next week, once Alixandra has confirmed the new security measures are stable."

"Next week?" I struggle to wrap my head around this. Marrying Cormac will give me access to his home, his office, his life. Everything I need and all that I hate.

"You will stay within the Coventry until security has prepared to transfer you here," he informs me. "Say goodbye to Amie while you're there."

"She'll be at the wedding, though?" My throat constricts on the question.

"Absolutely not," he snarls.

"Why punish her? She has nothing to do with this." My words are thick, coated in a mixture of fear and anger and disappointment.

"Someone tried to kill you tonight," he reminds me. "I won't put Amie in harm's way. End of discussion."

I'm frozen to the spot, trying to understand why Cormac Patton cares about what happens to my sister. I know there's something missing, but I can't quite add it up. "She's not in danger."

Cormac's fist slams against his chair. "I will decide that. Amie will not be risked."

"So you can use her against me?" I guess, glaring at him as my fingers twitch inside my gloves.

"Not everything is about you, Adelice."

"What reason do you have to care about my sister?"

He presses his index finger to his temple. "You think I'm heartless, but perhaps you'll finally understand me once we're married. Thankfully, we'll be married within the week."

I gasp at this further change of plans. "I'm not ready."

"It's time to grow up, Adelice."

"I don't expect you to understand," I say in a quiet voice,

not to be argumentative, but because it's the truth. I thought I would have more time. Time to forget Erik. Or at least time to find another way to stop Cormac.

"Why? Because of your *destiny*?" he mocks. "Because you're the Whorl?"

"I didn't ask to be."

"You think because some madman gave you a nickname it makes you special?" he demands. He grabs me and shoves me against the wall. "I determine who is special in this world."

"What you do is far worse than a simple determination." I brace myself against the plaster behind me. I can no longer keep it from spilling out. "You twist, Cormac. You twist the truth, nature, and worst of all, people. Especially yourself."

"And now the Whorl will stop me, right?"

I consider this. I want to stop him. I need to. "I'm not sure anything could stop you."

Except one thing.

My fingers lash out and grab for his strands. If I can catch them correctly, I can control him.

The only thing left is to manipulate him. Once he's under my command, I can even unwind him. The possibilities are endless. All it took was realizing that he would never redeem himself—that he doesn't want to.

But my fingers catch on his shirt.

Instead of ripping through it and down into the very matter that composes him, my fingers catch, fire bursting through them. I fall back as the flames dance inside my skin. I try to pull off the satin gloves, but Cormac grabs my wrists, pinning them in his strong grip.

"Do you think I would be stupid enough to remain unprotected around you?" he asks.

"They're gages?" I say, and Cormac nods. "So much for trust."

"Don't flatter yourself, Adelice. This is not a relationship based on trust. It never will be," he says. "More gloves await you at the Coventry. You will always wear them in my presence until a more permanent arrangement can be reached."

A tremble races through me at his threat. "And if I don't?"

"I'm protected. Remember that," he warns me.

"You have no idea what I'm capable of."

"What is your plan? Are you going to kill me? Take my face? Alter my memory?" he asks with a laugh, stumbling back toward the mantel.

So he's known all along that I planned to alter him. I showed my hand when I attacked Kincaid, and Cormac was smart enough to protect himself even after our arrangement. "You still want to continue this charade?"

"You cannot possibly understand how far I would go for Arras." Squatting down, he reaches past the grate and places his hand in the fire, withdrawing a remnant of wood as I stare, unable to move.

He stands to face me, crushing the smoldering wood between his hands. It turns to ash, blackening his burned palms. He's beyond anything mortal, like pain. He's evolved past it.

Instead of staying pressed to the wall, I saunter toward him and jab a finger at his chest. "There will come a day, Cormac, when no amount of technology will save you, and not only will I be there, I'll feel your life in my hands."

"You have no idea who you're dealing with," Cormac growls,

but he doesn't touch me again. Instead, he calls for his valet to bring him renewal patches. Security arrives shortly after to escort me to the rebound station. Before I leave, Cormac looks up from his wounds and smiles at me.

"Good night, Adelice. I'll see you in the morning."

The farewell is almost sweet, so I nod, confusion churning inside me. As I climb the stairs, trailed by a guard, the emotion inside me shifts to fear.

If I was truly the Whorl, I could hold things together. Instead, everything is unraveling. Even Cormac.

SIXTEEN

AMIE MILLS ABOUT MY QUARTERS WHILE SERVANTS bustle in and out, packing my trunks in preparation for the wedding, which will take place in the Northern Sector. She does a good job of looking excited, but the joy doesn't reach her eyes. Immediately after I returned from the engagement gala, Cormac sent her a telebound with the news that she wouldn't be coming to the wedding, leaving me to deal with her disappointment for the past two days. His message explained she was too young to attend a political function.

For once, he's calling something as it is. Our engagement *is* politics, after all.

"You aren't missing anything," I tell her. "A bunch of snooty ministers and their wives, each vying to be the biggest suck-up."

"Oh, I know," she says, but her words are punctuated with sighs. "I can watch on the Stream. You'll be on the purple carpet. Cormac promised the whole event will be filmed."

Admiration colors her words and I cringe. I'm no longer

the girl who watched the purple carpet with glee in her living room. Now I know about balancing on heels and fending off drunk ministers with grabby hands. But one look at Amie's face, and I suddenly wish I could enjoy it. I pretend to be giddy—if only to cheer her up for a moment.

"What if I trip?" I ask, dropping onto my bed and widening my eyes for effect.

"You should practice." Amie plucks a pair of heels from a loaded rack and tosses them next to me. "Show me how it's done."

I slip them onto my feet, left foot first. I watch for some sign that Amie has noticed this old ritual of our mother and grandmothers, but there's no recognition on her face.

"Gloves?" She holds up a pair of petite white gloves.

"They're back in fashion," I say in a tight voice.

"I'll have to get some," she says as she lays them back on my bed.

I bite my lip so hard I taste iron on my tongue. Cormac's orders were clear. As soon as I leave the walls of the Coventry, I am to wear them. There's been no more mention of the permanent solution that will forever cripple my abilities, and for now I can only hope the gloves will pacify him. Either way, after I leave here, I will never touch again. Not really. He'll rob me of my strongest sense—with a pair of gloves or an alteration. All I will have is the memory of the weave tingling across my fingertips and of the hot pressure of Erik's fingers threaded through mine.

"Will you return here?" she asks, drawing me back to this moment.

"Cormac expects me to live with him in the Northern Sector," I tell her as I blink back tears.

"Oh." Amie deflates a bit in front of me and I grab her hand.

"You can stay with us as soon as this wedding nonsense is over."

"Promise?"

"I do." I mean it. If I go through with this, maybe I can rebuild my family a little, but still when Pryana enters the room, I look to her, hopeful she's come to pass along a message from the Agenda. They must know of Cormac's plans, but she shakes her head slightly as though she can read my mind. No one is coming to help me.

"Pryana!" Amie jumps up and rushes to greet her. "Adelice says I can live with her and Cormac in the Northern Sector."

"Good for you." Pryana's words are forced and when our eyes meet, recrimination burns behind her irises, although she does her best to hide it. I'm taking another sister from her.

"Come with marital advice?" I ask in an attempt to keep the mood light. "Speak now or forever hold your peace."

"No, I came with a gift." Pryana hands me a small wrapped box. "Open it in private. I don't want to *embarrass* your sister."

Amie pretends to cover her ears, but I swat her hands away and fake a laugh.

"Thank you," I say to Pryana, who gives me a tight smile.

They stay until Amie's eyelids droop, and then Pryana forces her onto her feet. I wrap my arms around my sister, who's as tall as me, and try to find a way to say goodbye.

In the end the words were there all along. "I love you, Ames."

She nods through her tears, releasing me after a few minutes and stepping away, but her eyes stay locked on me as though I might vanish. She doesn't remember what happened the night of my retrieval, but the wounds are still there.

Pryana gives me a short, awkward hug. "Open the present somewhere safe."

I nod, wide-eyed as my pulse begins to race. I walk them to the door, torn between sadness and hope, and as soon as it locks behind them I retrieve the box. My fingers tremble as I carry it to the bathroom. I rip into it, discovering another box tucked inside the first—like a toy I had as a child. When I pull it out, the only thing inside is a crystal cube with a delicate, shimmering strand of silver frozen inside.

The next morning I find myself crammed into a tiny rebound lounge with a party of twenty security personnel and assistants. Despite the large number of people, no one speaks to me. My aesthetician for the trip is bubbly and bright, mindlessly chatting with the other girls who've come along to assist her. Alixandra watches from the corner of the room, aloof as usual. Not only from me, it turns out, but from everyone. The guards whisper and stay alert. Tension cuts through the room, needling everyone's nerves. It's only been a few days since the attack at the gala, making it feel as though there could be another attack at any time.

The Western Coventry's rebound station is prepped for our departure and there's not much waiting around. Half of the security team is going in advance, with the other half following behind. I've been briefed a dozen times on the schedule and on contingencies to the schedule and on contingencies to the contingencies.

I don't even pretend to care. I am going to marry Cormac.

I will never use my gift again. These words echo through my empty mind, threatening to destroy what little I have left. All my energy is spent on staying sane.

We wait for the first set of rebounds to finish and I sit alone, hoping to catch bits of news from careless lips. This is what I've become. A wisp. A nothing. Forced to latch on to gossip—as if it will ever do any good.

"Can you imagine sending any other Spinster with this entourage?" a girl says in a lowered voice. She's not quite whispering—she clearly wants to be heard. Her words are tainted with a listen-to-me tone.

"I thought we were in a state of austerity, but I guess not if you're the prime minister's wife."

"Future wife," a girl corrects her in an almost hopeful voice.

"I heard Patton's gone crazy," the girl says. "I think this whole thing proves how paranoid he's become."

"Oh, I heard that, too! But they're saying he's a shoo-in for the next election."

I want to ask who they are hearing these things from, but I keep silent.

"I think something strange is going on," a girl says. "Patton isn't just going crazy. It's like he's a different person."

"Well, that person is going to win reelection," chirps another.

"And I assume you are all on such familiar terms with *Minister* Patton that you're comfortable sharing such factual accounts," Alixandra says, stepping out from behind the group. Her face is blank and I want to know what she thinks about what the girls are saying. But as usual, she's removed and professional—and utterly unreadable.

"No harm in a little gossip," one of the girls says, tacking on a nervous giggle as if to imply they were only being silly.

Alixandra leans in and sizes her up before shifting back onto the heels of her boots. "There's a lot of harm in it, but not for the person being gossiped about, if you catch my drift."

Most of them nod, but as soon as she steps away their faces turn nasty behind her back. I'm certain Alixandra can feel their expressions, even if she doesn't see them. I recall the sensation of tiny daggers in my back, a feeling familiar from my testing. Unlike me, Alixandra doesn't seem bothered by it.

But I have learned one thing, at least. I'm not the only one concerned about changes in Cormac Patton. It sounds like the rumors are becoming more widespread. People everywhere are talking about it. What effect will this have on his plans? If faith in Cormac has already been undermined, what purpose can the wedding really serve?

"We're ready for the next party," the stewardess says, checking a list on her clipboard.

"That's us," Alixandra says, taking hold of my elbow and steering me toward the rebound chamber. We aren't using the ones I've rebounded through before, but instead a new, larger chamber. I expect Alixandra and I to rebound on the same platform, but there are two platforms adjoining each other instead.

"I thought we would rebound together," I say to Alixandra.

"We are, but two people need to perform the procedure for optimal safety." Her voice takes on the same annoyed tone it always does when I ask a question—as though everything that comes out of my mouth is completely stupid.

"I see."

"Minister Patton wants to be sure of your physical safety as well as your security."

"I bet he does," I say. My glib comment is rewarded with a scathing look. My sense of humor isn't growing on Alixandra.

The stewardess prepares each of us, going through the same speech full of warnings and reminders I've been given every time I've traveled via rebound. I nod, barely paying attention to what she's saying. I'm not surprised when she cuffs my arms to the chair.

"What, no scary metal helmet?" I ask.

The stewardess blinks.

"You will be alone during part of the process," Alixandra says, settling comfortably into her chair. "We'll be able to see each other, but technically we'll be in separate spaces. I want to be certain you are secure."

"Where am I going to go?" I point out. There's enough danger inherent in the process without me jumping off the platform in the middle of it.

"You've managed to pull off some incredible escapes in the past. You can't blame us for being cautious," Alixandra says.

"How long is the rebound?" I ask the stewardess.

"It will only take an hour," she answers as she stuffs a pillow behind my back. I want out of these cuffs and away from this awkward angle.

The pillow *is* helping, though. I remember the first stewardess who attended my rebound—on my retrieval night. She had been kind, too, trying to ease my panic about being tied down and taken to a new life. I didn't ask her name.

"Thank you . . . ?" I leave the invitation hanging between myself and the girl helping me.

"Diana," she says.

"Thank you, Diana."

"It was my pleasure, Miss Lewys," she says, pausing to add the obligatory, "and best wishes on your marriage."

"Thanks," I say. Her eyes meet mine and I see understanding in them. She knows, as everyone in Arras must know, that this isn't a marriage of love. Cormac is taking a bride. He's taking me.

And before I can wrap my head around it—around the fact that I'm on my way to be married to Cormac Patton—Diana has left the room and the countdown on the clock begins.

"Will I be able to talk to you during the rebound?" I ask Alixandra. Rebounds still make me a little nervous.

"Why would we want to talk?"

"Never mind," I say.

"Do you need to tell me something, Adelice?"

"I get a little bit of motion sickness," I admit, "and it might help if I had someone to distract me."

She looks pained at this suggestion.

"Like I said, forget it." I hadn't needed Alixandra's company before today. I didn't need it now.

"Adelice, it's my job to protect you, not only for Cormac," she says, struggling for the right words. For a moment our eyes meet and her carefully controlled composure slips to reveal vulnerability.

"Who are you doing it for, then?" I ask.

The mask slides back into place as she picks up a *Bulletin* from the table on the platform. "The people of Arras, of course. You've become something of a symbol to them."

"I don't believe you," I say, but Alixandra only shrugs. I can't expect answers from her.

And how am I supposed to feel about being a symbol, anyway? First, it's for the wrong reasons. What would my parents think if I came to represent the ideal of womanhood in Arras? Or Erik? Or Jost? Or Dante? How would they feel if I stepped into the role of perfect wife and obedient citizen? It wasn't supposed to turn out like this.

It won't.

I focus on that thought as the countdown clock reaches zero and the first changes shimmer through the room. I wonder what Spinster they've deemed talented enough to rush the rebound process and I hope her fingers are as skillful as they claim. It's not my idea of a good time to be torn in two by someone integrating my thread into another section of Arras.

The smooth white walls of the room flicker and fade in and out of my vision, and my belly flips as a rush of vertigo surges through my body. I turn to watch Alixandra, who is absorbed in her *Bulletin*. I can see her, but it's as though I'm watching through a sheer, stretched fabric. We are in the same place and yet we aren't.

"Alixandra," I test, but she doesn't respond.

I'm on my way to marry Cormac Patton.

Only a month has passed since he asked me to marry him. I thought it would be far in the future, but now it's happening.

There will be a state dinner and a series of Stream interviews. Fear is starting to settle into my blood. This seemed like a good idea when I agreed to it. Having unlimited access to Cormac would give me the chance to alter him *and* gain access to the Coventry. But now I know having unlimited access to Cormac means he'll have unlimited access to me. I also know he'll find a way to diminish my power, possibly for good. My skills are nothing against him now that he's found a way to protect himself from alteration, and soon, I'm certain, he'll alter me into the perfect wife.

It's only beginning to sink in that I will be his wife. On the happier nights since I was taken from my home in Romen, I'd allowed myself to imagine marrying. I'd pictured what it would be like to lie in bed with my husband. When I returned to Arras, I tried to let go of that, but Erik always invaded my thoughts in the quiet moments before sleep. I tried to deny myself the fantasy that somehow Erik would be the one in my marital bed, because I knew this day would come.

I knew it would only hurt more when I faced down my wedding to Cormac.

I was right.

A tear tickles down my cheek and I try to wipe it away, forgetting the cuffs over my wrists. It lingers, turning to salt on my cheek—an invisible line that no one can see, but I can feel it clinging tight to my skin. Love has left its marks on me in a hundred tiny scars that aren't visible, only felt. Erik's face floats into my memory. I squeeze my eyes shut and try to see him, but no matter how much I try it becomes harder. My mind is stealing him from me, hiding him away to protect me from the ache that burns in my chest and seizes my limbs.

When I open my eyes, I see him more clearly. It's as though he's standing in front of me. I realize that if I want to keep Erik, I can't lock him away. I can't ignore the memory of him or I will lose even that. Because when I embrace the pain of our separation—when I free his memory—he becomes real again.

Erik smiles at me and I smile back, tears streaming down my face. It becomes too painful and I turn away.

Alixandra is off the platform.

I stare at her. She's not supposed to leave the platform. That's rebound rule number one.

At first I think she's waving at me and I shake my head to let her know I have no idea what she's saying. I can barely move my hands, but I point a finger at her chair in case she's suffering some type of temporary insanity that can be cured by a simple reminder that she should be sitting down.

That's when I realize she's trying to tear the sheer barrier separating her rebound platform from mine. I look more carefully at her room and notice that it's fading farther and farther into the gray walls of the Cypress Station. Soon Alixandra begins to fade with it.

It isn't possible. We're rebounding together. She shouldn't be fading from my sight, because we're going to the same room, the same station. Alixandra told me I wouldn't leave her side during this process, and as that realization settles into place, she flickers completely out of view.

But my last vision of her isn't one of screaming or grabbing. For the split second before her rebound completes she looks past me and nods as her hands fly up once more to tear at the barrier.

I whip around and see the dark outlines of a rebound chamber. The clock on the wall is dead. The room is chilly.

But standing in the middle of it is something that warms my blood.

Erik.

SEVENTEEN

I CAN'T MOVE UNTIL THE FINAL PIECES of the room settle into place. Erik is real. Erik is here.

He takes a cautious step toward me.

This time I manage to say his name. "Erik?"

He races forward and unlatches my cuffs, pulling me up and into a tight hug. But before I can even enjoy it, he releases me.

I don't know where we are or how I've gotten here. The chamber is silent and abnormally cold. These facts collect in my mind but they don't add up to anything.

"Follow me." It's little more than a command, and for a moment I'm frozen to the spot. But when he walks out of the room, I go after him despite the shock and confusion warring within me.

I step out into an office. No, not exactly an office. More like a large meeting room dimly lit by lamps and handlights. Before I can react, Valery throws her arms around me.

"They did it," she says in a breathless voice.

I'm not entirely sure who they are or what they did or how

it happened, but I nod as she clasps my hands in her own. She looks the same, but she's free of cosmetics and her black hair is cropped to her chin.

"Do you like it?" she asks, fluffing her bob.

"Yes. It suits you." The whole conversation is surreal. The last time I saw Valery she'd admitted that she betrayed us on Alcatraz, but now she is here. That doesn't exactly explain where *here* is, though.

"Get those off." She points to my gloves.

It takes a moment for the suggestion to process, but when it does, I rip them from my sweaty hands and throw them to the floor.

"Thanks," I say to her over a lump in my throat as it begins to settle in that I'm free.

A dozen people gather around a table, poring over blueprints of some sort, and when a man stands up to leave, I see them.

Dante and Jost.

They're both here.

"Where are we?" I ask Erik, grabbing his arm. He removes my hand quickly but I don't think I'm imagining a gentle squeeze as he does it.

"We got her," Erik calls out, and everyone stops to stare at me. There are a few cheers. Some eye me with curiosity. Others look unimpressed. But all that matters is the grin that splits across Dante's face, because for a moment I feel like I've come home.

He strides forward and grabs me by the shoulders. He's still wearing the jeans and shirt he wore to Alcatraz, and he looks tired.

"You look different," he says.

"I've been busy preparing to become Cormac's little woman," I say, but I can barely focus on what he's saying to me. I'm too busy scanning the room, trying to process the incredible shift in my circumstances. Not even an hour ago I was on the way to my wedding, and now I'm here—wherever this is.

"But you aren't married?" Erik asks, and I think I hear a tinge of anxiety in his tone.

"No, I'm not."

"Thank Arras. I was worried we missed the blessed event," Dante says.

"Were you hoping to give me away?" I ask.

"I was planning to object."

"You weren't the only one," Erik says.

"You were just in time," I tell them. "I was on my way to the wedding."

"We had less time to strategize until we got here," Dante says. "Relative timelines, remember?"

"Yes, but where *is* here?" I ask. I turn around and take in the whole of my surroundings. I can't help but notice a line of framed portraits along a far wall. The room is average. It could be any meeting room in Arras, but that doesn't explain how my friends managed to set up in Arras. "Are those prime ministers?"

"You're in the Eastern Ministry offices," Dante explains.

"The Eastern Sector was destroyed."

"Do you believe everything Cormac tells you?" Dante asks. He drags me to a window that overlooks a courtyard. When I spot the elephant fountains, I know he's telling the truth.

I was here a little less than a month ago, but now it's been entirely transformed into an Agenda barricade. Only the shell of the room reminds me it was once Guild territory before Cormac destroyed it—or rather, pretended to. "Why would Cormac lie to me? He told me he destroyed the whole sector. He made me watch."

"To scare you." Valery's voice is soft as she speaks. "Fear is control."

She's right. How often had I demurred to Cormac's wishes to keep him calm? I was afraid of the havoc he'd wreak on the innocent people surrounding us. I hadn't considered that it might be a ploy.

"Cormac severed the sector, which means it will die soon enough," Dante tells me. "He didn't have to bother with destroying it. The sector can't self-sustain for more than a few months without the Spinsters. If the mines on Earth fail, it could be years—possibly decades or centuries—before their loss threatens the entirety of Arras. The Eastern Sector has considerably less time, though, because Cormac left no Spinsters and the looms are mostly destroyed."

"How long have you been here?" I ask.

"That depends," Dante says, gesturing toward Jost and Erik. "We followed you immediately, but it took us a while to get word to those on Earth. We're only beginning to get a handle on the situation. Thankfully the Agenda has spread throughout most of Arras, so we managed to regroup quickly."

"So you've been here since the severance of the Eastern Sector?" I ask.

"We arrived not long after. You were already gone. Cormac

practically handed the place over. It's allowed us a safe place to plan, but some of us only arrived in the last few days. Falon got here yesterday."

Falon glances up at the mention of her name, meeting Dante's eyes and then quickly looking away. She flips her dark hair over her shoulder so that it covers her face like a curtain. Although Falon was the first person we encountered on Earth, I'd spent little time with her. Now I couldn't tell if the cold shoulder she was giving us was aimed at me or Dante. She'd made it clear to me the last time I saw her that she didn't appreciate Dante not keeping her in the loop. If she hadn't known where he was until a few days ago, I understood her anger.

Dante had been here for weeks, along with Jost and Erik, and I hadn't even known. I wonder for a moment whether Pryana and the Agenda at the Western Coventry had any clue. Probably not, I decide. The risk to the heart of the Agenda would have been too great. The more important an operation is, the more secret it needs to be, I suppose.

It seems Falon might not have known where Dante was either. I recognize the cold shoulder, especially since Erik is giving it to me, too.

"I have lots to tell you," I say, trying to focus on something important instead of the ice spreading through my body in reaction to Erik's dismissive behavior.

"Soon," Dante says. He gestures for me to join him at a nearby table and as people clear a place for us I see that Einstein and Jax are there, too, discussing a complicated-looking equation scrawled across a sheet of paper. They're busy making adjustments, each bickering about the other's changes. It's quite the sight—lanky young Jax taking on Albert with his lined face and decades of wisdom. Jax worked for Kincaid on Earth, but he'd been using his considerable intelligence to help the Agenda. He might have met his match with Albert though.

"Hello!" I call out, waving excitedly to them. Despite the surprise of all this and of Erik's strange attitude, I'm genuinely pleased to see both of them.

"My young Whorl," Albert says, his bushy eyebrows rising with his smile.

"It's only been a month since you told me I was the Whorl, but I still don't understand what it means," I admit as I sink into the chair next to him.

"In time," Albert says. "There is much to discuss."

Like why Erik is acting as if he doesn't know me. Or how the Agenda set up its headquarters in the Eastern Sector without Cormac even knowing about it. I'd especially like to know how they managed to rebound me away despite the security assigned to me.

"I'm sure you have a million questions," Dante says, dropping into a seat across from me. "But we're in the middle of an operation right now. We had to adjust our strategy to capture you when we got the intel you'd be rebounding."

"How did you do it?" I ask. "I can barely go to the powder room by myself these days. My rebound should have been secure."

"It's nearly impossible to breach a secure rebound session," Dante says.

"I know. But if it's impossible, how did you do it?" I ask again.

"Nothing's impossible for a Creweler," a familiar voice says behind me.

I spin around in my seat, knowing that *this* is the one thing that should be impossible—even for a Creweler.

"I learned a few new tricks while you were away," Loricel tells me.

"Such as how to come back to life?" I can't keep the shock out of my question.

"Not even I can achieve that," she says. Loricel purses her lips and stares like she expects better of me. Without her smart suit and done-up hair she reminds me of my grandmother. She looks smaller than the last time I saw her, as though the weight of things has deflated her. But I still have no doubt: she's the most powerful woman I've ever known. "Did you think Cormac had the guts to terminate me?"

"He claimed he did," I say.

"He tried, but you know Cormac. He's a hoarder. If something shows the least bit of usefulness to him, he'll keep it around just in case." Loricel gives me a wink that's anything but amused. I can tell she wants us to continue this conversation in private.

I want to ask how she escaped, but I decide to wait until she brings it up herself.

"What's this mission?" I ask, recalling Dante's statement.

"We've managed to gather some important intelligence from local sources and public records," Dante tells me.

"Is it regarding Protocol Three?" I ask, hoping to finally have some answers.

"No," Dante says slowly. "What do you know about Protocol Three?"

"It's something I overheard Cormac say. It's probably noth-ing to worry about," I say. Dante doesn't look convinced.

Jost speaks up behind me and somehow, despite everything that's happened between us, I feel the fluttering of tiny wings in my chest at the sound of his voice. "We know where Se-brina is."

I turn toward Jost, unsure what to say to him. His blue eyes meet mine and there's fire in them. There's an electricity in the air around him, waiting to be unleashed. Finding Sebrina is all he's ever wanted, and even now, I want it for him.

"I remember she was rewoven into the Eastern Sector," I say. I'd found the information on the night we escaped from Arras to Earth. Even then Jost had been separated from her for almost three years, believing the whole time that she was dead—a victim of the Guild's warning to Jost's hometown. I cried for them both the night Cormac severed the Eastern Sector.

"They destroyed most of the files when they cut this sector off from Arras," Jax says, cracking his fingers as he speaks. "I had to get into the Guild's mainframe to recover the informa-tion. It took me a couple days. "

Jax gives Jost an apologetic look, but Jost waves it off. "The important thing is that we found her."

"Is she still here?" I ask in a small voice.

Dante steps forward and nods. "We have every reason to believe she's still within the Eastern Sector."

"Even ministers that evacuated left their families," Jax says.

I nod my head, already knowing this. I wonder for a moment if Grady left. "I watched Cormac tell a man to abandon his family because he could get a new one."

"You were there?" Erik's jaw tenses as he asks.

"I didn't want to be," I snap. He must know I tried to stop it.

"It's pretty clear that Protocol Two quarantines everyone in the sector who isn't a high-ranking Guild official."

"They must protect their secret," Loricel says in a soft but cutting tone.

I take a step back and meet Loricel's eyes once more. Does this mean she knew about the officials all along? Had she seen it before, herself?

When I first met Loricel, I wondered how old she was. I thought I had an idea after her short mentorship of me at the Coventry, but now I'm no longer sure. She still has paper-thin skin, creased with age, and the same silver hair. At some point, she allowed herself to age rather than maintain the charade of perpetual youth.

"Older than you think," she says.

It's clear Loricel remembers every moment that's transpired between us. And as she says the words—words she spoke to me at our first meeting—I realize she's been telling me the truth the whole time.

I just didn't hear her.

She knew about the Guild and how far renewal technology could go, but she hadn't told me. Loricel had covered up the Guild's biggest secret: they made themselves immortal at the cost of other people's lives; their own life spans were extended using the time strands of people whose lives the Guild had cut short.

"If Sebrina is out there," I say, trying to focus on the task at hand and not on the questions burning through my brain about Loricel's secrets, "we need to go after her."

Despite the chaos and strategizing going on around us, Dante grins at this. He looks a bit maniacal. It's how I know we're related.

"That's our next order of business."

EIGHTEEN

THE STREETS ARE DESERTED, AS THOUGH THE citizens are still abiding by the quarantine Cormac placed on the sector before he severed it. I can tell people have been out of their homes, though. Glass crunches under our feet from the shattered remains of storefront windows. The food co-op is devoid of rations. I wonder how many mothers and fathers fought one another for the little bit of food stocked on its shelves. I wonder how many people have run out of food entirely after the Eastern Sector's time in limbo. This is how Cormac left things. When he severed the sector in front of me, I thought he was a monster. But knowing that he left millions of people to starve in the dark makes me question if the word *monster* can even begin to describe him.

I trade my traveling suit and heels for something more practical—boots and jeans. Valery's shorter than I am, and her jeans and tunic are a bit too short and tight on me to be comfortable, but it's still better than running around in a skirt and stockings.

"We have to move quickly because we estimate resources will run out in as little as two weeks here," Dante explains to me.

"And what happens then?"

"People will start to die." He blows out a long sigh of frustration. "We need to evacuate everyone between now and then."

"Dante," I whisper. I'm not sure I want Jost to hear what I have to say. He has to be worried enough about Sebrina as it is. "Doesn't it seem too quiet to you here?"

Dante gives me a quick bob of the head that the others don't see. "On the one hand, it follows the pattern of behavior of the people left behind on Earth after the exodus. There's clearly been looting. Most food supplies are compromised. But you're right. On the other hand, it's too quiet."

"What do you think is going on?"

"I'm not sure," Dante says. "But it's not a coincidence if the Guild's involved."

Jost and Erik walk a hundred yards ahead of us, watching for danger. Valery trails between us and the Bell brothers. I want to ask her to join us, but I need to talk to Dante and I'm not sure I trust her yet. She may have proven herself to the others somehow, but her betrayal is still fresh to me.

Watching Jost and Erik in the distance, I can't help but think they're both avoiding me, and yet the sight of them working together makes me smile. They've become friends again in the time I've been gone.

"And those two?" I motion toward the brothers.

"They seem to have reached some sort of agreement after

174

Cormac took you. It was pretty obvious since they stopped bickering all the time. Bit of a relief, actually."

"Cormac didn't take me," I correct him.

"It's pretty hard for a man to admit when a woman's sacrificed herself for him," Dante says. "It's pretty hard for a father to admit it, too."

"What a waste of energy," I say.

"Says the one worrying about semantics." Dante shines his handlight over his face and raises an eyebrow. "You have a point."

Jost holds up a hand for us to stop. We slow down and wait as he moves forward a few steps into an alley. His figure disappears behind a building, and Erik follows him. Both brothers are swallowed by darkness and before I can call out to her, Valery goes in after them.

"Do they think that I'm going to wait around here and—"

A piercing scream shatters the night.

Dante and I race toward the alley, skidding to a stop at its dark mouth. Ahead of us is a figure, barely visible under the blacked-out sky. Dante flips on his handlight and the beam scatters across the figure. It's Erik. He waves for us to put the light away.

"Remind me to speak with him about hanging out in dark alleys without handlights," Dante mutters. He doesn't turn it off, but instead points it at the ground.

"Deal."

We approach Erik cautiously, unsure what to expect, but as soon as we're even with him, Dante's light reveals Jost crouched near the wall of the alley.

"What's he—" But I don't have to finish my question because as my eyes adjust to the darkness I see that Jost is not alone.

"Shhh!" Erik warns, and that's when I hear the voices. One is calm and reassuring, but the other comes in fits of words punctuated by giggles and wails.

I move closer to Jost but the woman he's speaking to startles and scuttles farther down the alley.

"Don't come any closer," Jost warns.

He calls out to the woman, but she only scrambles farther away from us in fits and jerks.

"What's going on?" Dante asks, and then he flashes the handlight in our direction. The woman screams as the light hits her and I realize she's not a woman. She's a girl not much older than me.

But everything about her is wrong. In the light her pupils are wide and black, and that's not even the most frightening thing. The whites of her eyes have gone red and her skin droops into giant jowls from her jawline. Some of it has detached entirely and something under the surface ripples. No, *crawls*. She hisses and wails and laughs as she scratches her fingers across the brick walls. It's as though she's decaying while she's still alive.

"Jost," I say, loud enough that he can hear. "We should go."

I take a careful step forward and touch his shoulder.

"She needs help," he says, flashing me a disappointed look.

"We can't help her," I say.

"Dante can help her," Jost corrects me, "and Erik."

So Erik has finally admitted to his brother that he's a Tailor.

"Then let's talk to them." I pull Jost's arm, urging him back to the others.

When we reach them, Dante and Erik are discussing something in grim voices. Valery hugs her arms to her chest and I place a reassuring hand on her shoulder. She doesn't look up, and Dante's expression is grave.

"That girl needs your help," Jost says. "I know you can patch."

"Jost." Erik places a hand on his brother's shoulder. "I have basic patching skills. I don't think I can do anything about that much . . . damage."

"I alter by feel," Dante says apologetically. "I don't have the medic training or equipment for such a severe case of . . ."

"So that's it?" I ask, frustrated by how unfeeling they both sound. Beside me Jost straightens a little in response to my indignation, as though he's physically backing up my moral stance.

"It's not only that." Erik pauses. "I've never seen damage like this before."

"That doesn't mean you can't fix it," I say firmly.

Behind us the girl bellows out a groan that grows strangled as she gasps for air. Jost takes a step toward her, but Erik grabs him, holding him back from helping her.

The girl's skin sags as she lifts her hands out to us, her flesh falling in sickening lumps to the ground. Her cry grows weaker, echoing from some pit deep inside her, until she is silent and still.

I can't tear my eyes from her body. I did nothing to help her. I only watched her die.

We stand in mute shock as we try to process what we've witnessed.

"Didn't she remind you of anything?" Erik asks us finally.

I don't have to think hard. The frenetic speech pattern, the animal-like responses, and most of all, her strange appearance.

"A Remnant," I say. "But Remnants are more controlled than she was, and her skin wasn't scarred."

"I don't think she was altered," Erik says. He speaks in slow, measured words. "This is something else entirely."

I shiver at the thought. I want them to help her, but I can't deny this is something we haven't faced before. "It was like she was decaying."

"I think that's exactly what happened to her," Erik says.

"Do you know something about this?" Dante asks him. "From your work with the Guild?"

Erik holds his hands up. He doesn't look guilty but it's obvious Dante doesn't trust him yet. "There were a lot of rumors flying around the Coventry. I never knew what to believe. The Guild was always testing new weapons and alterations. If I had to guess, I think that's what we're dealing with. But I have no experience with *this*."

"Did you touch her?" Dante asks Jost.

"No, why?"

"Until we know what it is we need to assume it's contagious."

"I saw it," I tell them. "It was like a swarm of insects."

Dante looks to Erik, who nods slowly. I know he saw it, too.

"It's possible," Erik says. "They altered people to create Remnants. It wouldn't be that hard to manipulate animals or insects in similar ways."

"You think it was an altered bug?" If he's right there's a good possibility I'll be seeing these things in my dreams.

"They dictated what came into Arras. They could eradicate

entire species, or . . ." Erik trails away, leaving us to our imaginations.

"Or create weapons," Dante finishes.

"We should keep moving," Erik suggests. I nod in agreement, but before we make it out of the alley a man appears at its end, blocking our departure. He has the same decaying appearance as the dead girl.

"We need to get out now," I murmur.

"You want to run past him?" Dante asks. He has a point. "We need a distraction."

Erik rummages through his rucksack but comes up empty-handed. "We can shoot him," he suggests weakly.

I don't even know what to say to that suggestion. But I don't have any suggestions of my own. In this strange severed existence, I cannot be sure my powers will work. I could do more harm than good.

"We don't know how the disease travels. We don't want any of his blood flying around. It's too dangerous," Dante says.

"I'm out of ideas," Erik says.

If we touch the man, we could become infected. But how are we going to get past him without touching him or hurting him?

Dante motions for us to huddle together, but as we come closer, I notice something is off. Our group is smaller.

"Wait. Where's Val?" I ask, but I'm afraid I already know. I pop my head out of our cluster and immediately spot her. She's no longer waiting silently by us. I know what she's doing. And I know why. Valery, so in need of validation after her betrayal, so eager to prove herself, is going to sacrifice herself. It is too late to stop her.

"Val!" Jost shouts, trying to call her back, but she's already only a few steps from the decaying man. She turns just as his arms close over her frail figure. When the man opens his mouth, a swarm of insects spills out, engulfing Valery. They cover her skin in a teeming black coat.

"No!" I yell. My fingers whip through the air, trying to latch on to the weave around us, but Dante grabs my hand.

"Stop," he commands me. It's only then that I see the tear I've left in my wake. The weave around it frays, unraveling into thin, brittle strands. This world is dying. Valery is dying. And I can't do anything to stop it.

Valery calls into the dead night, but her words are soft. The only one I'm sure I understand is, *"Run!"*

"It's too late," Dante says, dragging me beside him. I know he's right. As we rush past Valery, the insects have vanished, but then I see them trembling along under her skin as it puckers and bubbles until the bugs begin to strip her flesh. Even through her agony, she manages a small smile.

My fingers reach toward her, but Dante pushes me out of the alley and away from her.

"Did anyone touch the girl?" Dante demands.

I can't bring myself to answer his question. Valery will be dead soon. There's no way to stop it. If one of us is infected, we all will be soon.

"Ad!" Dante shakes me.

"She's clean," Erik says. "If any of us were infected, there would already be signs. You saw how quickly it infected Valery." He places a protective arm around my shoulder, and Dante turns his attention to the rest of us. No one shows signs of infection. We have to hope we're safe, but the truth is that none of us knows what we're dealing with.

We keep our lights on and move in a huddle. No one talks. A sense of shared urgency pulses among us.

"Why would she do that?" Dante finally says. His words are a mix of disgust and admiration, and I'm almost certain he's not looking for an answer.

"Guilt." Erik answers anyway, though his eyes never waver from the street ahead of us. "She betrayed us. This was her way of making it right."

I want to thank him for this obvious answer, but I know I'm looking for an outlet for my anger. I want to crack a joke and make the ache in my chest go away. But it's not going to be that easy this time. If it was ever that easy before.

"She didn't have to get herself killed." Erik's words are few, but full of meaning.

"Sometimes death is the only absolution," Dante says.

I shake my head. I don't buy that for one minute. "There is no absolution in death, only escape."

"There's absolution in sacrifice," Erik says softly. I hear it in his voice—the pain of his own sacrifice. But what has he given up, and why?

"Sebrina's house should be another block," Jost says, switching the topic to something practical to distract us from what we've lost.

"What if she isn't there?" I ask, immediately wishing I hadn't.

"She's there," Jost says. There's not a trace of doubt in his voice.

I wish I had that kind of conviction. I wish it were as simple as deciding to believe—in our plan, in the future, in who I am. My world is so tinged with little gray lies I can't be sure I know what to do or what to believe in anymore. The Eastern Sector is playing tricks on my mind.

The darkness creeps around us and I'm reminded of the world I left behind at the Coventry. But here the monster we face cannot be outwitted. It's simply a matter of being faster than it.

It's as simple as not being touched.

NINETEEN

THE STREET IS FULL OF HOUSES THAT blend into the night, each perfectly plain and unobtrusive. The trees are dying, their thin branches drooping like broken limbs to the clumps of grass and remains of plants in each yard. What was once precise and pleasing is now a neighborhood of ghosts. Any of these houses could be infested by whatever the Guild has unleashed. There's no vitality to the weave. Tarnished time threads knit through the brittle, frayed threads that make up the world around us. Only a few hours ago I believed there was no Eastern Sector. Now that I'm here I know that, without looms, there won't be one much longer. Everything here is dying as time and space slip back into the universe.

We quietly pass each house and I realize I'm holding my breath, waiting for the next attack.

None comes and that almost makes it worse.

The space between fear and anticipation is a waking nightmare of recrimination and doubt. I'm perpetually trapped in the knowledge of my own inferiority.

Could I make the sacrifice Valery did?

Would it even matter in the end?

The farther we walk in silence, the more questions tumble through my head. I have no answers and the lack of finality breeds more doubts until my mind is numb, overstuffed with questions I can never answer. It is a table of plates with no food—a feast of famine to gorge my mind on as we move closer to Sebrina.

I focus myself on this mission. I *can* effect change. I *can* save Jost's daughter.

I can.

I can.

I can.

I repeat it over and over in my head, but I come no closer to believing it.

Jost stops in front of one of the houses and we wait for him to give us instructions. After a few minutes I realize he's as stuck as I am, caught in a loop of self-doubt.

I take his hand and hold it. "Let's get Sebrina."

But he doesn't move, only turns to look at me. There's something imploring in his eyes. "What if she's dead?"

"She's not." I channel his earlier certainty and try to sound as confident as he did then.

"She won't know me," Jost says. "I'm a stranger, not her father."

This time Dante is the one to speak. "You will always be her father. Nothing can change that."

A lump grows in my throat. Poor Dante is the closest to understanding how Jost feels.

I know what scares Jost. He's worried that after everything

he's gone through to find her, Sebrina will reject him. How do you swallow the truth after a diet of lies?

"Let's check it out," Erik says, pushing past us.

I want to stop him because I can't bear to watch another person walk into the unknown. Instead, I follow him, circling the house to check for signs of people.

The house appears deserted.

"I think it's abandoned," I say to Erik.

He gives me a grim look and he doesn't have to say what I know he's thinking. *Or they're dead.*

"We won't know until we go in," Jost says, moving toward the door.

It's locked. His hand balls into a fist, but before he can knock against it, the door opens a crack.

"Are you the doctor?" a small voice asks.

Jost drops to his knees until he's level with the child peeping through the crack.

"We've come to help." His voice is husky and I can hear the tears he's holding back.

"My parents are sick," the child says. "They won't come out of their room."

My stomach turns over. They have the virus.

Does Sebrina?

I bend down and smile at her. "Can we come in and help?"

There's a moment of hesitation, but the girl nods.

As I stand up, Dante whispers in my ear, "Don't touch her."

I don't like that he said it. Not only because I hate what he's thinking, but also because I worry what will happen to Jost if Sebrina is ill. And because this is now an introduction layered with fear instead of joy.

The door opens and there she is. Already half my height, I know she has to be nearly five years old with the time we've spent on Earth. I expect to see the same calculation in Jost's eyes when I turn to speak to him. But it's not there.

Sebrina was a baby when the Guild took her from Jost. Now she's a young girl, self-sufficient enough to open the door for the doctor. She has wide, curious eyes that are the same blue as her father's. But her hair is dark and curly. She wrinkles her nose and crosses her arms as she takes us in.

"You don't look like doctors," she says.

"We're not," I say, gesturing to Jost but adding quickly, "They are."

As Tailors, Dante and Erik are as close to doctors as it's possible for any of us to be right now.

"What are you doing?" Dante whispers in my ear. "We can't save her parents. We have no renewal patches and no medicine. They're probably already dead!"

Sebrina's eyes flash up to his and her lower lip trembles.

"How long have your parents been sick?" I ask her, ignoring Dante's paranoia and taking her small hand.

"Father left to get food. He said it was too dark for me to come along, but I miss going outside and I miss the sun." She speaks in the rambles of a young child, trying to get the information out as quickly as possible, but getting distracted along the way.

"I know." I squeeze her hand. "When did your father go out for food?"

"I don't know," she says, tears welling in her eyes.

"Ad," Erik calls, and I find him in the kitchen. "He managed to find some." On the counter sit a few boxes of co-op instant dinners.

"Who knows how long they've been there, though," I say quietly to him.

Sebrina perks up. "I've only had one. I made it last until I fell asleep."

The pride is evident in her voice, even though she has no idea how much she's really told me.

"He must have gone out in the last few days," I say to Erik. "Maybe not long ago if she's only had one."

"Then her parents could still be alive," he says. To the right of us, Jost draws in a long breath and I remember that Sebrina still has one living parent and immediately feel guilty.

"We should bring her with us," Dante says. "Even if they're alive, they won't be much longer."

I'm not sure what to expect Jost to say in this moment. He's waited for years to get his daughter back. He lost too much time trying to find her, yet he doesn't sweep in and scoop her up. Instead he shakes his head. "I want to talk to her . . . parents."

"They're infected," Erik reminds him.

"I don't expect you to understand. I barely do myself. But what the Guild did—these people had no part of it," he says slowly, as though he's working through it himself. "They took care of her when I couldn't. I need them to know she'll be cared for now."

I can't pretend to understand his feelings. It's the barrier that's always stood between Jost and me. I've never felt anything as deeply as he does.

"Where are your parents?" Jost trips over the word as he asks.

Sebrina takes his hand and leads him into a short hallway. The house reminds me of my home in Romen. Simple and efficient. Bathroom, kitchen, dining room, living room, and two bedrooms. Sebrina is the only child, so they wouldn't need a bigger house. The Guild gave her to them for being steady and responsible and to make up for something the government couldn't control. But this is how it will end for them: victims of the government they obeyed.

Sebrina stops in front of a closed door and looks up to Jost with large eyes. He crouches down next to her. "I'm going to talk to your parents now. I want you to wait out here."

I move forward to take her back into the other room, but Erik beats me there. Before I can react, Erik picks her up and takes her away from the bedroom door.

Jost's eyes meet mine and I raise an eyebrow. Things between them have certainly changed since I left.

"Come with me?" he asks.

"Always."

He raps softly on the door but there's no response. He knocks again, more loudly, and the door shakes as something bumps against it.

"Jost . . ." I say in a low voice.

He raises a finger and we wait, our breath in our throats.

"I'm here to help," Jost calls. "Your daughter says you're sick."

"Go away." The voice coming through the door is rough and shallow.

"Please," Jost says, more insistent. "I need to talk to you about your daughter."

The door opens a fraction, but we can't see the person behind the door. "Is she safe?"

"Yes. I can explain if you'll open the door."

"No!" the woman cries. "You mustn't come in here. You have to take her away."

"I will," Jost promises. "But there's something you should know. I'm Sebrina's father. Her biological father. I've been looking for her for a long time."

There's a long pause before the woman responds. "The Guild told us she was an orphan."

"They told me she was dead," Jost says. "I wanted to—"

"I didn't know!" The woman's voice is a shriek and I can hear how hard she clings to control as illness ravages her body.

"I wanted to thank you," Jost says, placing a hand on the door. "And I wanted you to know she'll be safe with me."

"There's no safety left in Arras." A choking sound accompanies the words.

"I'm taking her away from Arras. She'll be safe. I promise you."

I think of Amie, rewoven as Riya, and wonder who Jost's daughter has become. "What's her name now?"

Jost gives me a look that shows this never occurred to him before. But when the mother answers, it's not what I expect. "We call her Sebrina. We were told that was her name."

"It is," Jost says. "It always will be."

"Look after her." The mother sounds calmer now, as though

knowing Sebrina will be safe has given her enough peace to cope as she dies.

"Goodbye." I leave the farewell lingering between us as Jost turns and takes his daughter from Erik. She doesn't fight him. It's as though she somehow knows he will care for her, even though she can't remember him. Sometimes love survives everything, even the darkest hours.

TWENTY

On Dante's order, the Agenda members left at the Guild offices place the facility on lockdown as soon as we enter. As it's a former Ministry complex, there are plenty of controls in place to ensure no one can get in or out without permission. But I can't help feeling as though we've locked ourselves in a cage.

"Where's Valery?" Jax asks as we enter the room.

Jost shoots him a warning look. Sebrina is in his arms, nearing sleep, but trying to keep her eyes open. I don't blame her for wanting to see where she's being taken.

"Do we have anything for her to eat?" Jost asks.

Jost refused to take the rations Sebrina's adoptive father managed to bring home. He claimed they were unsafe. He might have been right, but I knew that he wanted to make sure Sebrina's adoptive parents had food as well. Not one of us dared to tell him it was a pointless waste.

Jax manages to find some rations and the remains of a chocolate stash hidden in one of the ministers' offices. Sebrina bites off the candy in huge chunks, sighing contentedly while the rest of us watch.

"I'm going to find her somewhere to sleep," Jost tells us, gathering his daughter in his arms.

As I run my fingers along the glossy wood of the tabletop, I can't help wondering about the important decisions officials made here. In Arras there are three more tables like this, all full of officials meeting to discuss the problems Arras faces. I wonder if I'm on the list today or if Cormac has managed to cover up my escape.

"Valery?" Jax prompts as soon as Jost leaves.

I shake my head. "We were attacked. She didn't make it."

"Attacked?"

"There's something out there," Erik whispers. "A disease or a virus."

"A swarm," I say, thinking of how it descended upon Valery, disappearing into her skin. "Valery sacrificed herself so we could escape. It works quickly. She was already infected before we could reach her." Thinking back on the attack, I'm more certain than ever that we aren't dealing with a natural phenomenon. The Guild is up to something.

"You're sure you're clean?" Jax asks. He doesn't take a step back from us, but I sense that he wants to.

"Trust me," Erik says. "You can see it. Plus, it infects quickly. By the time we saw the first victim, the woman's skin was rotting off. She hardly looked human."

"She reminded me of a Remnant," I admit. I can't get my last image of Valery out of my head, nor the words she whispered as we passed.

Valery and I had a trying relationship on Earth, but we had

been friends once, in the way I had been friends with Enora, my mentor and her lover. We were kind to each other, helpful even, but neither of us truly shared who we were until it was too late. Standing here now, I realize we weren't so very different. We both lost loved ones. Neither of us ran until it was too late. The only thing that separated us was my skill. It bought me time and chances I deserved no more than Valery.

"You say their skin was rotting off?" Jax asks as we find our places at a long conference table.

"I've never seen anything like it," Erik tells him.

"I can't believe she's gone," Jax tells me in a soft voice. "She wanted to make things right with you. We talked about Enora and what she could remember. I tried to help her reverse more of the alterations they'd done to her."

"Were you successful?" I ask. Perhaps Valery's legacy would live on in helping us save the Remnants or the people affected by this disease outside.

"A little. Altering in reverse is tricky."

I think of Amie and how eager she is to remember our mutual past, despite having gone through multiple alterations.

"Whatever these things are," Dante says, "they aren't natural. They infect quickly. We encountered several infested people on our mission, all at varying stages, even the girl's adoptive mother."

"But the mother didn't hurt you?" Jax asks.

"It doesn't make any sense," I say.

"The Guild considers it genetic warfare," Albert says, settling into a seat across from me. "Why waste valuable material if it can be used to fight your enemy? A common pest becomes an ally in warfare, even something as simple as *Tineola bisselliella*."

"What?" Erik asks.

"*Tineola bisselliella*—a common fabric moth," Albert explains. "I'm afraid this is my fault. When we considered initial concerns regarding the Cypress Project—theoretical issues and such—we discussed whether certain species on Earth might negatively impact the artificial weave. I made a joke about fabric moths."

"Do I want to know what a fabric moth is?" My stomach churns as the conversation recalls the memory of Valery's final moments.

"An insect that eats away at fabric."

"Let me guess. In this instance we're the fabric?" I say.

"I'm afraid so."

"But why? Why unleash something like that here? These people were already as good as dead," Dante points out.

"The Eastern Sector was rebelling. This ensures no one here can fight back," Loricel says.

"How was anyone in the Eastern Sector going to fight back?" I ask.

Loricel gives me a grim smile from across the table. "Cormac is a thorough man."

That's an understatement.

"And yet you escaped him," I point out.

"Patton can't stand to waste resources," Dante says.

"You knew she was alive then?" I ask, gesturing to Loricel.

"I guessed. *Alive* is relative to a Tailor, anyway. Cormac's like Kincaid in that way. When he thinks people might be valuable to him, he keeps them around." Dante shrugs as if to say this isn't a big deal.

"But how did you rescue her?" I ask.

"That's an exciting story that makes me look really good. Unfortunately, I'll have to tell you another time," he says.

"I'm not going anywhere until someone tells me what's going on!"

"I see you're going through the ungrateful-brat phase," Dante says. "We saved you. Show some gratitude."

"I had plans," I tell him. "I was going to alter Cormac, maybe take on his appearance. But now I have no chance of ever getting close enough to him again. I'll never save the rest of the Remnants or slow the drilling on the surface. I'm sick and tired of people trying to rescue me, of everyone thinking and acting like I can do nothing right. I had enough of that from Cormac."

"Valery did it," Dante says, finally ready to answer my question. "We had enough information to guess where Cormac was keeping Loricel. With a little alteration and a lot of luck, we got in."

"And why couldn't you just tell me that?" I ask him.

"She didn't want you to know."

"Why?" I can't think of a single reason for her to keep this from me. Valery had a long way to go before she would be able to earn back my trust. Her participation in rescuing Loricel could only help in that regard.

"We barely made it out of the storage facility . . ." His voice fades away and slowly I begin to understand.

"Things got out of hand. I made a mistake." Dante's fingers tremble as he runs them over his cropped hair. "It's gone."

"What's gone?" I ask him in a hollow voice, afraid I already know the answer.

"The storage facility—and everything inside it."

My body goes cold and numb with shock. There's no chance to save the Remnants now.

Except my mother, Meria, whose thread is tucked safely away in my baggage. Baggage that didn't escape with me.

"I'm sorry," he says in a soft voice. I know he is sorry, because to him it means Meria is lost forever. I saw how he looked at her when he freed her from Kincaid's estate. Some things change with time, but others never do. Love like that leaves an imprint. It might fade with time, but it's always there, waiting for you to catch it in the right light.

"Right now they have something to show us," he reminds me. I become aware of the uncomfortable glances of the others in the room. I can't bring myself to tell Dante I have Meria's soul strand, not when he destroyed our chance at saving the others.

Jax looks for confirmation that he should begin, but my father can only manage a tight nod. A beam of light catches my attention as it bursts across the far wall, illuminating a screen with the image of Arras, and I'm grateful to think about something besides dead friends and a lost mother. The image is a basic map I once saw in academy. A rectangle with four points for the northern, southern, eastern, and western sides: the coventries. It's strange to see it now, knowing there's more to Arras than a map. This world isn't flat. Arras isn't limited by four corners. Now I see it as it is. Arras wraps and engulfs the Earth like a beautiful but deadly parasite.

Jax stands up, holding a digifile and looking a bit nervous. "This is how Arras is presented to the general population."

"I'm not sure I got that far in school," Erik says.

"Ignore everything he says," I tell Jax, motioning for him to continue.

"Okay." He swipes across the face of his digifile and the image begins to morph. "What the map doesn't show is the *dimensions* of Arras."

The map shifts into a half sphere and then a model of the Earth appears below it. Even though I've been to the other planet, I'm still in awe. It's large and blue and round. Arras hovers over about a fourth of it.

"Arras exists over Earth," Jax continues.

"We know that," Dante says, but Falon shushes him.

"As I was saying," Jax says, shooting Dante an annoyed look, "the two worlds exist relative to each other. However, Arras only exists because of Earth."

"Okay, now you've lost me—" Dante admits.

"Dear boy, you've seen the mines. Use your imagination," Albert interrupts him. The scientist is busy jotting notes. I can't figure out why. I know he understands things we can't quite grasp. But then he holds up the sheet in front of him, revealing a series of complex equations.

"I think I speak for everyone—except Jax—when I say *what*?" Erik says.

"I'm with Erik on this," I say.

"Oh never mind," Albert says. He crumples the paper into a ball and tugs off his sweater. He digs into its loose weave and begins pulling out a thread. It unravels until there's a small hole in the arm of the sweater. "I could take this yarn and make a new sweater, correct?"

I nod.

"But if I did," Albert continues, "I would destroy *this* sweater."

"So Arras is unraveling Earth," I say, "but we know that."

"Unfortunately, the existence of Earth is more vital to the universe than my sweater is," Albert says dryly. "If I unravel this sweater, it has no great effect on space-time, except to make me a bit colder."

"What happens to the universe if Earth unravels?" I ask.

Jax jumps in. "A singularity." But then he looks sheepishly at Albert as though he's spoken out of turn.

Albert waves off Jax's interruption. "No, explain with your images. It's much easier to understand."

"I got the sweater bit," Erik says to Albert.

"What's a singularity?" Jost asks. I'm surprised he's here given that he finally has his daughter back. I suppose her return is a reminder of what he's fighting for.

"Well, it's sort of like this," says Jax.

On-screen the image shifts. We watch Arras grow from the Earth, leaving behind a hole in its wake. Although Arras stays the same, the lines of light flowing into Arras from Earth leave a larger and larger hole. Eventually the hole grows so large that Earth begins to collapse into itself. A final bright flash of light leaves nothing more than a large black circle in its wake.

"What the Arras was that?" I ask.

"That's a singularity," Albert says in a grim voice.

"Basically, by taking Earth's resources, Arras is jeopardizing Earth's existence in the universe," Jax explains.

"But where did it go? Where's Earth?" Erik asks.

"In the event of a singularity, Earth will cease to exist. A massive well of gravity will pull everything—even light—

inside the singularity, destroying Earth *and* Arras." Jax pauses to let this sink in.

"What happens inside a black hole?" I ask.

"We don't know," Jax says. "Gravity is infinite in one, so it's impossible to tell."

"Meaning?"

"*Nothing.* Nothing will exist."

"So in this scenario," Erik asks slowly, "everyone dies?"

"Yes. Death. No doubt. The atoms might survive somehow and somewhere, or rather the leptons, quarks, and other subatomic knickknacks." Albert says the words with a fair amount of annoyance, as though this is all perfectly obvious. But even hearing him say it doesn't make it feel any more real.

"Cormac must not know this. Even he wouldn't be so foolish as to destroy *everything*," I say.

"He knows," Jax says. "More and more of the Guild Tailors and scientists have been defecting—fleeing to Earth and seeking us out. We believe he's planning a controlled demolition."

"What does that mean?" I ask slowly.

"If he can mine enough resources from Earth and then control its destruction, he might be able to prevent the singularity."

"Might?" Erik says, shaking his head. "Fantastic plan."

"There has to be a contingency for this," Dante says, running a hand through his hair.

And then I realize there is.

"Protocol Three." To my surprise it's Loricel who speaks.

"What is Protocol Three?" I ask Einstein. He has to know, with his intimate knowledge of the Guild.

"Cormac mentioned it. Well, actually, he sort of threatened it."

"That does not shock me," Loricel says. "Protocol Three is the ultimate threat response."

"Stop speaking in riddles," Dante demands.

"There are three protocols for dealing with trouble in Arras," she says.

"Protocol One is alteration," Erik says. He shrugs at me, mouthing, *Misspent youth.*

"The Guild employs Protocol One to contain information and deal with troubling behavior," Loricel explains.

"They used it here," I tell them.

"But the dissent was widespread and Protocol One became ineffective in coping with the situation," she continues. "Which leads to Protocol Two."

"They sever an entire sector from Arras," I say.

"Have you ever wondered why it is the Guild of Twelve Nations?" she asks.

I swallow hard on the question and nod.

"Only four sectors remain of the original twelve," Loricel says.

"The others were severed?" Jost asks.

"Yes. When a sector became too progressive, it was separated from the whole, or when a disease broke out, or if one wanted its independence. Protocol Two was how they dealt with these situations," she explains.

"So Arras was larger?" Dante asks.

"It was more divided. Once a separated sector ran out of resources and unraveled, we extended the remaining sectors to take its place."

"And no one noticed?"

"Over time as sectors were detached, we simplified the map and revised history to reflect that there were only four sectors. Because of education control, it was easy for the Guild to ensure the people only knew what they were told."

"But it was happening all around them!" I can't believe this, and yet I know it to be true.

"It's easier to focus on the life around you than to see the whole picture," she says.

"Then what will happen to this sector?" I ask. "What do you mean by 'unraveled'?"

"Extermination?" Jost asks with disgust.

"The disease in the streets only increases the rate of the sector's decay."

"We need to get everyone out of this sector," I say.

"What do you think we've been doing?" Falon asks in an annoyed voice.

"It's been weeks!"

"Do you think you could have done better?" she asks.

"This is getting us nowhere," Dante says. "We're working on a plan, Adelice. We expect to have survivors out within a week."

"What about the sick?" I ask.

"We can't take them," he says.

I can't help but feel disappointed in Dante. He had once set my mother free even though the Guild had turned her into a monster, but now he was turning his back on the people of the Eastern Sector.

"Unfortunately, if what you say is true, the virus progresses so rapidly we have no time to find a cure," Loricel says. "But the diseased represent a clear and immediate threat to our operations here."

"It doesn't sound like we'll be safer on Earth," Erik mutters.

Next to him Jost has gone pale. No doubt he's wondering how to protect Sebrina. I want to kick Erik right now.

"Can we prevent the singularity?" I ask, trying to focus on something positive.

"That is what Protocol Three is for," Loricel explains.

If the first two protocols alter people's psychology and destroy whole metros, I'm not sure I want to know what Protocol Three does.

Albert is the one to finish the explanation. "Protocol Three will end the Cypress Project."

"End it?" I echo. The Cypress Project was once an idea— the theory that with machines men could manipulate the most basic strands of the universe to create a perfect world. Now that idea was Arras itself.

"The men who created it were scientists. It stands to reason we would create a termination procedure if the experiment was deemed a failure," Albert says.

"And Arras is a failure?" I ask, feeling slightly insulted.

"It will be a failure if it results in the death of two worlds."

"But the people in Arras—"

Loricel holds up her hand. "Protocol Three will allow for total evacuation of every metro in Arras before the world unravels."

"And that's it?" I ask. "We press a button and then poof! No more Arras?"

"That oversimplifies things a bit, but—precisely," Albert says.

In a way it's what I wanted, but I've seen Earth and I know the hardships generations will endure rebuilding that world.

"You would let Arras go?" I ask Loricel.

She laughs at this. "I've been trying to let it go for hundreds of years."

I can't help it. I don't want to see Arras destroyed. Does that make me the same as Cormac?

"You spoke to me once of the greater good," I say to her.

"Age understands what youth cannot," she replies, but she offers no other explanation.

"How do we do it?" I ask.

Jax and Albert share a look and my stomach clenches.

"That's the hard part," Albert says.

TWENTY-ONE

According to Jax, we pretty much have to bust into the Guild offices in Cypress, hack their controls, and start evacuation procedures. Which will work—if we don't get caught. Returning to Guild-controlled Arras unnoticed won't be simple, especially if we need to break into the Ministry offices. But then there's still the matter of the self-destruct code—a code only Cormac knows.

Because we wouldn't want this to be too easy.

"I can get it out of him," I say finally.

"I would love to know how you're going to do that," Falon says.

"You have to let me go back. I can claim I was kidnapped and escaped."

"He's not going to believe that," Jost says.

"I don't care if he believes it," I say. "I only need to get close to him."

Cormac might be eager enough to continue the wedding

charade to go along with my lie, and I'd only need a little time to get him alone.

"No way." It's Erik who speaks, which surprises me, considering the distance he's kept since I arrived. But one look at his face and I know he's serious. I'm not sure how I feel about that.

I open my mouth to argue with him, but Dante raises his hand. "It has been a long day. Adelice should rest. We should all rest."

As soon as he says it, I realize I am tired. More tired than I've been in weeks. I can't quite stifle a yawn.

"We need a plan," Falon says.

"And we can come up with one eight hours from now. But we aren't going to come up with anything if we're tired and arguing," Dante says in a gentle tone.

"I believe you should all spend the evening with those you love," Albert advises. "Our time here is growing short."

I don't want to ask him what he means—whether our time in Arras is growing short, or our time in general.

"I'm going to see to Sebrina." Jost looks at me and then at his brother. The two share a very serious nod. Have they perfected an entire secret code while we've been apart?

"We created some bunkers in abandoned offices. You can sleep there," Dante says to me.

Dante leads me up a narrow flight of stairs and Erik trails behind us. Dante stops at a door and gives Erik and me an appraising look as he opens it. "I think I'm supposed to give you a lecture or something. As your father."

"About?" I ask, moving inside the room.

He laughs at me, and it hits me.

"Oh."

"You two should talk." Dante turns to leave, looking back once but finally throwing his hands up in the air, and mumbling to himself as he leaves Erik and me alone.

The door shuts too slowly behind him. Erik's arms are around me immediately, pulling me in to him. The distance I felt before is gone, replaced by urgency.

"I thought—" Then his lips cover mine.

Erik breaks away, his hands cradling my back. "You thought I'd changed my mind?" he guesses.

I nod, suddenly overcome by emotion that creeps hot up my throat, moving toward my eyes. I can't hold it back and it spills onto my cheeks. Erik brushes away my tears, kissing my cheeks where the tears fell.

"Never," he says in a quiet voice. "I was trying to be . . . professional."

"Professional? That's new," I say a bit too coldly.

"When my brother is around, I don't want to upset him. He's lost a lot. I had to focus on helping him rescue Sebrina. I owed him that."

"You're being thoughtful," I realize out loud. Of course our feelings for each other would threaten whatever peace Erik and Jost have found in my absence.

"But I hurt you." Erik's hands fall away from me, and I miss his touch immediately.

"No, I understand," I say, shaking my head as the petty anger I felt minutes before releases me. "I should have known what you were trying to do."

We linger for a moment in silence, neither of us sure what to say. But I can feel the pulse of my heart throbbing through my blood, stirring me to life, willing me to close the space between us. Erik and I were friends for a long time, but this is new. We're still learning how to be together and what we're willing to share with the rest of the world.

"While they were talking about strategies," Erik says, taking a strand of my hair in his fingers, "I could only think about kissing you."

I try to hold back the smile that jumps to my lips, but I can't, not entirely.

"Unfortunately, the strategy room isn't the place to make up for lost time," he says, a smile curving onto his face.

"We're not there now," I remind him.

He doesn't need any more incentive. The bunker's emergency lights flicker around us and with one smooth motion Erik flips the generator switch, flooding the room in darkness. I can't see him in the blackness, but I sense his presence and I feel his heat radiating as he draws me to him. His lips move along the curve of my jaw and linger at my ear.

"I love you, Adelice," he whispers.

Time slows as his words light upon me, but in my chest something bursts into a million fragments that melt back together instantly, remaking me into someone entirely new.

"I love you, too."

His lips close over mine at the affirmation and we slip into each other. Each of us evolving in the other's arms—a person stronger because of the other, but more vulnerable as well. His fingers grip the hem of my blouse and he pauses.

"Yes," I whisper into his chest even as I find myself in danger of exploding from the sensations crowding my body. He fumbles a little as he finds my buttons, and I laugh.

"I didn't expect you to be nervous." My words are too high-pitched and I realize how anxious I sound, but Erik laughs as well.

"This is a first for me, too."

"Erik," I say softly, and he stops. His face is a sketch against the darkness, the lines of it smooth and fluid, but his eyes are silver as they wait for me to speak. "I'm scared."

His hands cup my face and he gives me a sad smile. I don't have to tell him what I'm scared of. The war, what will happen next, Amie's change, Cormac's descent into madness. And most of all, who I will be after this moment, because this love is fresh and raw. I can already feel its wounds written across my body, singing with the tenderness of newborn skin.

"Don't be," he whispers. His hands don't leave my face. They are warm and steady as he waits. Finally, I pull them down and clasp them into my own. I take a small, but deliberate step backward. And another. And another. Until my calf bumps into the wooden frame of the bunk. I lie down and Erik climbs in beside me. Our bodies press together as he brings his lips to mine.

Erik isn't aggressive, even if his touch is urgent, and I understand because I've been holding this at bay for a long time, too—since that first night in the courtyard when we danced under the moonlight, and I kissed him because he dared to give me hope. Everything fits with him. The way his lips are soft but full on mine. The way my body locks into his. Our first kiss flashes through my mind. The silver moonlight, the trees etching the dark courtyard, dancing without music. But as we find each other now the world lights up around me, haloing Erik in brilliant life, and the music of time weaves around us, filling the air with a gentle, slow harmony that builds toward a soft cadence.

He's careful and kind, waiting for my cues. My nerves sing out where he touches me, sparking to life, and then his skin is on mine and my body bursts into fire and longing until there's no space left between us at all.

TWENTY-TWO

I WAKE TANGLED IN ERIK'S ARMS AND peer across to him, my eyes adjusting to the dark, his blond hair a mess across the pillow. I'm torn between pulling the crumpled sheet up over me and waking him. But while his eyes are closed, I can keep the ache niggling in me at bay, so I watch him sleep and wonder how I'll feel when those blue eyes eventually open. I draw my fingers through my hair to see if it's as untidy as his and then let them trace my own face, feeling for a change. Confusion churns deep inside me. I'm exactly the same, but everything is different.

Slipping from the bed, I wrap the sheet around me and examine myself in the window. Outside the glass, the world is black and my pale silhouette is reflected in it. I let the sheet fall open and study my body. It's still mine. There's no sign of a change, but it's there. I can't see or touch it, but I feel it somewhere, instinctually. Somewhere outside the bunker, a floodlight bursts on, and I back away, catching flashes of a woman in the pane's reflection. It looks like my mother but then I realize it's me. As the light streaks across the room, it slants through the windows and lights silver on Erik's face, causing him to stir. He's beautiful in his sleep, but soon his eyes flutter. The first wave of uncertainty rolls through me, catching my breath. He gets up gracefully, rubbing sleep from his eyes, unaware of the profound shift in the room.

"You are beautiful," he murmurs, reaching to pull me back to him and kissing my neck as I tumble into his arms.

I stare at the window, watching the reflection of two lovers as I try to comprehend the evolution of our relationship—what we've shared. Erik's mirrored eyes meet mine, and he doesn't speak. He doesn't have to—his gaze says it all. In the window, he looks like a man. Lean and tall. The angles of his jaw more defined under a thin layer of stubble. I still look like a girl. Too thin. No curves. But there's something in my face that makes a different case. The couple in the glass share a secret. Will it be obvious to everyone when they see us? Will everyone know?

I don't have time to decide, because the office door swings open and Jax's head pops in.

"Knock!" Erik yells at him as I clutch the sheet closer to me.

"Sorry," Jax says, turning his head away. "But we have a problem. Dante needs you both downstairs now."

"What's going on?" I ask, tripping over the sheet to get to my clothes.

"Alixandra is here," he says.

"What?" I stop scrambling and stare at the back of Jax's head.

"I'll explain. Tell them we're coming." Erik pushes the door shut.

"Get dressed. I'll tell you on the way down," he says, handing me a boot.

"Tell me now."

"Please," he says, turning the full force of his blue eyes on me.

I make a face at him, but pull on the boot like he asked.

Before I can open the door, Erik grabs me and pulls me to him. "I have a feeling I won't have many chances to do this soon."

His lips press into mine, igniting a fire in my chest. I want to stay here, pressed close to him. When he pulls back, we linger in the moment, looking into each other's eyes.

"'Love alters not with his brief hours and weeks, but bears it out even to the edge of doom,'" he whispers, quoting the sonnet we'd read together on Earth. It seems like a lifetime has passed since that night.

"Is that your idea of a pep talk?" I ask.

Erik's lips curve into an almost-grin. "I just want you to remember that."

"Always," I say. He leaves one more soft kiss on my lips, but then we have to go.

In the corridors, people rush past us with bags and folders.

"What's going on?" I ask Erik with dread.

"Come on." He grabs my hand and we race back to the strategy room. As soon as we're through the door, he drops my hand, shooting me an apologetic look. I wink at him.

"Gross," Falon says.

"Good to see you again." I smile sweetly at her, but then my gaze lands on the woman behind her.

"What are you doing here?" I demand.

212

"Nice to see you, too," Alixandra says. "I'm sorry to interrupt your honeymoon."

I blush furiously at this but keep myself otherwise composed. "Let's try this again. What's stopping me from ripping you in half?"

"Remind me not to save your life in the future." Alixandra glares back at me.

"Will someone explain what in Arras she's doing here?"

"I thought you were going to tell her," Jost says to his brother.

"We were . . . preoccupied," Erik says.

Dante covers his eyes and turns away from us. "I don't need to hear about this."

"We were talking," Erik says.

"Is that what they're calling it these days?" Falon asks.

"You!" Dante points at her. "Cut it out."

"I was under the impression that there was an emergency," I remind everyone.

"And you are right, dear girl," Albert says, shuffling into the room with Jax's help. I can't help but notice that Albert is looking worse than yesterday. As though all his stolen years were catching up with him at once. "But young love is equally thrilling, I think."

Erik's hand flies to his mouth and I know he's covering a smirk. I smack him on the shoulder. "Get serious."

"I guess we know who wears the pants in this relationship," Alixandra says.

"Why are you my best friend again?" he asks her.

"Wait! Alixandra? Alix?" I can't control the volume of my voice.

"That took you long enough," she says.

"But Alix is a boy," I say, trying to work through this confusing turn of events. "Alix has to be a boy."

"Why?" Erik asks.

"You g-g-grew up together and Alix w-w-works for the Guild," I stammer out my answers in spurts of confusion. "What about segregation?"

"All those things are true," Erik says, "but she's still a girl."

"You could have mentioned that," I say, smacking him again.

"It didn't occur to me."

"Thank you. That's very flattering, Erik," Alix says.

From his seat, Jost props his feet on the table and watches us with a giant grin.

"You are enjoying this too much," Erik says.

"Yes, I am," Jost says, folding his hands behind his head. "I told you, Ad. Saxun doesn't segregate. I married Rozenn the day she was released from testing."

"There is an actual emergency," Dante snaps, pushing Jost's feet off the table. We all look to Alixandra and she pulls a digifile from her bag.

"Cormac has initiated final termination of this sector," she says.

"Like, Protocol Three?" I ask.

"Protocol Three allows for evacuation before the sector is destroyed," Jax says. "This isn't Protocol Three."

"But why now?" Erik asks. "He's already infected half the population, there are no resources left. It's only a matter of time."

"He knows we're here," I say, looking to Alix for confirmation. She nods.

214

"He wouldn't pass up the opportunity to destroy the Agenda," Dante says in a grim voice.

"Does he know *I'm* here?" I ask, wondering if I can message Cormac. Maybe if he discovers I'm here, he'll stay his order to terminate the sector.

"He knows," Alix says. "I bought you as much time as possible before I had to get out myself."

"I guess the wedding is off," I say.

"Good. You can get rid of that ring," Erik says, and I realize I'm still wearing it. I tug it off my finger and throw it across the room.

"What do we do?" I ask Dante, feeling lighter and ready to take on Cormac.

"We evacuate," he says.

"But what about the citizens?" I ask. "Not everyone in the Eastern Sector is infected."

"We don't have time," he says.

"Where will we go?" Jost asks. "Back to Earth? It won't be long before it's unstable there."

He has a point. "It won't do us any good to run," I say. "If we waste time going back to Earth, Cormac will be more prepared than ever for our return. We have to ensure that the singularity can't occur."

"And how will we do that?" Falon asks.

And now I know that I can never save both worlds. I have to make a choice. This is what being the Whorl is truly about. I can't hold both worlds together any longer, not as this one spins further out of my control.

"We have to initiate Protocol Three," I say in a soft voice.

No one speaks for a moment, all of them digesting this

idea while in the same instant realizing I'm admitting defeat. For those of us who have lived most of our lives in Arras it feels unbearable, but I take solace in the promise of Earth. If we can initiate Protocol Three and evacuate the citizens of Arras before this world begins to self-destruct, we can rebuild the planet we left behind.

"Don't we have to get into the Northern Sector to do that?" Erik asks.

"I hate to interrupt, especially with bad news," Alix says, waving her digifile. "I know you don't have time to read this report, but Cormac has blocked communication between all sectors."

"Even if we initiate Protocol Three—" Dante begins.

"The evacuation calls won't go out," Alix confirms.

"Then we have to find a way to evacuate the population."

"It's too late—" Falon is cut off by the entrance of Loricel.

"Cormac can't be trusted. I've known him for hundreds of years, but his behavior shows signs of madness," Loricel states in an imperial voice.

"He has to be stopped," I say. "We can't go back to Earth and come up with another plan. We can't let him continue."

"I agree," Albert says, and everyone turns to him. "I created this world to put an end to violence, and while I struggle to see it come to violence now, I can't deny that Cormac Patton has become a threat to the very existence of the human race."

"So we agree," Erik says, "but I'm still not sure how we're even going to get into the Northern Sector."

"Leave that to me," Loricel says. "I got Adelice out. I can get you in."

"We can't all go," I say.

"She's right," Dante agrees. "We need a group to get the word out to the resistance leaders in the other sectors about what's happening. The ministers can initiate the evacuation procedures. All the protocols are in place for the ministers to open loopholes throughout Arras."

"What about the people here?" Jost asks, and I know he's thinking of Sebrina.

"A group needs to stay and get everyone out. If we send someone through the loophole, we can get the rest of the survivors evacuated in minutes," Albert suggests.

"Are you sure?" I ask.

"I'll make sure," Erik says, stepping in. Our eyes meet and we both know that our talents are needed in too many places at once to allow us to go together now.

"But the second they rebound into the other sectors, their personal identifying sequences will be flagged," Falon points out. "They'll have you ripped in minutes."

"We'll use a veil," Loricel says. "The veils will mask your personal identifying sequences. We might as well use the talents of the Tailors in the room."

"I don't have the materials to make a veil," Erik says.

"You have me," Loricel reminds him.

"How long do we have?" Dante asks Alix.

"About an hour," she says.

"Arras time or Earth time?" Jost asks.

"That's relative," Albert says.

"What does that mean?" Jost demands.

"It means that in this set of circumstances, we have an hour. We'd better get to it."

Everyone rushes in opposite directions, and I don't have time to say goodbye to Erik before Dante has pulled me to the side. We're leaving with Jax and Falon.

"That's it?" I ask. "How are we going to do this with only four of us?"

"Jax will stay with you the whole time, Adelice," Dante says.

"I'm not much of a bodyguard," Jax points out.

"You know how to initiate Protocol Three and Adelice claims she can get Cormac to tell her the pass code," Falon says.

"That was before I knew he'd ordered my death," I point out.

"Be extra sweet," Dante advises me.

"And the other sectors?" I ask, ignoring Dante's helpful advice.

"We will have several minutes in each sector before the coventries detect an anomaly," Loricel says. "You must get word out before I start the next rebound."

"We should go alone. Cover more territory," Dante says.

"I can handle two of you at a time, but past that, things will get tricky."

"I'll go to the Western Coventry," I volunteer. "Pryana will help me get the evacuations going, and I have to be sure that Amie gets out."

"We need to focus on the population, not the coventries," Dante argues.

"I'm not negotiating on this," I tell him. "I need to make sure Amie gets out, and Pryana is Agenda. She can notify others."

"Amie will be safe, Ad," Jax says.

"If the evacuation measures are in place," I say. "There are four of us. We can cover all the sectors and the Western Coventry, too."

"Fine," Dante relents. "Loricel, can you do it?"

"Absolutely," Loricel says.

Dante nods, his eyes flicking to each of us as if to gauge our readiness.

"Then Falon will take the leader of the Southern Sector, Jax the Northern, and I'll take the Western Sector, and then we'll all meet in the Northern Ministry to deal with Cormac together."

I nod, my pulse building to a frenzy. From this moment on we are on borrowed time, but before I can even consider how much danger we're rebounding into, Erik appears.

"I hear you need disguises."

TWENTY-THREE

I ALWAYS EXPECTED THAT HAVING MY FLESH altered would hurt, but other than an initial prickle across my nerves, I don't feel much.

"How are you doing?" Erik asks me.

I don't bother to look at him, because then I'll see what he's doing and I definitely don't want to see.

"I'm great," I say as enthusiastically as possible. "I'm still not sure what you're doing, though." I never mastered my Tailor abilities past basic alteration, and my work was overseen by Dante or Erik every time. This is well beyond the scope of my skill.

He snorts, but I'm telling him the truth—it doesn't hurt. "Veiling creates an alternate pattern of information in a person's personal identifying sequence. If you tried to go back in without it, it would only be seconds before a security alert was activated. One of the many unfortunate side effects of having total control over an artificial world is how easily anyone can be found."

As a child this information made me feel safe. Now that I'm the person being hunted, I can see the problem with this setup.

"But one of the perks," he adds, "is that what they see on the security looms can be manipulated."

"And what they see in person?"

"That doesn't change, and unfortunately, I don't have time to alter your appearance. Not that I want to," he adds.

"So this isn't an actual disguise?"

"Only for the security looms."

"Shoot," I say, trying to lighten the mood. "I was hoping to get rid of these freckles. I guess I'll have to settle for some funny spectacles or a big hat."

"I love those freckles." Erik leans in and brushes a quick kiss over my bare shoulder, straightening up again when Jax turns back toward us.

"How long does veiling buy us?" I ask.

"Depends." Jax sounds skittish and when I look at him, his skin is gray. It could be the lighting, but I tend to think he's actually getting sick.

"You okay?"

He gestures to my arm, and without thinking I look down at it. Erik's fingers are in my flesh. There's surprisingly little blood, but I suppose there's not been much blood any of the times I've witnessed alteration. Still, it's unsettling to see his fingers inside my arm, with my skin draped open like loose fabric.

"That's appetizing," I say.

"To answer your question," Jax says, tapping his foot in a nervous beat on the floor, "when we enter, we won't be flagged automatically because of the veil over our personal identifying sequence. But eventually they'll realize that there are unidentified sequences in the patterns of the sectors."

Dante reappears, chewing on some rations. I don't know how he can eat. "That's why we need to get in and out of the other sectors and then into the Cypress offices before they catch on," Dante says.

"We could have minutes or hours," Jax says with a shrug.

"I will be moving you within five minutes of the first rebound," Loricel informs us.

"That won't be enough time! What if we can't find anyone?" I ask.

"We don't have long before the destruction of the Eastern Sector," she reminds me. "I can work quickly, but I won't have a place to work for much longer."

"Wait. If you're staying here," I say slowly, piecing together what she's telling me, "then you won't make it out."

"Probably not," she says, but she doesn't seem upset.

"You'll die."

"I know that," Loricel says. "Don't be sad for me, Adelice. I've had more than enough time to come to grips with the inevitability of my death. Too long, actually."

"But . . ." I know she's right, but the thought of Loricel staying here to die while helping us escape makes me sick.

"I won't be alone," she says softly.

"Who?" I ask.

But then I spot Albert lingering in the corner behind her. She winks at me and I have to suppress a laugh. I'm still sad, but if the two wisest people I know want this to happen, then I have to believe they're right.

"What happens when we get in there?" I ask Jax.

"Once we breach the Ministry in Cypress, I'll access the system and begin Protocol Three."

"But what about the pass code?" I ask.

"You get Cormac to fess up," Falon says, folding her arms over her chest. She clearly doesn't think I can do it, which makes me want to hand deliver it to her.

"Once the protocol has been initiated, the system will begin the self-destruct process as soon as Cormac says the pass code," Jax says.

"I only have to get him to say it?" I say. "That shouldn't be . . . too hard."

"Yes, but he has to be the one to say it. It's voice-encoded," Dante says. "It won't work unless it's him saying it."

"Okay," I say slowly. It won't be as simple as raiding his office if Cormac fails to comply. "What if he's not there?"

Dante exhales heavily. "We have to assume he is. He gave the order to destroy this sector from his office."

"I don't like the idea of Adelice running around risking her life if we aren't sure Cormac is there," Erik says. He's finished with my arm and he squeezes my hand before he starts on Jax.

"It's a suicide mission any way we go about it," Falon says. She sounds like this barely bothers her. "You two need to say goodbye now."

I know I'll probably never see Erik again. I know I'll probably die today, but I don't need Falon to point that out at this moment.

"Falon," Dante says in a low voice. It's meant to be a warning but she rolls her eyes.

"What good does it do to lie to them or give them false hope? Let them have a minute alone."

"There's no time for that," he says.

"There's never any time for that," she says. She turns on her heel and walks out of the room and that's when I realize what's bothering her. She isn't as doom-and-gloom as she pretends to be. She's angry with Dante, because it's too late for them. They've spent too long fighting instead of taking a moment to be together.

"You know," I whisper to Dante, "she's in love with you."

"Falon?"

"You didn't realize that?" Erik asks.

"I don't assume everyone is in love with me," Dante retorts, but his eyes dart toward the door.

"Go on, idiot," I say, and Dante rushes out of the room.

We have minutes left to live a lifetime. We should make every second count.

TWENTY-FOUR

WE HAVE TO LEAVE TO MAKE THE rebound into the various sectors as quickly as possible, but Erik catches my arm and pulls me into a dark hallway, away from the people rushing to make the final arrangements.

"I have to go and get these people out of this sector before Cormac terminates it," he says.

There are tears pooling in my eyes, but I blink them away.

"This is not goodbye, Ad." He cradles my chin and forces me to look him in the eyes.

"You don't know that," I say.

This was a possibility. But now that we're facing it I can't quite catch my breath. The more I look at Erik, the more scared I become. What are the chances that we'll both come back from this? I only got him back yesterday and now I'm losing him again.

I run my fingers along the faint scar where he applied my veil. "'Love is not love which alters when it alteration finds,'" I murmur faintly, recalling his favorite sonnet. "I love you."

"I love you," he says with a smile, "'even to the edge of doom.'"

He kisses me goodbye then and I melt into him, wishing for one more night or even a few minutes more, but it's over before it begins.

An uncomfortable cough startles us apart and we look up to see Jost standing in the shadows, his thumbs hooked in the pockets of his jeans.

"I'm sorry. I don't mean to interrupt," he says.

"We were . . . done," Erik says, dropping his hands from me.

"Stop that," Jost says.

"What?" Erik and I ask at the same time.

"Pretending like you aren't in love," he says. "It doesn't bother me."

How can that be possible when it bothers Erik and me so much?

"I'm sorry," Erik says.

"Don't be. Love is one thing no one should ever be angry over," he says. "And without you two I wouldn't have Sebrina now. Thank you for that."

Embarrassed, I murmur, "You're welcome."

"You don't have to thank us," Erik says with a shake of his head. "You would have done the same for either of us." I realize he's right. Somehow, in the insanity of our time together, I managed to find a family, crazy and mixed up as it is. This is my family.

"I need you to promise me something." Jost pauses, searching for the right words. "If anything happens to me, please take care of Sebrina."

"You don't have to ask that—" I begin.

"No, I do. Not because I don't trust you, but because I need to know that if anything happens to me, Sebrina will be safe with you."

"You're coming back," Erik says in a firm voice. "That little girl won't lose another father. I swear on my own life."

"I see you're going to be a protective uncle." Jost's voice breaks as he speaks. He tries to cover it with a laugh.

"You're our family," I say, and Erik's arm slides around my waist. "She's our family, too."

Jost gives me a genuine smile this time. Not the wicked grin he shares with his brother. This smile is warm and full of hope and it goes all the way to his eyes.

"Come here," Erik says, waving his brother toward us.

He wraps an arm around each of us and we embrace, knowing this is probably the last time we'll ever do so. I only know one thing: one of us has to survive for Sebrina.

"If I don't make it—" I begin, but Erik shushes me. He seems incapable of accepting this possibility.

"No, please listen," I continue. "Find Amie. She can take care of herself, but she'll have questions. I need her to know why I did what I did."

"She knows you're a good person," Erik says.

"Am I?" I ask.

"Yes," both Erik and Jost say at the same time, and for the first time in a long time I believe it.

One of us has to live. To tell our story. To write it down. We're the closest to the action of this tragedy—if it's even a tragedy. I don't think it is anymore. I think it's a story of hope, unlikely as I once thought that was.

"I'll leave you two alone," Jost says, pushing Erik's arm toward me.

But before we can linger in our goodbye, Dante appears, yelling for us to get going.

In the end, no more words pass between Erik and me. There is no final kiss. Only a look, worth more than any whispered farewell.

Loricel has set up in the makeshift rebound room they brought me through when I arrived. There's a wide loom in front of her, larger than most I saw at the Coventry, including her personal loom in the high tower. It sits empty and I wish I could see the weave of Arras one more time, before it's too late. I know it's too dangerous to pull it up before we go, but there's an ache building slowly in me at the thought of never touching the precise, wondrous strands on a loom again.

"How are you going to do this?" I ask her, staring at the instrument panel.

"It will be like when you rebounded through the various stations," she says, adjusting gears in preparation.

"But that took an hour."

"Because less talented people were at the looms and they had to wait for bureaucrats to tell them it was okay to start the process. Then, they were watched the whole time—"

"Okay." I surrender. "I get it."

"You're in good hands," she says.

"I wouldn't trust anyone else to do this," I say.

"That's a shame," Loricel says. "You must learn to open your heart again, Adelice."

I think of Erik and Jost. I think of the little girl who might be dependent on me one day, and of my own sister. "I do trust people," I say.

"I made you believe once that love is a liability." Her eyes flicker to Albert.

"It is," I say softly. I feel like half of myself is outside this room, going off on a dangerous mission I can't control. I don't allow myself to think about it for long because the tears creep up my throat, shredding my will to do this. But even as the fear grows in me, there is certainty. This is the right thing to do. Erik and I both know that. We wouldn't be able to live with ourselves if we didn't try.

"Perhaps," she says, "but love also gives us the strength that we never knew we had."

"I'm glad you'll be together," I tell her, looking over at Albert. "I wish you had longer."

"Who can count the minutes she spends with the person she loves and not feel lucky?" she asks.

It's easier to say that, knowing she'll be with her love at the very end. Erik and I . . . I don't want to think about. "I want one more minute."

"You have it," she says firmly.

"How can you know that?" I ask.

"I know," she says. "Look closely."

Before I can ask her what this means, Albert's hand settles on my shoulder. "A final word?"

I nod, eyes stinging from the goodbyes. He leads me to a quiet corner and waits for me to speak. "I still have questions."

"And we have run out of time for answers. That is a sad fact about life, Miss Lewys. If you'll pardon the double entendre, not everything can be tied up in a neat bow." His soft eyes sink under the weight of his years.

"Why does everyone believe I'm the Whorl?" I ask. "Because I can weave *and* alter?"

"It's not your skills that make you special, it's that you chose to fight. The Kairos Agenda called you the Whorl because they needed someone to believe in. All rebellions have men of words, few have men of action," he says as his lips curve into a small smile.

"But they believe I was destined for this."

"You know better," he says. "We make our own destinies. Never forget that." My mouth opens, but the questions die on my lips, because I'm pulled away from him and into the chair we're using for the rebound.

This is unlike the other rebounds I've experienced. This time the bottom drops out from under me and the room shifts so quickly that my stomach flips, as though I'm falling. My hands fly to my sides as if my body is out of balance. They meet only with air. The world around me is a riot of color and sound. A clash of metallic strings shrieks through the space about me as though time is moving too quickly, throwing reality out of joint.

And then I find myself in the vermilion corridor of the high tower where I once lived. I race forward and knock on a door. No one answers and I rush to the stairs. I don't have time to wait for the ancient brass elevator.

I burst through the exit on the next floor and into the lounge of the high tower. I skid on its marble floors, nearly tripping over a leather wingback. At the same moment, the elevator doors *ding* and slide open to reveal Pryana. Her eyes widen at the sight of me.

"Adelice?"

"Where's Amie?" I pant the question.

"In her room. It's in the lower tower," she says. "I can take you there."

"There's no time!" I cry. "You have to initiate evacuation procedures. Contact the Agenda. Everyone needs to get out of Arras now!"

"What?" Pryana asks.

"You have to get the citizens out and to the surface," I say, "or everyone will die. Please. You have to get Amie out."

Her eyebrows knit together. "I don't understand. I haven't received any intelligence that Cormac is taking action."

This stops me cold. If the information had filtered to Alix, how hadn't it reached other members of the Agenda?

"Adelice, who told you—" She cuts off as a figure sweeps into the room.

The woman's eyes widen even as her mouth curls to reveal a toothy smile. Another Spinster might be surprised to see me, but Maela only looks delighted.

"As I suspected." She speaks in a low hiss, her words full of the venom she's stored up toward us.

I step forward, my fingers tingling at my side, as I plan my next move. All of Maela's weaknesses are psychological. I don't have to raise a hand to her when I can destroy her with a word. But before I can find the correct one, my body trembles and my stomach drops. Loricel is moving me again.

I lunge forward, hoping to grab Maela and drag her along on the rebound. She can't prevent Pryana from warning the Coventry. I won't let her. Pryana steps in front of me, her fingers squeezed into tight balls.

"Let me——" I start.

"I'll finish her," Pryana promises me as Maela's head falls back in laughter. The sound races through my body and I try to push past Pryana as the world sparks and cracks around me. I'm moving again, and my last glimpse of the Western Coventry is Pryana charging toward Maela. If she wins, there's hope for the Coventry, but if not, there's no promise of help for my sister.

This time I land in a crumple next to Dante.

"That's why we sit down," Dante grumbles, getting to his feet and brushing off his pants.

"Are we in?" I ask him. I spring to my feet.

"I think so," he says, pivoting to check out our surroundings.

"Wait," I say, "this is it. I was here a few weeks ago. But where are the others?"

"I'm sure Loricel can only move so many of us at once," he says, but his eyes dart around as we wait for Jax and Falon to join us.

After a moment, a figure rips into the room, crashing onto the floor. Jax rolls over with a groan. "That was not pleasant."

We wait a few more minutes before I start to realize no one else is coming. "Dante," I say softly, "Falon will chew you out if she shows up and we're waiting around."

Jax takes my lead. "Yeah, man. We can't wait."

"You're right," Dante says, but his eyes never meet mine. He keeps searching the air, waiting for her to appear.

Jax distributes a number of devices that look like digifiles to me, but they're smaller.

"What are these?" I ask him.

"PTDs. Portable telecommunications devices," he says.

"Like a walking companel?" I ask.

"It's more like a complant, but I don't have to embed this one in your brain. They're given to lower-level officers in the Guild. We'll be able to communicate with one another through them," he explains. "But if you get caught, smash it."

"Smash it?"

"Heel of boot and floor," he says. "Otherwise it will lead security straight to the other two . . . three of us."

If Falon joins us. There's still no sign of her.

"What first?" I ask.

"I need to get to the mainframe and dive in while you get Cormac to say that pass code."

"How will we know when you've initiated the protocol?" Dante asks.

"You'll know," he says. "This whole building is wired to alert everyone of the impending protocol."

"Are you telling me an alarm will go off?" I ask.

"Yes," he says with a sheepish grin.

"There goes our low profile," I say with a grimace. Now that we're here, my bravado is evaporating quickly. I might have been able to guess Cormac's code or find it somewhere in his office. I already knew all his favorite things—cigar boxes and decanters. If it was hidden somewhere, I could find it. But talking it out of him was another story, especially if I would have to wait for an alarm to signal me that it was time for him to say it.

"Nothing about this mission was going to stay secret for long," Dante reminds me. We race through the halls, following the blueprints Jax has uploaded to his digifile.

"I'm down here," Jax says, motioning to a door on his right.

"Good luck," I say, and without thinking I lunge forward and hug him.

"No time for that," Dante says, but the two shake hands with a meaningful nod to each other.

"Cormac's office is on the third floor," Jax says.

"I know." Despite my claim that I can get Cormac to talk, as we maneuver the halls of the Ministry dread builds in me, overflowing into a frantic energy that spills through my body. It's quiet here, so quiet our footsteps echo off the white tiled floors. Every door we pass is shut, and we haven't encountered a soul yet.

"You okay?" Dante asks.

I nod, but I can't hide the tremors rolling through my body. Everything depends on getting Cormac to do one thing for me. And Cormac has never done anything for me before. I don't know why I expect he will now. As we round the corridor that leads directly to Cormac's office, a pair of thick hands grab me from behind.

"Look what I found," a gruff voice teases in my ear. Hannox. Of course. I kick back against my captor, but between being out of breath from running and a little wobbly from the rebound, my feet meet with air. And the man laughs.

"Cormac is expecting you," Hannox says. He pushes me forward and I stumble up on my feet.

"I wouldn't drop by unannounced," I say, trying to keep the situation light even though my pulse is racing. I glance around, finally catching sight of Dante. He's been pinned by another security guard, who's holding a gun to Dante's head.

"Yet you're using a veil," Hannox says.

I bite my lip and stare him down. I have no idea how he can guess that.

"We found your friend. She put up quite a fight," Hannox says. "It shouldn't be long until they've locked in on all the veiled sequences in the pattern."

"What did you do to her?" Dante demands. Another guard is holding him steady, his arms locked behind his back.

"What we do to traitors," Hannox spits back at him. He gets up next to Dante's face. "We ripped that little girl. And now we'll rip her, too." He jerks a thumb at me.

Dante's jaw tenses, but before I can say anything to distract him, he smashes his forehead into Hannox's nose, sending a fountain of blood spurting into the air and the guard fumbling to control his gun.

"You bastard," Hannox says, grabbing his nose. His hand flies up.

"Stop!" Cormac commands. "This is no way to treat our guests."

"He broke my bloody nose," Hannox shrieks.

"Thanks for the status update," Cormac says. "Bring them into my office."

Hannox grabs me roughly and drags me toward the open door at the end of the hall. I consider the injuries I could inflict on him and for a moment my fingers itch and tingle, urging me to attack. But if I unwind Cormac's right-hand man, I'll never get Cormac to give me the pass code.

So I let them lead me down the narrow corridor and into the den of my enemy.

TWENTY-FIVE

"I'M SURPRISED TO SEE YOU CAN CONTROL yourself," Cormac says to me when Hannox shoves me into his office. Hannox and his men force us into chairs and tie our hands behind our backs. I don't even struggle. All I need is for Cormac to talk, and maybe he will if he thinks I'm incapacitated. Cormac shares a few quiet words with his right-hand man as one of the officers finishes tying us to our chairs. Hannox casts one long look at me before he orders his men to follow him out of the room.

We have Cormac alone. This should feel like a victory.

"I didn't try to escape this time," I remind him now that Hannox is gone. "I was taken."

"And yet I notice you aren't wearing my ring," he snarls. "And there is a glow about you. Spending time with young Erik? Or is it Jost? I can't keep up with you."

"We took Adelice," Dante says. "She convinced us to bring her back."

"Sell your lies elsewhere," Cormac says, tugging at his bow

tie. "I was heartbroken to learn young Alixandra is a traitor. I can't wait to get my hands on her—now that I'm through with her."

Through with her? I glance at Dante to see if he caught it, but his eyes are distant. Plotting.

"You came in veiled after rebounding into every remaining sector in Arras," Cormac continues. "You have someone very talented working with your group."

I keep my face stony. I'm not sure what harm it would do to admit Cormac is right, but I also know he hoards information, keeping it to twist for his own purposes later.

"Tell Loricel I said hello," Cormac says. "Unless . . ." He leaves the unspoken words in the air, niggling at me like an itch.

"Unless?" I can't help prompting him.

"Unless you came from the Eastern Sector."

"And if we did?" Dante asks.

"Then I'll be offering condolences soon."

I bite back a cocky smile. Cormac doesn't know that we know about his plan. He doesn't know that there was time to evacuate.

"Don't hide your smile, Adelice. I've always loved that *smug* grin," Cormac says. He strides over to his desk and pours himself a drink. "I especially love the moments when I get to wipe it off your *smug* face."

"Not this time, Cormac," I say.

"Do you think I didn't know Alixandra was going to betray me?" he asks.

He succeeds at wiping the amusement from me.

"You didn't set the Eastern Sector to self-destruct," I say in a flat voice.

"Of course not," Cormac says, "but by now your people will have herded themselves into a nice flock of sheep ready for the slaughter."

Erik. Jost. Sebrina. The list of people currently evacuating flashes through my mind. "Don't. I will do anything you want."

"But you've already done everything I wanted," Cormac says. "You rid me of a troublesome sector, put the rest of Arras into a panic, and managed to hand deliver the leaders of the Kairos Agenda. Do you think citizens will listen to strangers screaming that the sky is falling? Arras will look to me now and I am more prepared than anyone expected for the tragic events of today."

"You never wanted to marry me," I realize.

"Now you're catching on."

I wasn't a distraction for the citizens of Arras, I was a distraction for the Kairos Agenda. Because of me they walked right into Cormac's trap in the Eastern Sector. But worst of all, I'd been so caught up in guessing Cormac's next move in our staged plan, I never saw any of this coming.

"Pryana? Alix? You knew they were Agenda," I guess.

Cormac's lips curl as he nods. "I figured it out. They both proved quite useful. They were too busy thinking they were clever—"

"To realize you were feeding them information," I finish for him. That's why Pryana hadn't heard anything about Cormac's order. He had purposefully slipped the information to Alix, knowing she would pass it on to the rest of us.

"It was simple. Feed one rebel rotten information and she'll poison the rest of the group. Watch the lie spread and ferret out the traitors. Soon there will be no more Agenda infestation."

"And now the whole of Arras will believe you're their hero," Dante says. "Because there will be no one to tell them any differently."

"You've done a good job cementing yourself in the minds of the people of Arras," Cormac says to me. "When I share my heartbreak over your rebellion, they will feel the outrage that only betrayal can cultivate."

"And who will keep your looms running?" I ask. "What will you do when the Earth fails to produce your precious raw materials?"

"Once we remove the threat left below there, I won't have to worry about the interference of scum like you."

"And what if there's a singularity?" I challenge.

"That's a theory," Cormac says with a wave of his hand. "My men don't believe it's a threat."

"Albert does," I say in a low voice. "Keep harvesting and you'll destroy Earth *and* Arras."

"Aren't we taking our Whorl role a little too seriously?" His lips press into a thin smile. "There's no Whorl. It's only a legend passed between desperate men."

Nothing about Cormac's dismissal of me or the Agenda stings, because he fails to understand. Even now, I'm only beginning to comprehend it myself. "Those desperate men are your people, and they believe their *legend*."

"What good is belief? Perhaps saying that you believe in something helps you sleep at night, but you and I both know there is no power in that."

"It's not just the belief," I say as a sense of purpose plants itself in my brain, growing roots that lodge within my soul. "It's the possibility, and once people see what is possible, even in one tiny, insignificant moment, they're capable of imagining more. There is power in imagination. Undeniable, unpredictable, uncontrollable power. You're right. The Whorl might be nothing more than a dream, but the idea has given people the ability to dream again. You won't find it easy to control them now."

Cormac's jaw tightens, but there's no trace of anger or annoyance or even amusement. He's calling my bluff.

"But you already know that," I continue. "Girls and boys deciding not to marry. Spinsters refusing to stay at their looms. What will you do when all the Spinsters begin to dream?"

But he only smirks. "Every society must evolve."

He raises his fingers and trails them through an invisible pattern in the air. After a moment, a crack in the fabric of the room appears.

"What did you do?" I ask in a breathless voice.

"There are those who said men shouldn't have this power, but I disagree," Cormac says. "Not just *any* man should have this power. But I am not *just any man*."

"You've been altering yourself," I realize aloud. His erratic behavior. The scar I glimpsed. It makes sense.

"Isn't that why you kicked Kincaid out? For perverting the research behind the Cypress Project?" Dante asks. "Or did you kick him out to steal his idea?"

"Kincaid was a fool. He was always too busy showing off to consider what the people around him needed."

"Does that sound like anyone we know?" I ask in mock innocence.

"It takes one to know one," Cormac points out.

He might have a point. Even now I'm too busy showing off and talking back to consider what I need to do in order to ensure that the others survive this.

"So you're a Spinster—or are you a Tailor?" I ask. I pull against the rope binding my hands. I wasn't scared to be in the same room with him before. Now I am.

"I'm a thinker. A Tailor. A Spinster. A spy," he says. "But most important, I'm a Creweler."

"I don't believe you," I say, because I need it to be false. I need to believe he doesn't have these abilities.

"Oh, rest assured, Adelice. Thanks to your measurements, our scientists have been able to synthesize a genetic compound that has given me the same set of skills you possess."

I stare at him, trying to wrap my head around this. The thing is, it's not simply that Cormac has been altered to have these abilities. They've been synthesized, like in the earliest experiments with the serums on Earth. Experiments that had gone horribly wrong. The fact is, Cormac is merely a test case, which explains the unpredictability of his behavior and his erratic attitude in the past few weeks.

"I thought you seemed off," I say to him. "I wrote it off as stress, but it seems it was more than that. You've been running your own personal Cypress Project all along."

Cormac hadn't been losing his mind. He'd been warping it, pushing his own genetic abilities to the brink.

"I don't need your condescension, Adelice," Cormac says. "Nor do I appreciate it."

"You're insane," Dante says. "Can you appreciate that?"

"I'm powerful," Cormac says. "If I were insane I wouldn't be nearly as successful as I am."

"You have an entire world living a lie—"

"That they're eager to believe," Cormac interrupts me.

"You think lies are that easy to swallow?" I ask. "Arras knows you're full of it, Cormac, and soon they'll have proof."

"And who is going to show them?" he asks. "You?"

"Believe me, I'm up for the challenge."

Before he can retort, a shrill siren sounds. Jax has managed to trip the protocols and set off the evacuation alert. Now we merely need Cormac to say the pass code and Protocol Three will be initiated.

That shouldn't be hard, given his god complex.

"I see you didn't come alone," Cormac says. "What were you saying about wanting to come back and make things work?"

"I have no idea what's going on," I say, keeping my face blank. In truth, I don't know where Jax is.

Cormac holds up the PTD that Jax gave us to communicate and waves it at me. "Who's at the other end of this?" he asks.

"No one you know," I say.

"Not my dear Erik then? Pity. I would love to rip that nuisance right out of Arras. But it is someone you know, Adelice. You pulled a little trick once at the Coventry," Cormac says, "and I've often thought of it. You disregarded proximity standards. Do you remember?"

I know what he's talking about. I had called up the repository in Loricel's room and rewoven it into the strange screens in her studio, so that I could enter it and search for information about my sister. Because I was manipulating the space around me, I risked the integrity of the Coventry's weave. It shouldn't have been possible for me to do it, and it probably wouldn't have been if I had been using any loom other than Loricel's. Still, the loom had warned me by issuing a proximity alert. I have no idea what that has to do with the PTD that connects me to Jax, though.

"I've had them install a toy in my office," Cormac says. He presses a button, opening a hidden panel in his wall to reveal a gleaming new loom.

"That's your problem, Cormac," I say. "A loom isn't a toy. Arras is doomed if you think it is. You can't even access it within the boundaries of Arras." Now I know why he mentioned the proximity alert. It isn't safe to weave and do Crewel work within Arras. That's why the coventries exist between Earth and Arras—as a safety measure. And Cormac is disregarding that. I've spent too much time laughing off his drinking to realize his real addiction is power.

"Let's see what we can do with it anyway," he says.

He presses a series of buttons on the side of the loom and it whirrs to life. I strain against my bindings, trying to get a better view of the loom.

"You know how dangerous that is?" I ask in a quiet voice. "You've made your point."

"No, I have not," he screams, moving back toward me and getting in my face. "Because you still don't respect me. You don't fear me."

"That's what this is about?" I ask. "You want me to fear you? Well, you've got what you wanted. Seeing you playing with that loom with no regard for its power or the consequences of your actions frightens me, Cormac. And if you were sane, it would frighten you, too."

He's not the Cormac who picked me up on my retrieval night. That Cormac did what he thought was right for the greater good, even if his perception of what was best was warped. He's incapable of logic or consideration. He can't see anything but shades of gray.

And that makes him a danger to everyone.

Before I can react, a piece of the weave appears on the loom. In comparison to the protocol sirens blaring through the room, the blinking red proximity alert seems weak and inconsequential. But that doesn't mean it's not more dangerous.

"I've pulled the weave of this room onto the loom," he says with a smile.

And there it is. We're laid out in front of him and all it would take to destroy us is one careful sweep, if he has the talent for it. Could he have had that spliced into him or is he too arrogant to see he lacks it?

Without precision, he'll just take out the entire room. That would end the threat of Cormac, but it wouldn't solve our bigger problem. Arras is full of men too old and too set in their ways to change course. Another corrupt leader will simply rise in Cormac's place—and another and another. Perhaps it won't be any different on Earth if we evacuate, but at least we won't face the possibility of a singularity that could wipe humankind from existence.

Cormac picks up the PTD Jax gave me and presses the com button.

"You guys okay?" Jax's voice crackles over the speaker, and my heart sinks.

"It's a trap!" I yell, but it's too late. Cormac already knows where he is—now he wants to play with his prey.

"Adelice and I were visiting," Cormac says into the PTD. "You've been a busy bee."

"It's too late," Jax says. "I've locked the evacuation protocol and reopened communication channels between sectors. They know what you've done."

"Do you think they'll take the word of a rebel?" Cormac asks, practically screaming into the PTD.

"They won't have to," he says. "Loricel sent the communiqué."

Cormac curses into the PTD and drops it onto the floor. "Screen," he barks.

A wall screen bursts to life over us.

"I want you to see this," he seethes. "I don't know who your friend is. He must be quite bright to have breached our entire system."

"He is," I say, "and he's a better man than you."

"How touching," Cormac says. He barks a coordinate to the screen and the security stream for that section of the guild offices projects above us. Jax is moving quickly, checking over his shoulder. I want to yell at him, but I know it doesn't matter. He can't hear me, and even if he could it wouldn't matter anyway. Cormac knows where he is. Cormac has a loom.

Cormac can weave, which means Cormac can rip.

My stomach turns over and shoots bile into my throat, but

I swallow it down as Cormac returns to the loom and hesitates for a moment, staring at the brilliant tapestry laid before him.

"What's he looking at?" Dante asks. "It's a tangled mess."

I'm somewhat surprised Dante can't see it clearly for himself, but the minute differences between a Spinster and a Tailor have always surprised me. "It's here," I say, "he has this building on the loom."

Dante's eyes fly to the screen and he struggles against the rope binding him to the chair. Jax is his best friend and he can do nothing to warn him.

"You don't have to do this," I say to Cormac. "Everyone in Arras is evacuating. Come with us. Start over on Earth."

He ignores me, turning a gear to zoom in on the image.

"Go home," I add softly.

"I have no home," Cormac says, turning his attention from the loom for a moment and buying Jax a few more precious seconds. "You've destroyed it."

"Arras was never a home," I say. "It was a lie. It's time to let it go. What's the pass code for Protocol Three?"

"So that's why you've come," he says with a laugh. "So that Cormac Patton can betray Arras."

"No, I came to give you a chance at redemption," I say. "If Arras isn't unraveled, both worlds will be erased from existence. You have the power to stop it. You can be the hero."

"It's too late for redemption, and I don't have anyone to redeem myself to," he says, and then he turns back to the loom and, with the confidence of a well-practiced Spinster, plucks a single thread. It pulls out slowly and over us Jax is frozen in place, disappearing limb by limb, slowly being wiped from existence.

"Stop!" Dante yells, but it's too late.

I don't know how to feel. One moment Jax was there, racing through a corridor, about to escape. And then he was gone.

That's the evil of this system. It's insidious how easy it is to remove someone without their feeling a thing. Even watching it happen is unreal, as though Jax could pop back on the screen. But I know enough about this world to know that's not going to happen. The proof that Jax is gone rests in Cormac's hands.

"There was a time when this strand would be sent off for alterations," Cormac says.

"To make Remnants," I say. "Giving up your war on Earth?"

"Oh, no. We've developed much more effective ways to rid ourselves of the vermin on Earth."

My words are strangled. "Which means?"

"I'm sure you saw them in the Eastern Sector."

The moths. The citizens of the Eastern Sector rotting before our eyes, their strands being eaten slowly. "You didn't need to sever the sector," I accuse. "You wanted to test your bugs."

"And they worked as beautifully as we imagined they would."

"But then . . ." My words are lost to my thoughts.

"We were watching you the whole time?" he asks. "Of course."

"You severed the sector though," Dante says.

"Exactly. I severed it. I didn't destroy it. The sector still exists."

Dante and I exchange a look and I know we're both feeling the same thing. How stupid could we have been? This means he knows everything we've planned. He knew about Loricel and Albert. He knew about . . .

"How much did you see?" I ask. My voice is strangled.

"I saw everything," he says with emphasis. "So much for purity standards, eh?"

My chest constricts knowing that my time with Erik was on display for Cormac. It makes me feel hot and sick and angry at the same time.

"You son of a—"

"Be a lady," he says.

"Oh, I am well past being a lady." I spit the words at him.

A blur knocks past me, causing the world around me to spin. Before I can determine what happened, Cormac crashes to the ground. My eyes flash to the empty chair next to me and I see that the rope has been torn in two. The whole time we've been here Dante was slowly altering the rope with his fingers. It hadn't even occurred to me to try because I'd been distracted by my conversation with Cormac. That explains why Dante had been silent most of the time.

The room splits and light bursts across the space as Cormac and Dante tear at each other.

I tug at my own bindings, feeling their composition and pulling them apart. There's no point in trying to do it quietly. Dante clearly claimed the element of surprise.

By the time I stand up it's hard to tell what to do. Dante and Cormac are rolling on the ground and by now each of them is bleeding from superficial tears. Neither has managed to get a strong enough grip to incapacitate the other. But I'm pretty sure trying to grab either of them will end poorly. Each second there's more blood, and I know that most of it is

Dante's, because he has to work extra hard against Cormac's reinforced suit.

I head to the loom and trail my fingers along it, adjusting its scope to try to find this room on it. It's the only hope I have of helping Dante. If I can find the room, I can rip Cormac's thread. The loom shifts and pulls up one room after another, but I can't find this one.

I turn back to the pair grappling on the floor and consider lunging at Cormac just as Dante manages to pin him to the ground. I rush toward them, hoping I can help. Dante must not unwind Cormac—we need him to say the pass code before we can fully initiate Protocol Three. But Dante reaches for Cormac's chest anyway.

"Don't!" I cry. Dante's eyes flash to mine and it's only then that I realize what I've done.

I've distracted Dante.

It's only a split second, but that's all Cormac needs. I charge forward to stop him, but it's too late. Cormac's hand sinks into Dante's chest and I fall to the ground facing the golden strand clutched firmly in Cormac's hand.

"Please." It's the only thing I can say in this moment.

"Because you asked nicely," Cormac says, "I'll give you a second to close your eyes."

"You don't have to do this," I remind him. "You have a choice."

"Yes, I do." And with a wrench, he rends the time strand clean from Dante's body.

My eyes meet Dante's and he smiles. "Close your eyes, baby. I'm glad I met you."

I squeeze them shut and try to drown out the horrible

scraping noise of unwinding time, the unnatural dissonance of stolen years leaving my father's body too soon. We never had enough time.

"Open your eyes," Cormac orders me. I shake my head, my eyelids pressed down to hold back tears I don't want Cormac to see.

"I've seen you cry before," he reminds me.

I open them and let the angry tears roll out. They are tears of accusation and hatred, but I'm not entirely sure they're meant for Cormac.

I can't escape knowing that this is my fault, but that's not a new feeling and I've learned one thing.

It doesn't matter.

Mistakes ebb and flow like the ocean and if you linger in them, the tide will wash you out to drown.

TWENTY-SIX

CORMAC IS COVERED IN DUST AND HE brushes it off as though it's nothing, dropping the time strand on the floor at his feet. I reach forward and pick it up, cradling it in my palm.

"Keep it," he says.

I drop the strand and swipe at Cormac, but he sidesteps me and I crash to the ground.

"I want you to think about what you're doing," he says.

"I know exactly what I'm doing," I say, scrambling to my feet and preparing to launch myself at him again.

"You need me," Cormac says, "and you couldn't defeat me if you tried. Are you willing to let innocent people die because you were impatient?"

I push my arms down to my sides and stare at him. My tears haven't abated, and I don't care.

"Are you going to give me the pass code?" I ask, already knowing the answer.

"Absolutely not."

"You know," I say in a low voice.

"Know what?" Cormac asks. I lean across his desk and press my hands hard against the smooth wood, waiting for my moment to strike as he pours a drink.

"That both worlds are in danger. What *I* don't know is how you think Arras will survive without Earth. Albert calculates—"

"Have you ever considered that those are the ravings of a decrepit man?"

"Look who's calling someone else decrepit," I mutter.

Cormac ignores me, but he sets down his glass with unusual force. "What would you do? Repopulate Earth? That is madness. Only one can survive—Earth or Arras. Which would you choose, Adelice? A world where everyone has what they need or a dying planet full of criminals and deviants?"

"The people of Arras don't have everything they need," I say.

"And what are they lacking?" His lips smack on the final word.

"Freedom." I hold my gaze steady with his. He knows this and he can't deny it's something Arras doesn't have and will never have under the control of the Guild.

"That's a *want*, my dear," Cormac says without missing a beat. "No one *needs* freedom."

I guess we'll have to disagree on that.

"We could kill each other," Cormac says. "Right here and now and then what would come of Arras? Of Earth?"

"I'm not sure what happens if we both live through this," I say softly. I don't know if either of us deserves to walk out of here. And yet if we don't, what becomes of everyone else? The singularity Albert predicted could be another form of control, misinformation spread by Cormac to distract us from his plans and lure me here. But did Albert believe it? Because I'm certain he wouldn't lie to Loricel and me.

"It's not too late. We can still join together," he suggests.

"You just killed my father," I remind him. "Our relationship is built on body bag after body bag, Cormac. I can't think of anything worse than joining with you. Plus, you already admitted you've wanted to kill me this whole time."

"There is that." Nothing flickers in his cold black eyes. He's not amused. He's not calculating. His eyes are the color of the dark of night when the world lies in wait.

He's plotting.

"Then neither of us walks out of here?"

As though he's giving me a choice.

There are no choices with Cormac, only carefully laid traps. This is something I know too well.

"Arras won't survive, but if we initiate Protocol Three then we can still save the people," I argue with him. "As long as I've known you, you've always acted out of concern for the citizens, even if your methods were a bit warped for my taste." I'm putting this mildly, hoping to lure him in with honeyed promises and sweet words.

He laughs at me, clearly seeing through my act. "Don't try to placate me, Adelice. I've spent my career twisting words to get what I want. There will be no compromise on Protocol Three."

I look to my useless digifile. There's no one to call. Every channel leads to dead air.

"I see you're still trying to set things right. You can stop," Cormac says. "You've played your part remarkably well, Adelice."

I don't feel the ball of burning rage that usually builds in my chest when Cormac mocks me. No clever retorts float to mind. In their wake is something much more chilling: a dreadful emptiness that yawns inside me and makes me feel like giving up. How can you save the world from men like Cormac? There are too many to ever defeat them all.

Too many of them to even make it a possibility.

Cormac watches me with interest and a smile plays at his lips.

"What now?" I ask him.

"I find your reaction rather dull," he says. "I expected a fight. I find it tasteless to unwind someone who's sitting around doing nothing. If you aren't a threat, then what's the point?"

"If what you're telling me is true, then I've *never* been a threat to you."

"Touché, and yet . . . " Cormac pauses, tilting his head slightly. The companels in the room prompt us once more for the pass code but now the evacuation sirens feel like background noise. I hear the prompt, but it doesn't matter. "Hannox, initiate the troops in the Eastern Sector."

My eyes fly up to Cormac's and now there's a glimmer of amusement in them. He's made his puppet dance.

"Would you like to watch?" he asks.

"Is this necessary?" I ask him, reaching for any argument that might stop him. "The bugs will spread to Earth more quickly if you let the citizens go to the surface."

"Who sounds desperate now?" He barks a security clearance code at the screen and it begins to stream the Eastern Sector. There's a crowd of people gathered outside the Ministry offices. The camera's stream sits far off the ground but I spot Jost and Erik directing the group.

"Stop this. I'm asking you to stop."

"I can't!" He knocks his glass from his desk, sending its contents flying across the room. "As long as the poison is in the system, it continues to spread."

I set my chin defiantly and stare at him. "Then you'll have to kill me, too."

"It will be my pleasure," he says.

Cormac hasn't noticed the small changes I've made to my posture. He hasn't noticed that I'm not sitting but rather squatting over my chair and that my arms are locked and ready, so when I fly across the room, my feet pounding out the few steps that lie between Cormac and me, he doesn't have time to react.

I bound up the desk before he can move away and with one perfect, precise swipe, I'm holding his time strand in my left hand. It's golden and new, much too young for someone as old as Cormac. I knit it through my fingers, raising it up to my face so that Cormac and I are both staring at it hovering there between us. My fingers are red with blood, and it oozes onto Cormac's lifeline.

"Always lead with your left," I whisper. "All Crewelers know that."

"I guess this means that you win," Cormac says. His voice is breathless. Expectant.

"I never thought of this as a game," I say as I twist the delicate strand. I only have to pull it, but is it too late?

"Are you waiting for something?" he asks.

"You've always struggled under the illusion that one simply does or doesn't do something," I say, "but that's taught me to think about my actions."

"I suppose you expect me to beg for mercy."

"I would never expect that." And in truth I don't. Cormac is too proud to beg, but there's something else in his eyes now. It could be mistaken for dread, but it looks more like finality.

"The world tells us there is a black and a white. We're told people fall into those two categories, Adelice. Good and evil. Light and dark. But that's the real lie they sell us. Everyone exists in the gray. We're only capable of living within that shaded perception of truth," he says.

"So what you've done wasn't wrong?" I ask, thinking of my mother and my father. Of Dante. Of Erik and Jost, who are probably dying right now at his hands.

"It's wrong to you, but can't you see the gray?" he asks. "If you were me, could you turn away? From the power? From the possibility?"

"And leave innocent people alone?" I ask. "Yes."

"And yet plenty of innocent people have died at your hands," he says.

I stare at the time strand wrapped around my fingers and wonder how his perception has become as warped as the strand itself. It's no longer simply about the greater good. Cormac has made himself into a hero. He's given himself the power of the creator, after bestowing that "gift" upon others before him. He doesn't see himself as having committed any wrong, because he did what he thought was right.

And here I am, holding his life in my hands and knowing

exactly what it means to persist in a gray area. Cormac Patton deserves to die. Of that much I'm certain, but do I deserve to kill him? Does anyone have the right to kill someone else?

There is enough blood on my hands for a lifetime.

I could unwind Cormac and wait. Wait for the singularity. Wait for the Guild officials to find me. Wait to die one way or another. It hardly matters anymore.

Because no one wins in this scenario.

"Don't tell me you've had a sudden fit of mercifulness?"

"I'm thinking." I press the time strand tightly between my fingers and Cormac gasps.

"What is the pass code?" I ask him.

"I will never tell you that."

"You're going to die, Cormac," I say. It has already begun. His hair is slowly turning white and lines are appearing in his polished face. He won't be the handsome face of the Guild much longer. "And without us, there will be no Arras," I say softly. "So why not tell me the pass code?"

"Because I've lived over two hundred years and I will die alone," he says. "I will cease and no one will mourn me."

"You won't be alone." I realize then that fear is the barrier between us now, and only I can remove it. But I won't say I will mourn Cormac. I won't lie to him.

"You will die, too." Cormac's words aren't a threat. They linger somewhere between a thought and a question. As though he needs me to know this, needs me to acknowledge this.

"Everything has a beginning and an end," I say to him. I pull gently on his time thread, careful not to remove it entirely. I can feel the end of it barely holding on, still running through him. I could pull it completely out, unwind him, but instead, with a gentle twist, I snap the thread at his chest. Maybe he has seconds left. Maybe he has days.

"Why not unwind me entirely?" he asks.

"I want you to face your own end." By removing most of his time strand, I've taken back the life he's stolen from others. I could have unwound him entirely and watched as he crumbled to dust, but I want him to stare his death in the face, knowing he can't stop it.

But now that I've released my hold on him, he pushes me against the wall, his arm crushing my windpipe. I struggle to breathe, black spots blotting my vision, but I don't fight against him. And then he drops his hold on me and stumbles back, laughing. I gasp as my throat reopens and air rushes into my lungs.

"It doesn't matter. I will make certain you fade with me. Neither of us will be the hero of this story," Cormac says, falling onto his back and clutching his chest. "Authorization: Alpha One Destruct Three. Arras will be destroyed and you along with it."

Cormac isn't going to let me walk out of here, and I don't blame him.

"Now we're even," he says between heaving breaths. "We'll both die here. Neither of us wins."

His breathing becomes more labored and I know he's close to the end. The color drains from his face. This is it. The man who took everything from me is finally going to die. It hardly matters that he's found a way to kill me now.

"The evacuation has already started. The people are safe. It doesn't matter if I die," I say without flinching.

"You're prepared for this? To lose the looms? To lose the control?" he asks. "You could have lived forever."

"I'd rather die than continue with this lie."

"It takes a talented girl to do that," he says.

I regard him for a long moment before I answer. "I know."

His body seizes as the light fades from his dark eyes, and then he's gone. Standing, I walk to the window and stare out. There's no point trying to run now. There's nowhere to go. Whatever security forces are left here won't let me go, although I doubt anyone's sticking around.

The door bursts open and Hannox barrels in, nose still bloody, stopping to stare at Cormac's lifeless, withered body. I close my eyes and wait, both for retribution and for peace.

But nothing happens. When I open them, Hannox's gaze has shifted to me.

"He's dead, then?"

I can't read his face. It is entirely absent of thought or feeling, nearly slack with apathy. "Yes."

Hannox looks up to the ceiling and then lowers his head to nod once. "I've waited a long time for this day."

"You were his best friend," I say, hoping to prompt a reaction, because fear is starting to filter through my blood. I'm not sure I can fade away with the world. I'd rather die fighting.

"Duty and friendship are not the same thing," he says.

Outside, the sky is a shimmering web of color, loosening and blurring in a spectacular display of light. Closing my eyes, I listen to the discord of space and time colliding and crossing as the pattern of this world collapses on itself. I wonder what it will feel like to fade into the universe. I can almost imagine the numbness of nonexistence creeping through my limbs like a slow-moving drug, and yet I feel oddly at peace.

There's a crackle of sound in the room and I whip around to find myself standing face-to-face with Alix.

"How?" I ask, staring at her.

"No time for that," she says, tossing me a backpack.

I look at Hannox, and Alix freezes, drawing a gun from her hip, and in the same moment that I scream, "No," I hear one word escape from his lips.

"Please."

The shot is off before either word registers, and Hannox falls back against the wall. His eyes find mine and he smiles. It's then that I realize he wasn't asking for mercy, he was asking to be freed.

Alix shifts back on her heels. "I didn't know that he was an ally."

"I don't think he did either."

Alix shakes her head as if to dissolve her guilt. "We can't worry about it now. Put that on."

I examine the pack, unsure what to do with it until Alix groans and grabs it, holding out the straps. She slides them over my shoulders and pulls a strap around my waist. I buckle it into place and wait for her to give me any indication of what's going on.

"How did you get here?" I ask her when nothing happens.

"How do you think?" she snaps, pivoting around the room as though she's looking for an escape route.

"But Cormac destroyed the Eastern Sector," I say.

"Most of it, but Loricel is talented and she wasn't going

down without a fight." Alix spots Cormac's body and whistles. "I wish I could tell her about that."

"It doesn't matter," I say confidently. I'm enough like Loricel to know that the victory would be as hollow for her as it is for me. I wonder what we're waiting for, what impossible feat Loricel is going to pull off now.

And as I wonder a fissure of light splits the room, in the middle, like a seam ripping open. But there's no Interface beneath us anymore. It's already dissipated as Protocol Three unwinds Arras from existence. This is her plan? This isn't like my escape from Arras. Then the Coventry was in the Interface, closer to the ground. We can't survive jumping from here to Earth.

But Alix doesn't waste time considering this as she grabs me and throws us through a gash in the weave.

We're falling too fast for me to get a handle on Earth's strands. Alix points to her vest and tugs at a cord near the zipper. A balloon of fabric billows behind her. She jerks as it opens fully, but then her fall starts to slow. My own speed accelerates so quickly that she grows small in my vision. I search frantically for my cord, but my fingers find nothing, which is a problem since the ground is getting closer and closer. Finally, my hands close on the cord, and I yank it as hard as I can. The force of the chute jolts me, knocking the wind from my lungs, and I gasp for air I cannot catch. As my descent slows, I'm able to calm down enough to breathe deeply and by the time I hit the ground, I crumple into a ball, trying to ease the last waves of panic.

"You okay?" Alix calls, running over to me.

Note to self: it only took a near-death experience for her to show some concern for me.

I try to say yes, but I'm too overwhelmed. She pulls me up from the ground, but her grip isn't gentle and she drops my hand as soon as I'm steady on my feet.

"Loricel said this is your chance," Alix says. "She said it's the one she should have given you before."

I look up at the pattern moving swiftly across the sky. It's already growing fainter, like a strange cloud disappearing into rain.

Thank you, I think.

Alix turns on her heel and starts to head away.

"Wait!" I cry. "Where are you going?"

"There are millions of survivors," Alix says, facing me. "They'll need me."

Need her. Not me. Nothing has changed between Alix and me, even after everything else that's changed around us.

"The others?" I ask. "Did they make it out?"

"Nearly everyone left with the first wave. The little girl is safe," she says, but she stops short of telling me what I want to know and a knot tangles in my stomach.

"What about the boys?"

"They stayed to help everyone evacuate." She pauses for a moment and something flashes across her face. Like everything about Alix, it's completely unreadable. "That's all I know, but I wouldn't count on them getting out."

"Why?" I ask. "You did. They could have, too."

Alix hesitates before she answers. "They . . . they stayed to make sure Loricel could rebound me in to you. They held off the security forces Cormac sent in."

She takes a long breath before adding weakly, "I'm sorry." I don't believe a word she says, or maybe I can't believe it, because it means I'm the one who has to tell our story and I must do it alone. I will live a half-life, caught in a past I can never forget.

I don't ask Alix to wait for me. Instead I turn my eyes to the sky as numbness washes through me. It's exactly how I imagined I would feel as Arras faded from reality. Although I'm here and alive, I feel as frozen and dead as I expected.

Arras has become a web of color written across the sky in lines of lace and luminescence. The sun breaks through the growing holes and for the first time in decades its heat touches the Earth. It's hot on my face and I think of emerald leaves and possibilities lost. There will be no schoolgirl to tug my hand earnestly toward home. There will be no boy to take me in his arms for a moonlight dance. It's the end of my world and the beginning of my life.

I've never felt more alone.

TWENTY-SEVEN

THE CAMP IS A MASS OF FAMILIES CLUTCHING together and speaking in low voices. They sit on coats and bags. No one was prepared for this and as the new sun wanes over Earth—the day far too short for a history of darkness—the group I've stumbled on barely notices me as I shamble into their presence. A few cast suspicious eyes in my direction, but otherwise I feel invisible. And for the first time in a long time, I am no one. I can't fix this world at the touch of a loom.

I am free. I am possibility.

Something crushes my heart as I take in the survivors. It grips me with thin, cold fingers and I can't shake them loose.

"Do they have that radio system up and running yet?" a man shouts to another.

"Not yet, and who knows if anyone else will have one."

"We still need to work on it," he says as he stops to converse with a family. He's tall and strong and he looks like my father. This is what Benn would be doing right now. Making plans, helping others.

It's what I have to do. Be helpful. Be strong. I must move forward.

"Are you okay?" someone behind me asks, and I turn toward the voice, but I sway with the movement and collapse into her.

"Does anyone have any water?" she yells. There's a clamor of activity around me and a few moments later a cup presses against my lips. I hadn't realized I was thirsty, but I drink it and I let them lay me back against a bed of jackets.

"Do you know where you came from?" the woman asks me as a half dozen concerned faces peer over me.

I look at each one and try to decide what to tell them. In the end I settle on the simplest story. "I was in Cypress."

"What's your family's name, honey?" she asks. "We'll pass the word around. They must be worried sick about you."

"Lewys," I say. "But I was alone."

No one recognizes the name—or me—without Cormac at my side. Without the beautiful clothes and pinned-up hair, without the cameras, I'm only another girl. I'm only another survivor. No one asks why a girl of my age was alone or what happened to my family, but I can't be the only orphan here tonight.

They are remarkably calm, but as the woman strokes my forehead, someone asks in a low voice, "Have they figured out what happened yet?"

No one speaks, but finally a man shakes his head. "There are theories, of course," he whispers, but as he begins to share them I slip into the darkness pressing heavily on my eyes.

I have no need of theories.

*　*　*

I wake to an old lullaby and for a moment my mother's face swims into my vision, but when I blink she is young and fair-haired.

"Amie!" I gasp.

"You're awake," she says, relief flooding her voice. She waves to someone and Pryana hurries over and helps Amie sit me up.

"You won. You got out," I say in a weak voice.

Pryana shrugs, even though she grins a little. "Did you have any doubt?"

"Thank you." The words feel too simple slipping from my lips, but they weigh heavy in the air between us. It's all I can offer to a girl who owes me nothing and to whom I owe everything.

"I'll leave you two alone." Before she goes, Pryana bends down and wraps her arms around me, squeezing me in a tight, awkward hug.

I swallow and nod once, afraid I will cry. I can never repay my debt to her.

"How did you find me?" I ask Amie after she's left.

"Pryana got me out," she says. "She suspected you would go to Cypress. To find Cormac."

Amie waits for me to confirm this, but I only nod. I'm not ready to talk about it yet.

"Is he dead?" she asks me in a flat voice.

"Yes."

Amie's face contorts and I recognize the pain of confusion. "Did you kill him?"

I can't lie to her. Not anymore. Lying has never protected her. "Yes."

She presses her lips into a thin line and neither of us speaks. My reasons for killing Cormac won't absolve me of what I've done and her forgiveness won't either. But she doesn't leave my side. We sit in silence like two strangers who have nothing to talk about.

TWENTY-EIGHT

THE REFUGEE CAMPS ARE FULL OF THE broken and the bruised, the angry and the grateful. Each camp is a press of bodies—living, working, and healing together. Although there are no elected leaders, the strong step forward to direct and guide until there is a working system. I stop at each camp, checking the wounded; the bodies have been buried by volunteers. The bodies that made it to Earth before Arras faded into space. The evacuation was dangerous, but the days after were worse. Peace is still a fragile reality here.

But in the camps along the eastern coast of America, they tell me stories of the ones who came to save them. They tell of the brothers with the same eyes, who fought the Guild forces when they came.

No one has seen them.

Amie travels with me, choosing to leave Pryana behind at the first camp, and I'm grateful for her company. Without transport, we walk, and the days become weeks until our new reality no longer feels new. We've been on the surface a little over a month, and Amie hasn't questioned why I won't stop looking.

I think she wants answers that I cannot give her—about what happened in Arras. But those memories are too tangled with grief for me to separate them into words, so we are mostly quiet as we travel. I am bound to a promise and haunted by hope. Alix said Sebrina made it to the surface, and I have to find her for Jost. But I'm on the east coast, about to give up, when news of an outlying camp on the northern end of the seaboard reaches us. We speak to one of the self-appointed leaders, hoping he can point us in the right direction.

"That outpost is a two-day walk," he explains to us.

"Amie"—I turn to my sister—"you should stay here while I go to check it out."

"No, I'll come with you." Despite leaving a life of luxury, Amie hasn't complained once about the conditions on Earth. Our weeks here have been full of harsh travel as we walked in search near the coasts. I've spent so much time thinking of Amie as a liability—as a victim—that I never saw how strong she has become in the absence of our parents. We've both grown up too soon.

One of the men from the camp comes over to us and whispers in the leader's ear. Their conversation is low and strained, but when it ends, he turns to us. "I can offer you two motocycles."

"We can't borrow them," I say. "We're heading west by week's end. I can't return them."

"It's a gift."

He doesn't look like he's in a very giving mood—this is clearly the other man's idea—and I shake my head once more, even as Amie squeezes my arm. She wants me to accept. I want to, too, but I also know how valuable a motocycle would be out here.

"It's a generous offer," I say, "but I can't take them from you. You need them."

"Miss Lewys, I don't know how you did what you did," the other man says. "And I know there are a lot of rumors flying around about what happened in Arras between you and Patton. Not everyone here likes you."

So I've been recognized. I knew it would happen as the survivors' shock dulled. I'd been on every screen in Arras only weeks before its destruction.

"Tell me something I don't know."

"I'm not one of those people, and I want to say thank you," the man says. He keeps his gaze level with mine; his eyes don't blink, as though he's challenging me to decline his offer again.

"Thank you." I don't say anything else. I know what it's like to feel like you have nothing to offer someone in need. I know how hard it is to even say thank you.

The motocycles are slick, large beasts, recovered from Guild warehouses near the abandoned mine sites. Chrome tubes twist along their bodies and even parked they look nearly as large as motocarriages. The man gives Amie and me a tutorial on how to ride them. I don't tell him that I've ridden one before or that I'm terrified of it now. Both because I don't want to look ungrateful and to set a good example for my sister. More than anything she needs to see that I'm strong and capable in this world. The engine hums to life between my legs, the vibration traveling up through my fingers and dying on their damaged tips, and I grip the handles tightly and kick off from the dirt. We roar forward to our last hope.

With the motocycles the journey to the outpost takes only a few hours. We have a compass to guide us, but it doesn't take us long to see signs of life. Now that the population of Earth has grown exponentially, travel between the new outposts is more common. And with the number of refugees and wounded on Earth, more and more people are reaching out to the fledgling communities that surround them. We pass two young men walking down the road toward the camp we came from. They wave hello and I slow to speak to them.

"We heard there's a camp full of the wounded ahead."

"We have a few, miss. They were at the battle of Allia."

My heart beats hard, and I'm sure it can be heard over the roar of the engine. The Eastern capital. That was where Cormac unleashed his forces. I know Erik and Jost were there.

"Can we give you a ride?" Amie asks.

"No, miss." The boy smiles widely at her, and I realize, with more than a little apprehension, that he thinks she's pretty.

It's still hard to fathom that my baby sister is nearly as old as I am now. Or that she's grown into a young woman. It had been only months for me that we were separated, but it's been years for her. She grew up while I wasn't looking.

"We should go, Amie."

She shoots me an annoyed, if amused, look. Maybe I do know how to protect her.

The camp isn't far ahead and we park the bikes outside the tents.

"You know, there aren't purity standards here," Amie tells me, poking me in the arm. "I can talk to boys."

"It's not the *talking* to boys I'm worried about," I say dryly.

"I'm not the one stalking across half the world looking for a boy." Amie claps a hand over her mouth. I know she wishes she could take it back, but I roll my eyes, unwilling to betray the stab of pain in my chest. Her accusation hurts because it's true.

We don't talk about Erik. She hasn't asked me about him since we've been on Earth, but love is one emotion that leaves its marks on you. Even my kid sister can see them.

"That's why I'm worried about you," I say. "Trust me, this isn't something I want for you."

Amie stops me and studies my face for a moment. "You love him?"

No matter how I frame these trips as being about finding Sebrina, I hope to find him, too. And she can see that, so I nod.

"Why wouldn't you want that for me?" she asks. "We were lucky to grow up with parents who loved each other, Ad. It's okay to be in love."

I can only give her a tiny smile. I don't tell her that this is killing me. Not knowing. Pretending to be strong when I need to crumble. That this is what love is: vulnerability.

"About purity standards," Amie says, changing the subject.

"Yes?"

"Any chance you still meet them?"

"You saw Erik," I say, grinning despite myself. "What do you think?"

"Forget I asked."

Zigzagging through the tents, we stop to speak to survivors, looking for directions and tips like we've done in every camp thus far. At the base of one tent, a woman eyes us warily as we approach.

"Hello," I say, trying to sound friendly. "We're looking for some survivors from Allia. We think they might be here. Two—"

"Don't know anything about two brothers," she says.

I look at Amie. I hadn't said anything about brothers. I push down my mounting suspicion, but I can't bring myself to say anything. Or I'll want to accuse the woman of lying.

"Are you sure?" Amie asks. Her tone is naturally kinder than mine.

"Nope."

"Thanks anyway," I say, grabbing Amie's arm and dragging her off. I know the woman is watching us.

"What was that about?" Amie ponders out loud.

"They have to be here," I say through gritted teeth. My eyes dart between the tents and before I can stop myself I start lifting the flaps and looking inside them. More than a few people yell at me, but I wave an apologetic hand and continue looking.

"Why would she lie to us?"

"I don't know."

When I lift the next flap, I'm staring at Alix.

She's chopped her long blond hair into a bob and she's dressed in jeans and an old flannel shirt. No one would think this woman is a threat, but I don't know what to think of her at all. I know she's capable of force, and of deception. That's why I'm not surprised to see her here. I've thought Alix was hiding something since she showed up in Cormac's offices. Why else would she take off as soon as we reached the surface?

"Adelice," she says, but the shock in her voice is manufactured. She knew I would come.

"What are you hiding?" I demand, ducking into her tent.

"It's nice to see you, too." She stands to greet me, but I don't take her extended hand. She turns and offers it to Amie, who accepts it with an uncomfortable glance in my direction.

"Is he here?" I ask her. I know she had a history with Erik, but would she keep me from him after what's happened?

Alix turns away from me and rakes a hand through her loose hair. When she speaks, her voice is low and distant. "Erik is dead."

I die in that moment. Amie's arm wraps around my waist, but I push her away. I squeeze my eyes shut and try to erase the words from my head.

"You're lying," I accuse.

Alix rounds on me and there are tears in her eyes. "I wish I was lying."

And then I know it's true, because I can see her heart is broken. I hear it in her voice. I see it in the absence behind her eyes. I feel it in the hollow of my stomach.

"What happened?" Amie asks because I can't.

"I'm not sure. I wasn't there," she says, reaching down to retrieve a bag from the ground. "Come on."

We follow her out of the tent. Each step is automatic. I follow her because I should. I don't care where we're going.

"How can you know he's dead?" Amie asks her. "If you weren't there."

A spark of hope flares in my chest. Why hadn't I thought to ask that?

"I saw his body."

The tiny flicker dies.

"Where is it?" I ask.

"I buried it."

I don't ask her where. It doesn't matter. Erik isn't there any-more. I try to remember what Loricel told me about people who die naturally. A piece of them fades back into the universe. Had I watched him fade away with Arras as I stood on the surface of Earth? No, Alix said she buried him, so he must have made it here.

"Wait," I say, grabbing Alix's wrist and twisting it. "You told me you didn't know where he was. The night of Protocol Three."

"I didn't know where he was then."

"But when you found out, you didn't send for me?" I ac-cuse.

"This isn't Arras," Alix reminds me. "I can't shoot you a telebound. He's dead, Adelice. I can't change that."

She can't change it, and it's not her fault. But I need to be angry with someone, because the pain is building like an in-ferno desperate for oxygen. I want it to consume me and de-stroy me.

"Where are we going?" Amie asks, trying to change the subject.

Alix stops in front of a large canopy made of a variety of canvases patched together. She gestures for us to enter. Inside lie rows of makeshift cots full of the wounded and the recov-ering, and Alix marches down one. A few volunteers stop her to ask questions. Obviously Alix has stepped up to a leadership position in this camp.

"You were Agenda the whole time," I say finally.

"No, I was turned," she says.

"By whom?" I ask.

"I think you know the answer to that."

I want her to say it. Was it Erik who convinced her to betray Cormac? *How* had he convinced her? What promises passed between them? There were more layers to discover about him. Now I can only uncover those secrets through her.

"Adelice." Alix turns and stares at me. "I understand you have questions, but there's only one thing you need to know. Erik loved you."

"I know that." It's the only thing that feels real.

"Nothing else matters, then."

In the void left by his death this seems impossible to comprehend. Of course other things mattered. Because without answers there was only the aching absence of him. If answers could fill the void, I would keep searching for them.

But even as I thought it, I knew that they never would.

"Nothing I can say will bring him back to you, and there are other things to consider."

"Like what?" I bark. Alix has had weeks to deal with this loss. But it's a naked wound for me and I don't need her to lecture me on how to handle it. Maybe she can forget, but I can't. I've been asked to forget too many people already.

"Like him." Alix points to the cot she's stopped beside. I turn angrily to the bed and the sight sucks the breath from me.

He's badly injured, a thick wind of gauze around his head, dried blood coating the outside. I drop to Jost's side and push the hair from his face, revealing the telltale marks of battle already scarring along his jaw. He's healing quickly, but the damage is extensive.

"Jost?" My voice is barely a whisper over the pounding of my heart.

"You didn't lose everyone," Alix reminds me.

I am not alone to tell the story. This thought crowds into the empty space inside me, threatening to spill over into joy.

"Will he live?" I ask Alix, and as if to answer my question, Jost's hand jerks forward and grabs mine.

"Jost?" This time I'm calling to him, asking him to hear me.

There's a flutter of lashes and he opens his mouth, but no words come out, only a groan.

"He's in bad shape," Alix says, "but he's a fighter and he has a good reason to live."

"Sebrina," I guess.

"She's here. You missed her by about five minutes."

"She's staying with you?"

"I'm looking after her," she says, "until Jost gets better."

"I promised to take care of her. We've been looking for her for weeks. You disappeared before you told me where she was," I say.

"She's safe here," Alix says, but I shake my head.

Even if Jost recovers, this is my promise to him.

"Ad." The nickname is spoken so impossibly quietly that I think I must have imagined I heard it slip from his lips.

"I'm here." I lean down to Jost, placing my other hand over the one clutching mine.

"You have to take care of Sebrina," he says.

"I told you I would," I remind him softly.

"I don't think I can do it," he says. His hand begins to tremble in mine and a seizure rolls through his body. A medic rushes over and gives him a shot.

"I'm sorry, but he'll go back to sleep now," he explains.

"It's okay. I'll be here awhile."

"He'll sleep for a long time," he warns me.

"Will he get better?"

"His injuries are severe, and some of the work is extensive."

"Work?" I ask.

"It looks like a Tailor tried to heal some of his wounds," Alix says, stepping in.

"A Tailor?" I ask in horror.

"We're not all bad," the medic says with a wink, and I realize with some embarrassment that of course this man would be a Tailor. "Your friend will be fine."

"Thank you," I tell him.

"We should let him sleep," Alix says, placing a hand on my shoulder.

I pull away from her.

"I need a few minutes alone with him, okay?"

The medic and Alix exchange a look, but they do as I ask.

"I'll be with Alix," Amie says. She leans down and kisses me on the forehead.

Once they're gone I turn my attention back to Jost. Some of the scars are barely visible while others streak angrily across his shoulders. I pull the sheet down to examine his chest. The marks extend there. Whatever happened to him, it was serious. Despite the medic's reassurances that he will live, dread steals through me. How had he survived this? How exactly was he altered?

"Sebrina." Her name barely escapes his dry lips.

"She's fine," I say to him. "Alix is watching her."

"Promise me like you promised him," Jost mumbles.

I'm not sure what he's trying to tell me. The drugs they've given him must be making him delirious.

"Promise you'll care for her," he repeats.

"I promise, Jost." The weight of the vow is heavy on my chest, but he seems to relax, his hand loosening over my own.

"But you have to fight, Jost," I say. "For her. For me."

"Never stop . . ." His words are a maze of sounds, losing me in his drugged haze. "You."

"Rest," I command, placing a gentle kiss on his bruised cheek. He goes to sleep then, and I stand to leave him, wondering what he meant by "never stop you."

But the thought that haunts me can't be possible.

TWENTY-NINE

NIGHT FALLS, STEALING AWAY EARTH'S SUN UNTIL another day dawns. It always feels like the darkness settles too soon over this healing planet, but I'm grateful that the camp grows quiet. People return to their makeshift homes and tents. Amie falls asleep in the one loaned to us by someone with a kinder heart than mine, and I sneak out to the edge of the camp where the world is still and the air hangs like a heavy black blanket. This is where I can see the stars.

Alix appears, moving so softly through the darkness that I'm unaware of her until she's nearly by my side. She thrusts a tattered bag into my hands.

"What is this?" I ask her, tired of her lies and secrets.

"Open it."

"I don't want it." There is nothing she can give me anymore. Not answers or guidance, and certainly not hope.

"You aren't the only one with a broken heart," she says in a soft voice.

I don't look at her. It doesn't take much to know when

someone is in love, especially when that person is in love with the same man as you. It doesn't soften my feelings toward her, though.

"Is that why you won't tell me how he died?" I ask her. "Because you can't share his last moments?"

Alix takes a step toward me, and when she speaks her voice is low. "Do you think that he would want you to share that? He died for Jost, so that his brother could live."

Her eyes are heavy as she confesses this, full of a burden that I don't quite understand.

"Then why not tell me where Jost was? Why keep it hidden?"

"I'm sorry that I was presumptuous about Jost and his wishes," she says, skirting my question.

I stop her. "You weren't presumptuous. You were purposeful. Deliberate. You knew what he wanted. You knew I was alive. I know that. The only thing I don't know is why you kept the truth from me."

Alix opens her mouth but then shuts it again, turning back toward the camp.

"Take this," I call to her, holding out the bag.

"I have no claim to that," Alix says. "I'll be gone by morning. Take care of Sebrina. Jost will be strong soon."

I should argue with her, try to stop her, but instead I let her fade into the night while I consider her words. She felt she had a claim on Jost. That's why she kept him from me, but I'm not sure why. Except that he's the last piece of Erik left. I consider the growing ache that only exacerbates the hollowness inside of me instead of filling it. That's why she kept Jost from me and why she won't tell me about Erik's final moments.

Moments that are as much mine as they are hers. So what can she possibly give me now? What doesn't she have a claim on? I tip the bag upside down and let its contents fall to the earth. It nestles there catching moonlight and reflecting it like a beacon, unwanted but undeniable in its potential.

A small crystal box.

THIRTY

Buildings are born from scraps and found materials. Babies are born to mothers. Earth blooms into a world of promise instead of mere potential as each of us rebuilds from what's been left behind. I expected to find myself more alone than ever before. But there are people who fill my time with emergencies and concerns and even laughter.

I find a hodgepodge of rooms that I build into a home and I open it to my strange, collected family.

Sometimes in the crowded streets of our fledgling metro I think I spot my mother watching me. Other times whispers follow me. I don't go out for weeks at a time after those days, but I've started telling my story to Amie. She listens in our cramped living room, without questions. But every now and then she gasps at a revelation, and I'm taken back to our bedroom in Romen. To two sisters whispering gossip in the dark. I leave nothing out, because she deserves to know everything.

A day will arrive when others come for this story and I am determined to remember it.

I will face that moment to protect my family—Sebrina, Jost, and Amie.

And when I'm finally ready to believe again, I will pull a relic of a former life from the high shelf in my closet. A small crystal box—a gift from Pryana, the girl who gave me everything that I took from her, and salvaged by Alix, the girl with a broken heart—that holds the very humanity of my mother.

Maybe one day I'll seek the answers I haven't found—from the woman who spies on me from the outskirts of life. I'm certain she has those answers, just as I am sure that she watches Amie and me when she thinks we're not looking. But I'm not quite ready to hear that story from my mother.

But I share other stories—less dangerous ones. I read stories of heroes who don't wear faces I know. Stories captured by people long since dead. I slide into books and lose myself in pages.

"Read more," Sebrina begs as I shut the worn book. She could listen to stories all night.

"You have to sleep sometime, little night owl."

Sebrina makes a hooting noise and I grin at her, brushing her hair back and giving her a soft kiss on the forehead. We're settling into this quiet life at a rate I wouldn't have thought possible. It has its difficulties, but given the choice between tilling soil to plant food or facing the Guild, I'll gladly choose this life.

"Ad, when will Jost be better?" she asks me, and my heart skips a beat. She still doesn't call him *Dad*. I wish she would.

"I'm already stronger," Jost calls from the doorway, leaning against its frame.

"You two will have your own home soon," I tell her, "because your dad is healthier every day."

Sebrina screws up her face. "I like living with you. Don't you like living with Adelice?" she asks him.

There's a pained pause.

"Yes, I love it, but she might want her own space," he says.

"Do you want us to leave?" Sebrina's eyes are wide and bright. I think they look more like Erik's eyes than Jost's, and I shake my head.

"I want you to stay as long as you like."

I pull the covers up to her chin and tuck them tightly around her like a cocoon. Then I sing my mother's lullaby, aware that Jost is still here. I close the door softly behind me when Sebrina's breathing slows into a rhythmic snore.

"I'm sorry about that," Jost says when I step into the living room.

"There's nothing to be sorry about," I tell him, moving past him to sit down.

"She's getting attached to you."

"And you don't like that?" I ask him.

"No, I do." He dares a glance at me. There is a mournful sadness in his eyes. "I don't want you to feel trapped, Adelice. You aren't the one who's responsible for her."

"A lot has changed, Jost," I say.

But we don't talk about the gulf between us or the loss we've endured. There can be no moving forward for Jost and me. The past has left a wound in both of us that can never heal. We both know that.

And yet, things have changed. Jost has changed. He's quick with his smile and silly with his jokes. But the fire has gone out of his eyes. He's no longer consumed by guilt and duty. Now a calm wisdom reflects from them. Perhaps he's more like Erik than I realized. Maybe he needed Sebrina around to show me. But there's something else. Something I don't let myself think about even though it niggles into my dreams and lodges in my unconscious mind, playing tricks on me during the waking hours when I catch Jost looking at me.

"What are you thinking about?" he asks. He stretches out his hand and runs a finger along the outline of my techprint. The scarred skin tingles and something pushes against my mind—a thought I refuse to acknowledge even as it trembles through me.

I draw my hand away. "Ghosts."

Our eyes meet and a chill creeps up my neck.

"No ghosts," he says, extending his hand again. "Dance with me?"

"There's no music."

"I know," he says.

I take his hand, curiosity getting the better of me and something shivers through me at his touch. A familiarity. An instinct. I stare into his calm blue eyes and swallow the question that wanders onto my lips as he leads me into a sweeping waltz. He meets my gaze and I know him.

Love is not love which alters when it alteration finds.

THE END

Acknowledgments

First and foremost, I need to thank the readers for seeing this through to the end.

As this is my last chance to thank the people who saw this trilogy from beginning to end, this is going to be a long one. I have to begin by thanking my editor, Janine O'Malley, for being my literary doula through this adventure. We birthed one big baby.

Special thanks to the entire team at Macmillan for their enthusiasm and support of my books. Thank you, Simon Boughton, Allison Verost, Elizabeth Fithian, Ksenia Winnicki, Caitlin Sweeney, and the rest of the team. You are truly like family!

This book wouldn't be in your hands without Mollie Glick, who picked this story out of the slush, fought to represent it, and held my hand through the whole whirlwind. A big thank-you to Katie Hamblin, former assistant and forever genius, for many wonderful notes on all three books.

We wouldn't have shelves for books if not for bookstores. My utmost thanks to the many booksellers who have welcomed me into their stores, especially my hometown shops: Rainy Day Books and Liberty Bay Books.

Growing up, I got my books from the library. Now that I'm an author, I have even more love for libraries, particularly the Johnson County Library system. Here's looking at you, Joshua Neff!

If it weren't for friends, I would live in my own made-up world. Thanks for getting me out of my head: Lindsey Barjenbruch, Ashley Fuller, and Bethany Taylor.

I'm especially grateful for my writing friends, who understand that characters can break your heart and frustrate you to no end. Thank you, Michelle Hodkin, S. J. Maas, Lissa Price, Josephine Angelini, and Jen Armentrout, for words of wisdom and shoulders to cry on. I was incredibly lucky to go on this wild ride with some Fierce Sisters: Jessica Brody, Anna Banks, Ann Aguirre, Emmy Laybourne, Marie Rutkoski, Caragh O'Brien, Marissa Meyer, Lish McBride, and Leigh Bardugo.

To my inner circle of critics and cheerleaders, thank you: Bethany Hagen, Robyn Lucas, Laurelin Paige, Tamara Mataya, Kayti McGee, and Melanie Harlow.

And finally, I wouldn't be writing this at all if not for my family. Thank you to my parents for letting me read and providing me with transport to the library. Jessica, I think I'm responsible enough to check books out from your private library. Elise, I see amazing things for you. Josh, pop the question already! Thanks, Aunt Kristi, for sneaking me books and CDs under the radar. I'm blessed to have the best in-laws in the world. Jim and Robin, thank you for welcoming me as your daughter. To my oft-neglected children—James and Sydney, you are my world. And to Josh, who always believes. You are my patronus.

Photograph by Tessa Elwood

GENNIFER ALBIN

is the author of *Crewel* and *Altered*. She holds a master's degree in English literature from the University of Missouri and founded the tremendously popular blog theconnectedmom .com. She lives in Poulsbo, Washington, with her husband and two children. Learn more about her at genniferalbin.com.